In Good Spirits

HELEN JULIET

Also Available

BY HELEN JULIET

Contemporary Fairy Tale, Folk Tale and Classic Literature Adaptations

The Fairy Tale Collection Box Set (Beauty and the Beast, Cinderella, Rapunzel)

Daddy's Fairy Tales Box Set (Daddies and kink – Goldilocks, Little Red Riding Hood, The Three Little Pigs, Puss in Boots)

Sweet Tooth (Christmas – Hansel and Gretel)

Jacked Up (D/s – Jack and the Beanstalk)

Rise and Shine (Novella – Sleeping Beauty)

We're All Mad Here (Novella – Alice in Wonderland)

———

BY HJ WELCH

Paddle Creek College (Daddies and kink)

#1 Heaven Sent

#2 Yes, Sir

#3 Little Pleasures

#4 Four Play

#5 Hell's Kitten

#6 Make Believe

Pine Cove (Small town)

Complete Box Set

Homecoming Hearts (Former boy band)

Complete Box Set

Seasonal Daddies (International romance multi-author shared universe)

Jalen & Colby: A Daddy for Christmas

Arlo: A Daddy for Summer

Bears-4-U (Daddies and bears multi-author shared universe)

Keep Me

Content Warning

This book deals with overcoming grief from the sudden, accidental death of a loved one several years ago. There are no detailed descriptions of the accident, but the theme of grief, guilt, and finding happiness again is central to this book.

Despite that, I want to assure you that this book is as low angst as my others generally are. This story is full of so much love between these four men it's going to give you a toothache! I promise that all broken hearts will always get healed by the end of my books.

I wish you a merry Christmas, happy holidays, and all the best for 2025!

For Luna, the best corgi who ever corged

CHAPTER 1
Evan

I DON'T KNOW WHY I THOUGHT THIS WAS A GOOD IDEA. Because apparently, nowhere is safe from Christmas in December, not even sex clubs in Soho.

I sigh and toy with my glass of red wine, watching a couple of gorgeous men in nothing but red thongs and reindeer antlers doing an impressive routine on the poles to a perky festive pop song about baubles shaking under the tree.

It's December first. I really thought I'd be safe for a few more days.

If I wasn't such a miserable grump, their routine would probably have been very arousing. But all I can think about is heading back out into the darkness of London and trudging my way to my empty house. At least it would be quiet there.

Too quiet.

It's a familiar routine. The grief wells up in me, so I forcefully swallow it down. Preferably with a mouthful of rich, warm merlot, like I do now.

The dancers finish their display and take a bow as the watching crowd applauds. I've got myself one of the small round cabaret tables that's set around the sunken dance floor where people have been standing. It means I and any other seated patrons can still see the stage. That act was apparently the last one for the moment, however, as the lighting has changed and the music cranked up. I look around as the throng of mostly younger men below begin to thrust and gyrate to the new song.

I say 'young' like I'm old. I'm not even fifty yet, and not a bad catch, or so it seems. I can usually rely on Bootleg for a quick and easy hookup when the mood takes me. I've still got it in me to be the bossy older guy for an evening or even a whole night.

But once the morning comes, it's always over. In daylight, boys don't just want sex.

They want a Daddy.

And I can't do that. Not ever again.

My glass is empty. Nothing left to help me swallow down the crushing sorrow. The lights and the music are too much, as is the cotton wool fake snow and colourful tinsel that's been draped everywhere. It was foolish to think that maybe this year, things would be different. Or that somebody would be dazzling enough to distract me.

I haven't even had the enthusiasm for an anonymous quickie in forever. I doubt I'm going to want anything until the new year now, when life returns to 'normal'. Whatever that means.

Christmas is everywhere, and that means Beau is everywhere…and yet, cruelly, nowhere. My heart can't take it. Perhaps exposure therapy will work next year. But for now, I plan on sticking with what's protected me for the last several years.

Keep my head down until January. Start fresh, start anew, keep going, keep living. It's what he would have wanted. Not that I got a chance to ask. But it's what I need to survive.

I'm not hungry, but I promise myself if I leave now and

make the half hour walk back to Russell Square, I can place an order with the Indian restaurant nearby that I adore and pick it up en route. That and another glass or two of red wine should be enough to salvage my Friday night. At the very least, stop it from tumbling into utter despair.

Decision made, I rise from my table, already seeing a couple of different parties eyeing it up, ready to pounce. I wish whoever gets it the best of luck, and that they all have better evenings than me.

Now I have dinner plans with myself, I don't feel so hopeless. I'm reading quite a good spy novel at the moment, and that along with a long walk in Regent's Park don't sound like such bad weekend plans. At least I should be able to avoid most of the trappings of the season.

I stand and pluck my heavy woollen coat from the back of the chair I just vacated. As a lot of the patrons here enjoy wearing very little at all (and I often enjoy that on them, too) the heating is always turned up. But once I step out into the London night air, I'm going to need the extra layer.

Draping my coat over my elbow, I don't bother to look over my shoulder and see who manages to grab my table. May the best men win. But I do catch the bartender's eye as I walk past, giving him a nod. He's the owner's boyfriend—or kitten, I guess I should say. He's usually wearing thigh-high boots, a jock strap, fluffy tail attached to a butt plug, ears and a collar. Tonight, like most of the staff, he's also got a Santa hat on his head, although he has cat ears attached on either side of his, like they're poking through the material.

I expect him to nod back and continue serving drinks. Instead, his eyebrows rise, and he looks over to one of the booths. I follow his gaze to see the owner, Miller, who gives me a look of recognition before smiling and waving me over. He took over the place a couple of years ago and really poured his heart and soul into it. Before, there were a lot of safety concerns for the dancers, or so I've been told. I was in a constant haze of booze and drugs in those days, trying to drown my fresh grief, so it's all a bit of a blur.

But Miller is a good chap. In the bad old days, this place was famed for its anonymity with seedy types skulking around in the shadows. Now, he's made it more of a community, a safe haven for kinksters and queers. I wouldn't say the two of us are friends. But then again by this point I've pushed all my actual friends away, so I appreciate that he's at least friend*ly* with me.

"Heading out?" he asks as I approach. He's got his laptop open on the table, but he also has a cocktail, so I hope he's not working too hard on the Friday night.

I nod and look absently around. "Yeah…Christmas isn't really my vibe."

He blinks in surprise. "Oh, I'm sorry to hear that. I know it's not for everyone. I hope you're excited about tomorrow at least?"

Something cold ripples through my chest. "Tomorrow?" I'm drawing a blank.

As far as I'm concerned, I don't have any plans for the whole month. I know my niece will try and entice me over for some sort of gathering as she frets about me becoming a 'lonely old git'. Too late for that, Freddie, I fear. But even though I always make excuses, it's nice that she tries every year regardless.

But what on earth could Miller be talking about?

"Uh-huh," he says slowly. "Tomorrow." Unfortunately, he's looking as apprehensive as I'm feeling. This doesn't bode well. "The Secret Santa Daddy/little Dates? We matched you with Christian Prior and he's very excited, but then he mentioned you hadn't replied to any of his messages."

I feel my world tilt slightly on its axis. "Messages?" I repeat faintly.

As far as I'm aware, I've never met this young man, and I certainly haven't heard anything about whatever this blind date thing is.

Miller licks his lips. I feel bad and he's clearly concerned, but I have no earthly idea what he's talking about. I certainly haven't gone anywhere near the daycare room where the littles hang out since they created it. My heart wouldn't be able to take it.

"Yeah, we set up a special section of the website for certain holidays," he explains as he starts clicking and tapping on his laptop before spinning it around so I can see. "There's a messaging service as part of it. We're trying to match people up with various kinks on a more local scale than the big apps and stuff. It's okay if you didn't get the messages. Tian gave me his number to pass onto you as he figured something might be up."

Now he's got his phone out and he's scribbling digits on the back of a cardboard Bootleg branded coaster. My head is spinning, and my palms are sweating. "I didn't sign up for anything," I manage to utter. The red wine is churning in my stomach. A date? With a *little?* Just the thought of it is making all that grief claw up my throat again.

Miller holds out the coaster and gives me a questioning look. "Uhh…well someone else did in that case. I've personally gone through all the matches with a great deal of care. Your profile is quite detailed, and I think you and Tian could have a lovely time. Don't worry! Like I said, it's supposed to be tomorrow, so it's not too late. It doesn't have to be anything fancy."

I realise he's still offering me the coaster with the phone number on, and I truly think I'm going to be sick. "I'm s-so sorry," I manage to stammer. "No, I can't. I just…there's been a mistake. I'm not…this isn't…I…"

Tears are burning in my eyes as I look around at the

garlands of tinsel all around the club and the stars and baubles hanging from the ceiling. I can't do Christmas. I can't be anyone's Daddy. I certainly can't go on a date at Christmas with a little who…who…

A little who isn't my Beau.

Miller drops his arm slightly. He's not angry, but I see pity in his eyes, and that's somehow worse. "I'm sorry," he says genuinely. "I can see there has been some sort of misunderstanding. I'll tell Christian that you've had to cancel."

He goes to pocket the coaster in his shirt, but I find myself thrusting my hand out almost unconsciously. "No," I say firmly. "I'll do it."

I might be broken, but I'm not a coward. It's not this young man's fault this fuck-up happened. The decent thing to do is apologise myself. But there's no way I could possibly fathom going on a last-minute date tomorrow…

Before I can get too overwhelmed, I take a deep breath and do my best not to blink. Otherwise, the tears might fall. Miller presses the coaster into my hand with a sympathetic look.

"You sure?" he asks.

I manage a stiff nod. "Course. Perhaps there's someone else that can take him out, though?"

Miller doesn't exactly grimace, but his mouth does pull to one side. "Perhaps."

That means 'no' then. He said he personally worked hard on matchmaking everyone. Now, because of me, this Christian boy is going to be let down.

But that's *not* my fault. "You wouldn't happen to know who did put me up for this?" I ask, slipping the coaster into my trouser pocket.

Miller frowns and turns his laptop back around. "Let me check the email address and see if that can't shed some light on the matter for you." He's quiet for a few moments then lets out a groan I can barely hear over the music. "I should have looked more closely," he says apologetically. "Lots of people have emails that aren't their names, but this looks like someone else's name entirely. Do you know a Marlon Lee?"

I can't stop the sharp intake of breath that catches me out. I haven't heard that name for a couple of years now. Back in the early days of my grief, I would have called him my best friend. We probably drank and slept our way across London several times over before we naturally drifted apart. I can't even remember why now. I guess my mourning eventually took me in a different direction to him. He was always just out for the best time and didn't care about breaking hearts in the process.

"Marlon signed me up?" I ask incredulously.

"It looks that way," Miller says with a shrug. But then he rubs his chin and scowls at his computer screen. "I think we're going to have to redesign this if we do it again next year. I didn't foresee the system being misused in this way. I'm so sorry."

I shake out my coat and put it on, the movements helping distract me from my emotions. "It's fine, really," I say gruffly. If I wasn't such an arse, there wouldn't be a problem. "I'll fix it."

Miller lifts his eyebrows. "Yeah."

"Yeah," I grunt. I give him a nod, then turn towards the exit.

I'm not sure how I'll do that, but I do know that I'll be texting two different numbers tonight and getting to the bottom of this.

"Bloody Christmas," I mutter to myself. "Who needs it?"

CHAPTER 2

Sai

THE FRONT DOOR OF THE FLAT DOESN'T SO MUCH OPEN AS crash, bang *and* wallop. I blink and raise my eyebrows as I turn away from the risotto I've basically finished cooking. I look towards the corridor at the end of the narrow kitchen, then down at the corgi sitting not very patiently at my feet. "What's going on, hey, Bow?"

She gives me a little whimper then jumps to her feet, tail wagging in anticipation. As far as she's concerned, everyone is always delighted to see her, so why would there be a problem? I hear an internal door open and slam, though, so I think something must be up.

Looking down at dinner, I decide to turn off the heat and cover it. It'll probably keep warm long enough to discover what's going on. Or…at least not congeal so we can reheat up bowls in the microwave after whatever crisis has (hopefully) been averted.

The kitchen is situated in the middle of our single storey Clapham apartment. I wipe my hands on a tea towel before sticking my head out to look up and down the hallway. Like the kitchen, it's long and so narrow we have to breathe in if two people pass each other. But this place has been home for over five years now, so I'm very fond of it even if it can be awkward.

The front door opens directly into the living-cum-dining room, where the corridor then leads past the spare room, my office, the kitchen where I'm standing, the bathroom and separate loo, concluding in the primary bedroom where my husband, Jude, is also leaning against the doorframe, his expression one of confusion.

"Was that Tian?" he asks.

I shrug and look back down to the closed door of the spare room. "Must be."

Wordlessly, the two of us begin walking along the corridor, falling into step. Jude is freshly showered, having worked a day shift at the hospital. I love it when the three of us can manage a Friday evening together, but even though it's usual for Tian to use his key to let himself in, typically he bounces inside like the bundle of joy he is.

Locking himself in the spare room is definitely cause for concern.

Of course, we call it the spare room out of habit for mixed company. Its actual purpose is our playroom. We created it after we started dating Tian seriously. If we have guests, it's still possible to tuck most of the childish paraphernalia away, but that's quite rare these days. It's my boy's sanctuary where he can truly be himself.

Right now, he's using it to hide from us. I don't like that.

I knock gently on the door. "Tian?" I call out gently.

"Go away!" he practically wails through the wood.

I share a look with my husband. Jude crooks an eyebrow. "Someone's going to get their bottom smacked," he says with a snort.

Bow whimpers again and dances around our feet. "Hush," I tell him softly. "He sounds genuinely upset."

Jude bites his lip and nods. I know him well enough after so many years to tell that he was making a joke because he's worried. We both are. Bow, too. She's got a natural instinct to detect stress and always does her best to ease it by crawling into your lap.

Except, I'm also feeling a surge of protectiveness as well as concern. If someone has hurt my sweet boy...

"Tee," I call out more firmly. "Daddy and Jude are going to come in now, okay. We're here to make things better."

I don't hear a spoken response, but I'm pretty sure I catch a sniffle. Oh, if my baby is crying, I will break down the blasted door if I have to.

Luckily, Tian hasn't locked it, so I'm able push inside without incident. As usual, Jude is on the same page as me, and we both dart in but block Bow's way with our feet. It might be that doggy cuddles are precisely what he needs right now. But as his Daddy, I'm going to assess the situation first and that will be easier without a cold nose and digger claws trying to get into everything, or non-stop barking.

"Good girl, just stay there," Jude says kindly to her as we manage to close the door between us. She whimpers, but she generally knows if she's been shut out, it's for a good reason. We'll be sure and fuss her extra when we come back out or let her in.

The overhead light is off, but Tian has flicked on the lamp that looks like a hot air balloon. I know this space is for designed to encourage his age play, but I can't lie and say it doesn't give me a lot of comfort as well. Tian loves all things vehicular, so I worked hard on a travel theme, giving it an 'Around the World in 80 Days' feel.

My baby boy is currently sat on the rug that looks like a map of the globe, hugging an elephant stuffed toy with one arm and angrily thumping coloured wooden blocks on top of each other, trying to make some sort of tower that crashes down as Jude and I step closer to him. Tian makes a high-pitched noise before smacking several of the cubes away.

"Uh-uh," I lightly scold him. Crouching down, I take his free hand between both of mine, looking directly at his face until he meets my gaze. Eventually, he does, his eyes watery and his chin wobbling. "That's it. Good boy. We're not mean to our toys now, are we?"

Honestly, this behaviour is so out of character for him, I can't help but let my imagination run wild. Did he get fired? He loves his job as a PA. It's a smallish company, so there's always a chance they'd have to make redundancies. But I'd really hope not at the very beginning of December.

Lord above. What if he was mugged? Or maybe one of his housemates was a dick again. The old urge to insist he moves in with us rears up again, despite us all having discussed the fact that we don't really have the space here. But it's getting desperate. I'd move to a bigger place for him. The three of us are committed, and if he's having trouble at home…

I'm yanked from my tumbling thoughts as Jude scoots up next to Tian and hugs him tightly from the side. "Was someone mean to you, Tee?" he asks, deliberately using our baby's little name.

I watch as my boy starts shoving blocks around aimlessly, not looking at either of us. He shrugs. "Doesn't matter," he mumbles.

My knees can't take crouching for much longer, so I shift around and sit cross-legged in front of Tian. He clearly needs to keep his hands busy, so I rest my palms on his thighs and rub my thumbs against the material of his trousers.

"Of course it matters, darling. We love you and we don't like it when you're sad."

Jude nods eagerly, placing a noisy kiss on Tian's cheek. "Daddy and Jude take care of Baby Tee!" he declares, slipping into his more middle persona as well.

He doesn't age play the way Tian does. My husband is a pure soul who loves hard and fast, and always sees things through more innocent eyes. He knows when to be professional or mature around different groups of people. But people who know him well appreciate that if anyone's going to have a spaceship backpack or spend his free time playing video games, it will be him.

To my relief, the kiss gets a sweet little giggle out of Tian. He blinks wet eyes and looks between me and Jude. "I'm being silly," he whispers.

I shake my head and squeeze his knees. "Your feelings are always valid, baby. Daddy would really love it if you talked us through what's on your mind so we can help. Can you do that for us?"

Jude watches as Tian chews his lip, a look of adoration on my husband's face. We've been dating Tian for almost three years now and I know we both feel forever about him. If the law would let us marry him, I'm sure we'd be working on a proposal this very Christmas. We've also talked about making a big deal about asking him to move in, but a bigger place would be a financial strain on all of us.

Anyway, that's not the issue right now. He knows how we feel about him, and what we have is still wonderful. As uncharacteristic as this outburst is from my baby, I'm hoping we can sort it all out soon, then get back to enjoying our Friday night together.

I'm Daddy. It's my job to take care of both my boys, and I take it very seriously.

Tian seems to turn things over in his head a little longer, nibbling on his lip. "You know I love you both so much," he starts off tentatively.

I'd be lying if I said my heart didn't falter a fraction in my chest. But as panicked thoughts flash through my mind, the logical part of me knows this probably isn't a breakup.

Probably. Right?

"We love you, too!" Jude cries, sounding horrified that would be in question. Tian sighs and leans closer into their hug. That gives me a modicum of reassurance that this conversation isn't going to end in disaster.

"I just don't want you to feel like you're not enough," Tian mumbles, pulling at the edge of the rug.

Ah. Okay, right. I think I have an inkling of where this is going.

Jude and I have always been open in our relationship, whether that be seeking lovers individually or together to play as a threesome. That's how we met Tian and fell in love with him. He's the only man we've ever gotten serious about outside our own relationship, and we remind him how special he is all the time.

We don't necessarily have time to date or scene or hook-up with anyone else these days, but Tian has been really looking forward to this Daddy Secret Santa thing one of the kink clubs has organised this year. I think the Daddy he got matched with caught his eye some time ago.

Since we officially became a couple, he's never hooked up with another guy, let alone gone on a date. He's never even talked about fancying anyone else. So this Secret Santa thing is kind of a big deal that Jude and I have quietly been very interested in, but he's been very shy and private about it.

We only know it was happening because Jude overheard something at the club, Bootleg, when the two of them went out dancing the other night and the owner apparently talked to Tian about it. I'm not keen that he's being secretive, so we're overdue a chat anyway.

"What do we always say, baby boy?" I prompt him.

He sighs once more and finally meets my eyes again with his own. "We always come home," he says dutifully.

"And?" I ask.

"And we always communicate," he tells me, keeping hold of my gaze as he nods.

"That's right," Jude chips in earnestly.

"I know that you love us, and we love you," I say firmly. "Because we have a lot of love to give, don't we?" Both my boys nod. "And it's also okay to want to go play and have sexy times with other people if that feels good, right?"

"Right," they both agree, although Jude with far more conviction that Tian.

"So did something happen with your Secret Santa?" I ask him.

Tian screws his face up and wraps his fist around a block, banging it on the floor. Quick as a flash, I cover his hand with mine and hold it firmly. "Tee, if you keep treating your toys badly, you'll be getting a smacked botty. Do you understand?"

His lip trembles. "What if Tee *wants* a smacked botty?"

I feel myself soften. "Then you ask Daddy to help you. Is that what you want?"

He shrugs and looks away again. "I don't know."

"You have to use your big boy words and tell Daddy how you're feeling," I warn him.

Of course I want to help him. Everything inside me screams to. But right now, the best way I can do that is by getting him to work through what's got him so upset. I don't mind if the spanking is a punishment or for pleasure, so long as Tian gets what he needs. In this moment, I'm not entirely sure what's best.

"I *like* Daddy Evan," he blurts out suddenly, his brow creasing and his eyes pooling with more tears.

I glance at Jude who subtly shakes his head at me. No, neither of us have heard this name before, but I'm guessing it's Tian's Secret Santa.

"That's okay, baby boy," I assure him. "You told us you would be going on a date. That's fine."

However, he's still looking miserable. "Except I'm not," he says shakily, snuggling closer to Jude. His tone has changed and he doesn't sound so little right now. "I knew something was wrong as he hasn't been active on the website since we matched. He messaged me on my way here to say there's been a mistake and he never actually signed up for the date, his friend did it for him without telling him. But he doesn't want to plan something last minute. He said it's not a good time for him which means he doesn't like me back and…and…"

He's properly sobbing now, so I lean forwards and gather him and Jude in my arms, hugging them tightly and rubbing Tian's back. "You are amazing," I tell Tian firmly. "That's not fair if Evan's friend did this without telling him. But it makes sense if he can't commit to something with twelve hours' notice. I know you're disappointed, but you don't know what Evan's circumstances are."

Tian takes a few moments to calm his crying down before leaning back and wiping his eyes on his sleeve. I reach up and grab a tissue from the box on the bedside table, handing it to him before he can also blow his nose on his clothes. He obediently cleans himself up with it, then takes a deep breath and looks between Jude and I.

"I know he's lonely," he says with conviction. "I think someone broke his heart a while ago and I just wanted to try and make him happy. No one should be sad at Christmas."

My heart swells. Both my boys are so caring, always thinking about everyone else around them first. That's why they need me to be bossy and take care of *them*, otherwise I know they'd let their own desires fall by the wayside. Well, maybe not Jude. He'd brat his way through anything. But he wasn't good at asking for the aftercare he needs before we met, and I soon fixed that.

"I quite agree, baby boy," I tell Tian. "Have you tried talking to him? Perhaps you have an opportunity to get to know each other a little better now, regardless of who signed him up to the Secret Santa date."

Tian takes another deep breath, and I can see he's coming out the other side of his tantrum. "I just wrote back 'Okay' because I didn't want to say anything I'd regret."

I chuckle and lean forwards to place a kiss on his forehead. "Good boy," I tell him earnestly. "Daddy's very proud of you. Perhaps tomorrow Daddy and Jude can help you write out a longer message so you can explain how you're feeling to him. If he doesn't know it's upset you this much, then he can't make it better, can he?"

"What if he doesn't care?" Tian asks quietly.

"Then he's a wanker who doesn't deserve you," Jude answers hotly.

"Language," I warn him, but it's mostly for show. He knows he's not supposed to use bad words when we're having little time in the playroom. But I can't help but love seeing my husband defend my boy like that.

Tian laughs wetly. He's still shaking off his sadness. However, I can see a sparkle in his eyes again.

I genuinely don't know this Evan from Adam. He could be a decent chap who's equally a victim here. Or he could indeed be a wanker that callously hurt my baby's feelings. Right now, though, I don't care about him. I care about Tian and will do whatever it takes to make him feel better.

"That's settled, then," I say in my big Daddy voice. "We'll get more answers tomorrow. But right now, Baby Tee, I think Daddy and Jude would love nothing more than to make you feel absolutely amazing. Isn't that right, Jude?"

Immediately, Jude's cheeks are flushed and his eyes

dilated. It still turns me on so much to see how quickly my husband's lust takes over for our sweet boy. Naturally, neither of us would ever wish for Tian to be in any predicament or to be feeling low. But Jude thrives on taking care of him just as much as I do. His way is just a little different to mine.

"Yes, Daddy," he says breathlessly to me.

When it's just us, he'll either use my name or, depending on the scene, 'Sir' or 'Master'. Tian sways between liking more regular sexy times and staying little. When he's like that, Jude loves encouraging him by calling me 'Daddy' as well. I love that all three of us have our own unique dynamics with each other. It's one of the most beautiful aspects of being polyamorous.

Jude looks back at Tian. "Would you like that, Baby Tee? Can I kiss you and play with you?"

Tian's nuzzling his nose against Jude's as he nods, their hug becoming something more as their mouths find each other. "Yes, please, please," he begs.

I'm not sure what tomorrow will bring and how much Tian actually cares about this Evan guy. Perhaps he's just caught up in this moment of rejection. But now he's settled down, I intend to remind him exactly who he belongs to, even if it takes all night.

Especially if it takes all night.

CHAPTER 3

Jude

Having my husband by my side as we both fell in love with Tian was one of the greatest experiences of my life so far. We'd had plenty of sex with other people as a couple in the past. But realising that this sweet, gorgeous, feisty, adorable boy had captured our hearts in a more permanent way was incredibly special.

I suppose our relationship has fallen into a bit of a routine of late. There hasn't been much time for anyone to hook-up, especially when we each have two lovers waiting at home. But seeing my baby come to us crying like this has certainly stirred up the dragon inside me tonight. It's okay, he's got Sai and me to be his white knights in shining armour.

Yes, I can be both the dragon and the knight, because I'm precious like that. Sai says so.

Whatever. It's like a switch has been flipped and I've gone from feeling angry and protective to like I have to mark what's mine right this second. Perhaps I am more of a dragon. I just want to hoard Tian away and ensure he knows he's ours. Hopefully with lots of moaning and screaming involved.

We mostly keep sex to the bedroom when we're all in a more adult frame of mind. But sometimes, Tee likes to stay in little headspace, so we have a bed in the playroom as well. Of course, there are times he just wants to nap, or we have actual guests over and can turn this space into something more boring again pretty quickly. But at times like this, I'm very grateful there's a comfy mattress and a drawerful of lube and toys so we don't have to break the spell of the moment.

Tian's kissing me with a not small amount of desperation. It's easy to tell he needs this release, and I'm more than happy to help him with it. But I pause for a second, brushing a curl of hair from his forehead and a stray tear from his cheek. Then I glance at Sai, wanting—needing—him to take charge of us both.

"Clothes off, on the bed," he murmurs. Just those simple words send a jolt down to my throbbing cock and balls, excitement bubbling in my tummy.

"Yes, Daddy," Tian says eagerly. I help him to stand, and then we rush to strip each other as quickly as we can. Sai is still on the floor, looking up at us in awe. He hasn't given us any further instructions, so I start kissing Tian again and fondling his hardening cock.

"Such a good boy, Baby Tee," I mumble into his mouth. "So good, so perfect."

It's not like Tian had a tragic childhood or anything. His parents love him, and he has a nice albeit quiet family. But he's always been small and effeminate, and I think he got bullied a fair bit at school and struggled to find his footing initially with work. All that's to say, he really likes praise kink, especially when he's feeling vulnerable. Normally, a couple of compliments as we're getting it on will do. But I have a feeling he might need it laid on thick tonight, and I bloody love doing that. Sai does, too. But until he gives us more direction, I'm in the driver's seat.

"I love you, sweet boy," I continue between kisses, stroking his leaking cock with one hand and digging my fingers into his back with the other. "You're so good for me and Daddy. Our perfect little baby boy. So sweet and sexy. I want to fuck you so badly. Do you want that, too?"

"*Jude*," he practically sobs.

He had been fumbling with my cock, but tonight, I just want him to lie back and let us use his body to make him and ourselves feel so good. He shouldn't have to worry about a thing. So I bat his hand away and slide our members together in my grasp, kissing his mouth messily.

"Tell me what you want, Tee," I urge him. It doesn't matter that we've all been together for quite a while now, consent is always important. Especially when it's my gorgeous baby boy begging for it.

"I want...I..."

"Come on, sweetheart," I tell him between kisses. His body feels so good against mine. I'm already sweating and trembling. "You can tell me. I know you can. You're so good for me and your Daddy, aren't you?"

"Yes, yes, I'll be good," he whimpers.

"Then what do you want?"

"Please fuck me, Jude," he begs, gripping my hips and kissing my mouth like he wants to bruise it. "Show me you love me."

"Of course I will, Baby Tee," I promise him. "And Daddy, too? He gets to fuck your tight, delicious hole after me? Make sure you're filled up with both our cum?"

He lets out a proper sob and buries his face against my neck, shivering as I wank both of us off. "Yes, yes," he cries.

And then Sai is there. He's still dressed, and his T-shirt

and jeans feel so good against my skin as he hugs us both, kissing my temple, then Tian's.

"Good boys," he says, his voice low and full of lust. "Tian, Daddy wants to watch you suck Jude's cock. He's going to lay on the bed for you. That way, your pretty bottom will be in the air for me to give you a spanking. Do you remember why you're going to be spanked?"

I see a flash of almost panic in Tian's eyes. It's the kind of look that tells me he knows he has to do exactly what his Daddy says right now. Part of his instincts are frightened of that, but really, he loves that total submission. Of course, in reality, he's the one in charge and could stop everything in an instant with one word. But I know how good it makes him feel when we take control and fuck him into oblivion. He wants to let go of absolutely everything, and we're going to give him that gift.

He blinks as he looks up at Sai, his breathing ragged. "I'm going to be spanked because I was bad and threw my toys," he says with a tremor in his voice.

Sai's expression visibly softens. He reaches out and cups the side of Tian's face, brushing his thumb against his cheek. "No, baby boy. You're going to be spanked because you were *good*. You were a big boy and talked about your feelings, and then you asked Daddy if he'd spank you. So that's what we're going to do, okay? You're going to take everything I give you whilst you make Jude feel so, so good. And if you want to cry, you must. Big boys have a lot of big feelings and sometimes they need some help to let them out. Do you understand?"

His breaths are still sawing in and out of him and he's trembling. But he's also rock hard in my hand and looking up at Sai with reverence. "Yes, Daddy."

"Yes, what?" he asks.

"Yes, I understand, and yes, I want to be spanked and suck cock and cry."

Sai moves his thumb to run it along Tian's plump bottom lip. "You want Daddy and Jude to use you and fuck you and make you scream?"

"Y-yes."

"You want us to love you?"

He closes his eyes, making twin tears fall down his face. *"Yes."*

I kiss the tears away before they can drip down his chin. "We'll always love you," I say with all the sincerity I can muster. "You're our perfect Baby Tee. Are you ready to come have some fun with me?"

He lets out a shaky laugh and nods. Together, we glance at Sai.

He gives us both a kiss on the lips. Me first, then Tian. "Neither of you are allowed to come until I say so," he warns.

"Yes, Daddy," we both say in unison.

It's funny. I wouldn't roleplay with Sai like this by ourselves. Sure, I love being a brat and a tease and getting my own fair share of spanking and other games. But it's only with Tian that I really tap into that fun middle space and let go enough to call him by that name.

I crawl onto the bed and flop onto my back, groaning as Tian immediately jumps on all fours on top of me, swallowing down my cock like his life depends on it. I drop my head back and dig my heels into the mattress, sliding my fingers through his thick, silky brown hair. He looks cute with it this short back and sides style, but sometimes I think he keeps it this long on top because it's so good for pulling when he's getting fucked.

Sai positions himself beside Tian, casually reaching down and wrapping his hand around Tian's prick as well. "Remember," Sai growls in that low Dom voice that goes straight to my already aching balls. "Neither of you can come before I say so. If you do, you will be punished, and you won't like it."

Tian moans around my dick and I manage a grunt and a nod. "Yes, Daddy," I say hoarsely. Tian is already torturing me, but it's the most exquisite kind of torment. I can hold out.

However, Sai knows how to help edge me on for longer. He lets Tian's length go, then also cards his fingers through Tian's hair before gripping tightly and pulling him off my cock. A string of saliva trails obscenely from his swollen lips to my red, glistening head.

"I'm going to smack your bottom now, Tee," Sai rasps. Even though he's still dressed, I can see the bulge in his jeans from how turned on he is, too. "I'm going to make your pretty little botty red and shiny. Then, when I've decided you've had enough, I'm going to watch you ride my husband's big cock until he comes, then I'm going to fuck you hard and fast. Only then will I decide if you get to come."

"Yes, Daddy," he croaks. He already looks so wrecked, and we're only just getting going. "I can do it. I'll be good."

"I know you will be, sweet boy," Sai says warmly, giving Tian a kiss on the lips. Then he pushes him back down, his lips gliding over my cock and making me inhale sharply.

"Good boy," I whisper. "Like that. I love it. Don't stop."

Then Sai's right hand flies through the air and connects with Tian's cheek, a loud crack slicing through the air. Tian squeaks and whimpers around my dick, but he doesn't stop the blow job.

Fuck. I clench my jaw, grip the bed sheets, and screw up my eyes. I have a horrible feeling it's going to take a lot of self-control for me not to accidentally shoot my load.

The smacks ring out loud and clear as Sai beats Tian's arse and thighs red raw. Tian obviously falls into a kind of subspace as he times the bobbing of his head in between the blows. But after a while he's crying too hard and he just keeps his head down, sucking on my cock like a baby with a bottle. I run my fingers through his hair and tell him he's good and perfect and beautiful, all the while keeping myself hovering just on the edge of my climax.

I guess I fall into a bit of a trance myself, but when Sai shifts around the side of the bed and slowly pulls Tian off me, I realise he must be done with the spanking. Tian's face is covered in tears and snot, but Sai does just as he promised and tenderly wipes him clean, encouraging him to blow his nose on a fresh tissue and drink some water from a bottle he's produced from somewhere.

"You did so good, baby boy," he says with such warmth it makes my heart ache. "It's all over now. You did so well. How do you feel?"

Tian blinks and looks down at me, swaying on quivering arms. "Good," he slurs eventually. "Thank you, Daddy."

"You're so welcome, sweet baby. Now, do you want to come?"

"Please," Tian cries, his voice cracking.

Sai laughs, but it's not unkind at all. "Such a good boy. But you know you can't yet, right? When can you come?"

"When Daddy says," Tian tells him immediately.

"Exactly," Sai says proudly. "Good boy. Now I want to watch you suck my husband's cock some more whilst I prep your gorgeous hole for him. Jude, are you allowed to come?"

I smirk at him, feeling devilish. "I will if I want, Daddy."

Sai arches an eyebrow at me, and I swear I do almost explode right there and then. *"When* are you allowed to come, Judas?"

Ohh, he only calls me that when I'm a bad boy. I pinch my nipples and squirm, watching him lube up his fingers. Tian is still waiting patiently, hovering over me on all fours until he's told what to do next because he really is such a good boy.

I drag my lower lip through my teeth and moan. "I'm

allowed to come when I'm fucking our sweet, sexy boy, and our Daddy says I can."

Sai gives me a heated look that suggests he'd quite like to pound my arse into oblivion in that moment, but hopefully I can tempt him into doing that later. Tian might love being told he's good and perfect and special, but sometimes I just want to be pinned down and told I'm a filthy slut who's going to give it up whether he likes it or not.

My husband has many tools in his toolbox.

And yes, I might be horny as fuck, but that pun was very much intended.

Without a word, Sai pushes Tian's mouth back on my cock and gets to work stretching out his hole, going straight in with two fingers.

"That's it, good boy," he murmurs. "Take it just like that. Such a sweet, pretty boy. Your hole was made for our cum. We're going to fill you all the way up so you don't forget who you belong to, who loves you."

Tian moans, fresh tears dripping down his face, his cock straining as it bobs between his legs. I caress his hair and tell him how much I love watching my dick stretch out his lips and cheeks and how perfect he is. Then Sai is sliding his fingers out and whispering in our baby boy's ear.

"Ride my husband now, little Baby Tee. Like he's a show pony and you're going for the gold medal."

Tian is trembling from head to toe as he scrambles up the bed and lowers himself down. Before I can help, he's already guiding my cock inside him, so instead I run my hands up his thighs and over his belly, pinching and rubbing his pretty pink budded nipples.

"Yessss," I hiss as he impales himself, forcing my length deep inside him until he's bottoming out, eyes glassy as he looks down at me. "Does that feel good, baby boy?" I ask, jerking my hips and making him squeal.

"Y-yes, Jude," he stammers.

I look over to where Sai has already shed his clothes. He's got a lubricated hand around his cock as he stands over us, waiting to watch us fuck. "What do you want, Daddy?" I ask, using the word for Tian and sure enough, it elicits a delicious whimper from him. "Baby Tee and I will do whatever you want us to. He can ride me, or I can fuck him. It's your choice. We belong to you." That makes Tian sob, so I take a second to lean up and kiss his lips tenderly. "Good boy," I whisper just for him. "You're doing so well. I'm so proud of you."

Sai comes closer, letting go of his cock so it stands hard between me and Tian. Regardless of his sticky fingers, he runs them through both our hair, the lube making it tug painfully. I can tell Tian loves it just as much as I do.

"We're taking care of our baby tonight, Jude," Sai says warmly. "Make him see stars."

That's all the direction I need to grab his hips and start thrusting like I'm the one going for gold. "That's it, take it, gorgeous," I grunt as we look into each other's eyes. He holds onto my shoulders, but otherwise he's almost limp, letting me take care of everything. "Like that. You're so good. You feel amazing. I love fucking you. My sweet baby boy."

"You can come whenever you want, Jude," Sai says, leaning down to kiss my cheek.

After that, I screw up my eyes and chase my climax like it's the last hurdle at the gymkhana. I've been so close to the edge for so long now, it takes no time at all before I'm blowing my load and yelling all sorts of filthy curses that are sure to go in my favour when I goad Sai into fucking me roughly later.

For now, I manage to catch my breath and look up at the sweating, trembling boy still straddling me. I brush his wet hair back and smile at him. "You're amazing. Did you like that?"

"Yes, Jude," he says, sounding absolutely destroyed.

He's not done yet. But Sai takes mercy on him. Gently, he helps slide him off my softening cock, lifting his bum in the air so he's still on all fours above me as Sai positions himself behind him. I kiss Tian's swollen lips as Sai wastes no time in forcing his lubed-up cock inside Tian's already well fucked hole. My baby's eyes go wide as Sai no doubt immediately begins slamming against his prostate, lighting him up from within.

"You can do it," I tell Tian as I caress his face, kissing his lips, his cheeks, the tip of his nose and his closed eyelids. "You're doing so well. I know you can take it. I'm so proud of you. You look so perfect and beautiful when you're getting fucked. Our sweet, special boy."

Unsurprisingly, Sai was worked up almost as much as I was, so within a few minutes he drops his head back and starts letting out that low moan he always does before coming his brains out.

"You're so close," I urge my exhausted baby boy. "You're driving Daddy wild. He's going to fill you up with all his juicy cum any second now. Squeeze your pretty hole how he likes it. I know you can."

Above me, Tian grits his teeth, but when Sai snarls like a wild bear, I know Tian is clenching his muscles around my husband's cock. It always tips him over the edge, and sure enough, the next second Sai is digging his fingers into Tian's hips as his orgasm crashes through him.

Tian takes it all beautifully, his face, neck and chest flushed with desire and exertion. Sai uses his body to ring every last drop of cum from his cock before hastily pulling out. He reaches down next to us, grabbing the bottle of lube and slapping it in my hand.

"I want to see our perfect boy make a mess of you, you whore," he says with a wink.

I might not be in my twenties anymore, but Jesus Christ I could almost come again there and then. Instead, I tuck that delicious barb away for later, pumping gel onto my fingers and sliding my hand around Tian's poor neglected cock. As I do, Sai uses both hands to part Tian's cheeks and bury his face between them, slurping out both our messes as he eats out Tian's sensitive hole.

He screams so loud I briefly worry about our neighbours, But when I see the look of desperate bliss on my boy's face, I don't care. Anyway, they've got to be used to our shenanigans by now.

"Can I come?" Tian rambles. I rub him fiercely and Sai licks and sucks at his puckered entrance. "Daddy, please! Can I come? Daddy…Jude…I have to…please…I can't…I've been so good. I love you…I love you…*I love you.*"

Sai surfaces long enough to rasp, "Come, baby boy," and then Tian is howling and painting my chest, face and hair like he's been storing it up for weeks. Sai goes back to mercilessly eating him out, and I keep stroking until I've coaxed every single drop from him.

Finally, he collapses on top of me, pulling himself away from Sai's mouth and my hand. He's probably so sensitive it's painful, but I know Sai loves pushing both of us to the limit of what we can take.

Now, though, it's over.

I wrap my arms around Tian's back, squishing his jizz between us. I revel in the mess. He buries his sobbing face against my neck, and I stroke his hair and back as he shakes and cries. "Good boy," I tell him for the hundredth time that night alone. "You did so well. Such a perfect boy."

I glance over his shoulder to see Sai squirting soothing lotion into his hand that he then gently applies to Tian's bottom, red from being spanking and fucked hard. Once he's finished, he lays beside me. The bed is a double, so with Tian on top of me, he's got room. Then he throws an arm and a leg over us, cuddling us both tightly as he murmurs how Tian is a good baby boy and I'm a needy little slut. I grin and snuggle closer to him.

I don't know who this Evan guy is. I'm so sorry that he upset Tian like he did. But perhaps in the morning, my baby boy will forget all about him. Of course, the way our dynamic works is that we're free to follow our own paths. But if this other Daddy is just going to make Baby Tee cry, he can bugger off.

The three of us already have everything we need right here.

CHAPTER 4
Evan

THE GREAT EXPECTATIONS PUB ISN'T ANYTHING FANCY. IN fact, that's why Marlon and I chose it as our spot back in the day. Just a basic drinking hole with a few barstools to prop up its patrons. They barely sell packets of nuts, let alone crisps, and they certainly don't serve hot food. Many a night we'd soldiered our way through several pints, then hit up the kebab place around the corner before crawling home and somehow making it to work the next morning.

As I walk through the door on Saturday night, I expect a wave of nostalgia to hit me. Instead, I just wrinkle my nose at the scent of stale beer and old man cologne.

Am I an old man now? Is that what my aftershave smells like?

No. This place has a definite whiff of despair about it that either wasn't here before or I was too messed up to notice.

Over the music system, a Christmas rock song from the seventies plays at a low enough level that it doesn't disturb the people chatting. A few skinny lengths of silver tinsel are strung out above the bar. They look and smell like they're also from the seventies.

Well, this is where Marl wanted to meet, so there's no point in grumbling about it. In fact, I feel the tiniest glimmer of hope that I haven't wanted to spend my time here in a couple of years now. I'm still not the life and soul of the party by any means. But at least I'm not dwindling my days away here anymore.

There's no sign of Marlon yet. I manage to find two tall stools next to each other and catch the bartender's attention to order myself a house red. No point trying to ask if they have any decent wine—it'll just cost twice the price and taste as bad as the regular stuff. Besides, the point of the drink is to occupy me, not necessarily to sit and savour it.

When the guy asks if I'd like anything else, I pause, wondering if Marlon still has the same order. I figure getting a round in is the polite thing to do, even if I am here to chew him out for putting me in such a shoddy position. Part of me wants to tell him he can buy his own drink.

Then I think of Christian's sad, simple response of 'Okay' to my explanation text, and decide that both Marl and I are the fuck-ups here. The least I can do is be the slightly less shitty man.

I order the pint of bitter then nurse my wine until the door opens again, blowing in the cold and also my old mate.

It's hard not to react too obviously. But holy hell the last few years haven't been kind to him. His grey suit under his black coat is shabby and baggy. His hair is scraggly and his stubble several days beyond trimmed. The skin over his nose and cheeks is ruddy and not just from the cold. Even with his glasses on, I can see the bags under his eyes.

When we'd seen each other regularly, he'd always had a healthy robustness to his countenance. But it's as if he's soured in the time we've been apart.

Still, when he spies me, he musters a smile, lifting his hand in a wave. "Zegler!" he cries, shambling over and taking the free seat beside me. He points at the pint I got him. "Oh, you legend," he says appreciatively, clapping me on the back as he picks it up and drains half of it in one go.

"It's good to see you," I say, not sure if I mean it or not. He was a decent friend in my era of desperation. The kind of company I needed in that moment. But all I feel now at seeing him is sadness and a general unease. Whatever we shared back them seems to have evaporated now.

"Ah, no, it's not good to see me. You're pissed at me, I know." He grins and winks my way before polishing off the last of the bitter. I'm mildly shocked at his speed, but before I can say anything, he flags the barman down and jerks his thumb my way. "Another round of the same, boss."

The guy nods, quietly pouring our drinks as Marlon fishes a crumpled twenty out of his pocket and leaves it on the sticky counter.

"You know why I texted, then?" I ask. I messaged out of the blue last night asking to meet up, not sure if I was relieved or not when he said tonight would work just fine.

"You found out I signed you up for that blind date thing at the club, yeah?" His tone is strange, like he thinks what he did was hilarious but at the same time his shoulders sag and he's definitely…rueful? Sheepish?

"I suppose you had your reasons," I say diplomatically. I sip my wine, eyeing up the fresh glass that's been placed in front of me. I doubt I'm going to get through this one, let alone start that one. But I don't want to reject Marlon's hospitality.

"Seemed like a good idea at the time," my old friend says around the lip of his second pint before taking a gulp. At least with this one he's slowed down and doesn't look like he intends on necking it.

I sigh and rub my thumb against the stem of my glass. "I only found out about it last night. It's not something…I'm not interested in that, Marl. But the young man I was paired with…" I sigh. "It felt like a particularly twatish move to stand him up the day before."

"Yeah," he says glumly. "That wasn't my intention. Didn't think about that bit. Poor lad. Hope he's okay."

I frown. When we used to tear up the town, Marlon used to laugh at any boys if they showed even a hint of…what is it the youngsters say nowadays? Catching feelings? 'Love 'em and leave 'em' was Marlon's motto. It never sat well with me, but I was always very upfront with anyone I tangled with that it was strictly for sex. So I figured he was just doing the same in his own way.

Now he cared about Christian Prior?

Guilt swirls in my guts even though this mess isn't of my making. I genuinely don't know if Christian is okay or not, despite that being the word he used.

"Why *did* you sign me up? And on the sly?" That's my main reason for asking him out to the pub tonight. I thought perhaps he'd done it for a laugh or as an excuse to hang out again. But as I look at him picking at the edges of his cardboard coaster, I don't get that impression from him at all.

He sighs after a few beats, taking another swig of beer. "I was at Bootleg a few weeks ago."

"Really?" I raise my eyebrows.

He chuckles darkly. "Yeah, it's been a while, I know. I asked around about you. A couple of people said you still hadn't moved on. That you were a sad sack wasting the best years of your life."

I bristle immediately. "Hold on just a minute—" I begin, but he waves me off, like my indignation is boring.

"I know, I know. No one could ever replace Beau."

Ice rushes through me and I freeze in place. I want to tell him to get Beau's name out of his mouth, but he turns to me with such sad eyes, the words catch in my throat.

"And you're right. No one could, should, or ever would *replace* Beau. But that's not what it's about, mate. It's about…urgh."

He scowls and apparently changes his mind about his drink, chugging it down, his Adam's apple bobbing as a trickle of beer slips down his chin. He wipes it away irritably with the back of his hand and signals the bartender for another. Thankfully, he doesn't get me anything else.

"We were fucking idiots," he spits out. His leg is jiggling against the stool, and he starts ripping the coaster up, so the server gives him a fresh one under his new pint. "Breaking hearts like it was all a joke."

"I wouldn't say I exactly—" I try and protest, but he cuts me off again.

"I met someone."

I blink, too stunned to speak for a moment. "Really?" It's probably rude, but it was hard to imagine Marlon settling down back in the day, let alone now when he's looking so rough. However, I'm genuinely happy for him. "That's great, I—"

"No, *met*," he snaps. "As in past tense. Didn't you wonder why I stopped bugging you to go get pissed all the time?"

I did, but I honestly just figured I outgrew him as my grief became slightly less raw. Rather than ask him more questions, I sip my drink and wait for him to talk in his own time.

"He was beautiful," he says before laughing sadly and shaking his head. "Beau means beautiful, doesn't it? Anyway, he—my boy—was way too good for me. A clever clogs, sweet as candy floss, made the most incredible noises when I fucked him." I glance around, but the bartender is carefully not listening to us.

"So what happened?" I ask, unable to stop myself.

He scoffs and glowers into his pint. "Me, of course. I happened. I was terrified of commitment. I always said I never wanted to get tied down and I clung to that stupid notion like a fucking spectre clinging to the grave. I messed him around. Played games. Cheated on him. I was so busy getting him to break up with me so I wouldn't have to man the fuck up and marry him that he finally did. He dumped me, like he bloody should have. And when that last straw made him lose my number and disappear forever, then—*then* —I realised I'd lost the love of my fucking life and there was no way I was ever getting him back."

He takes another gulp of beer, licking his lips and trying not to make a big deal of rubbing at his moist eyes.

"Fucking *idiot*," he snarls.

The moment hangs between us for a heartbeat. "Marlon, I'm so sorry," I tell him sincerely.

He shakes his head and laughs. "Nah, don't worry about me. I'll be fine." He looks so far from fine I almost want to hug him. I refrain, though, sure he'd loathe that. "But you… you were always the gentleman of us two. The nice one, the kind one. You made it clear you didn't want to stick around but you'd always order them a taxi home or some bollocks. You had love. *Real* love. It's not your fault it got snatched away."

The lump rises in my throat, so I quickly take a mouthful of red wine to try and chase it away. It doesn't quite work. He's rambling, mixing up the guys I hooked up with and Beau, but I manage to follow what he's saying.

Marlon turns and looks earnestly at me. "You shouldn't be hiding yourself away still, Evan. You don't need to punish yourself for something that was in no way your fault. You deserve happiness as much as the next bloke. I just thought if I put your name in for that thing, it might give you a kick up the arse or something. Don't…don't be me. Or one day you'll look around and realise it's too late. That you let something incredible slip through your fingers like a fart in the wind. Don't be me."

I'm so stunned, I just watch as he shakes his head, downs the third pint, then slips off his stool to stand once more. He only sways a little, which is quite impressive given the circumstances. Still, I'm definitely worried about what he's doing to his liver.

"I won't bore you anymore," he mumbles. "Feel free to text me if you want. But I think I'm going to go and…and I don't know? Get my shit together maybe? New year's resolutions and all that bollocks you used to bang on about. You were always better than me. Don't shut everyone out before they even have a chance to get close. You deserve happiness. You're not trying to replace Beau. You just deserve to be happy. He'd want that."

And as if he hadn't just dropped the most devastating clanger of them all, he grips my shoulder briefly, then trudges towards the door, back out into the biting cold.

For several moments I just sit there, not really looking at anything, numb yet also prickling all over. With a jilt, my hand reaches out and seizes my wine glass almost of its own accord. Mimicking my departed friend, I gulp the rest of it down then take a deep breath.

Of everything I'd expected from this meeting tonight, it went in every other direction it possibly could have. I'm reeling enough without the wine hitting my system on an empty stomach.

Part of me wants to shake off his chilling warning and say I could never end up like him. But what exactly am I doing differently with my life? Barely letting anyone speak to me, let alone get close. Spending my evenings alone in my dark house. Trying my best to avoid the biggest, brightest holiday season of the whole year.

I was a parody of living. I might as well be haunting my own life.

Is that really what I think Beau would want for me? Is that how I should be honouring his memory?

I'm contemplating starting the second glass of wine after all, when my phone pings, telling me I've got a text. It pulls me from my reverie for a moment, enough to get me to fish my mobile from my pocket to see who's contacting me on a Saturday evening.

When I see the name, I almost drop the blasted thing. It appears, though, that Christian has more to say to me than just 'okay'.

CHRISTIAN: Hi, Evan. Thank you for letting me know yesterday that you were unaware we'd been matched for the Secret Santa blind date. I appreciate that you didn't choose to put yourself forward for it. However, I was excited to spend some time together. You seem nice, and my friend Charlie said you sometimes volunteer at Battersea Dog's Home, which I think is so kind. I felt like we could have enjoyed an afternoon today, even if it was last minute. I respect that you said you're not looking to date right now. I'm not necessarily, either. I just thought that since we got matched, it might have been worth exploring. I was really sad that you cancelled. If I don't hear back from you, I completely understand. But now at least you have all the facts. Enjoy your weekend, and if we don't speak again—Merry Christmas. Tian xxx"

I don't know how many times I reread the long message. At some point I realise that half of my second glass of wine has disappeared, and I push it away, worried if I don't, I'll get sloppy and do something I regret.

Christian—Tian—didn't have to write that. In fact, after the way Marlon and I mucked him around, I'd have thought he'd never want to talk to me again.

He thinks I'm kind?

I wasn't aware that anyone knew I tried to pop down to the big cats' and dogs' home at the weekend. I was planning on going there tomorrow, actually. Animals were simpler than people. I like letting them know that even if they've been abandoned or lost, they're still worthy of love.

Oh.

That lump rises in my throat again, and I recall Marlon's words just now.

You deserve to be loved. Don't be me.

I was abandoned, even if it wasn't on purpose. I've certainly been lost for a long time. If I was a dog, I wouldn't punish me for that. I'd say I deserve a good home to go to just like anyone else.

I'm not sure I want to take the metaphor that far, but the wine is certainly working through my system. I ask for a glass of water and decide to get some chips as soon as I leave. But before I do…I want to write another text. A good one.

Tian deserves that much.

CHAPTER 5

Tian

I DIDN'T EVEN EXPECT DADDY EVAN TO REPLY TO THE TEXT message I spent ages fussing over yesterday. In the end, Jude got a little impatient and told me to just send the bloody thing. Daddy Sai gave him a warning glare, but also gently agreed that I'd taken enough time over it and if I wanted to send it, I'd probably rewritten it as many times as I could.

But the response came less than half an hour later and I almost fell off the sofa in shock. He'd apologised again for the misunderstanding, which wasn't so surprising really. But then he'd said he'd been thinking about going for a walk in Regent's Park on Sunday and asked if I wanted to join him. He'd said he wasn't sure it would make up for any kind of date I'd been hoping for, but it would give us a chance to meet if nothing else.

I've always been monogamous and only dated one guy at a time before meeting Sai and Jude. So in many ways I'm still getting used to how we operate and I worry that by showing interest in someone else they might feel hurt, rejected or jealous no matter how many times they've told me that this is who they are. Still, when I confessed that I wanted to take

Evan up on his offer, I was taken aback by their delight and enthusiasm.

This is the first man I've been actually keen on since we became an official throuple. It's not like Sai and Jude aren't enough... sometimes they're too much if anything. I've never been lavished with attention like they do with me. So my life isn't lacking in romance or sex by a long shot.

But Evan Zegler just...I don't know. He's caught my sympathy like a fish on a line. I've noticed him several times at Bootleg, and the way he keeps his distance from everyone is so heartbreaking. He obviously doesn't want to be alone otherwise he'd stay at home. But I can't help but feel like he's afraid to connect with anyone in any meaningful way.

That's why when I saw he was doing the Secret Santa dates I jumped at the chance to sign up, specifically wording my application in the hopes that we'd get matched. When we did, I felt like I'd won a prize! But I guess part of me worried it was too good to be true because I never mentioned it to Daddy Sai or Jude. Jude found out accidentally at the club, and only then did I come clean.

I was wrong to do that. Keeping it from them made it feel like cheating, and that's not what it was or how we work as a polycule at all. Daddy Sai and I had a long conversation about that as we walked Bow on Saturday morning. I realise I'm still working through some hang-ups about my own feelings on us being open and all that.

But my Daddy is right, and the rules are quite simple. We always come home, and we always communicate. That's the only way our relationship will survive and thrive.

So it was actually quite fun to compose the perfect text with them to send to Daddy Evan, and even better to see how happy they were when he invited me out after all.

So here I am on Sunday afternoon in Regent's Park by the bandstand, waiting for Evan Zegler to arrive.

I decided to bring Bow with me, both because she's always up for a walk, but also as a bit of a shield. I won't feel quite so nervous if I've got my furry little four-legged protector with me. She's tugging a bit on her lead as she's eager to paddle at the edge of the lake, even though it's bloody freezing. But when I tell her it's alright and we have to wait here, she does settle down a bit.

"Daddy Tian is waiting for his new friend," I assure her. It is kind of hilarious that Sai is my Daddy, yet we're all daddies with a lowercase 'd' to Bow.

I wonder idly if Evan could be my Daddy as well.

Nope! That's against the rules I've made for myself. I don't want to put any pressure on this meeting. It's just a little wander around the park, that's it. A one-time thing. Evan might be *a* Daddy, but he's not *my* Daddy.

I appreciate that this is probably a big deal for him to come and meet me seeing as on Friday he freaked out and bolted at the idea of a real date. This is just…two people who share some common interests saying hello after the awkwardness of a misunderstanding.

Simple.

Yeah, right.

I notice him approaching when he's about twenty feet away. He's so handsome in a thick woollen black coat, his hands in his pockets as he looks out over the grass. There are a lot of people out and about despite the cold, but somehow, he manages to stand out. I study his profile and see in the light of day that his dark hair is just getting a hint of salt-and-pepper at the sides. He has a short, neatly trimmed beard that I want to rub against like a dog marking their territory.

Speaking of which, it's like Bow can tell I'm staring at him as she starts to bark and tug in his direction rather than towards the lake. I'd told him I was going to be in a blue parka with a faux fur lined hood. Also, that I'd have an excitable corgi attached to me. But I still wave eagerly as he looks my way. It's probably lame, but whatever. I've never been cool, and I barely qualify as an adult. It's why I enjoy being a little so much.

When our gazes meet, he pauses for a second. I remind myself that I might have seen him around at Bootleg before, but this is the first time he's actually laid eyes on me.

He's close enough that I can tell that his eyebrows rise. I swallow and try not to let my nerves get the better of me. I'm imagining that he's horrified by how pathetic I look and that he's just going to turn and walk away without a backwards glance.

Instead, a small smile tugs at his lips, and he continues moving forwards. "Evan?" I call out.

He nods. "You must be Tian, I take it?" He walks up as far as Bow's straining lead, then crouches down to offer her his hand to sniff. "And who's this sweetheart?"

His voice does something ridiculous to me, and I hope if he notices me shiver, he just thinks I got caught by a cold breeze. But it's so rich and soothing, I actually feel the opposite. Like I'm being warmed from the inside.

"Uhh, this is Bow," I croak eventually with a nervous laugh.

He looks sharply up at me, and for a second, I'm afraid I've already fucked up. "Bow?" he repeats.

"Yeah," I say with a nod. "After the Bow Bells. That's the area where she was rescued from, but it's also a fun Christmassy name—like what you decorate a present with."

Thankfully, Evan's shoulders drop, and he visibly relaxes. "Oh, B-o-w," he spells out. "I used to know someone…never mind. She's gorgeous. How long have you had her?"

"Well, she's not technically mine, although I guess she is."

I wrinkle my nose and remind myself that other people's

hang-ups are not my concern. If Evan is going to have an issue with my relationship status, it'll be better to realise it now and move on.

"Did you see in my profile that I'm dating a married couple? We've officially been together three years."

Evan stands and slips his hands into his pockets and begins to walk. Without thinking, I fall into step with him, and Bow happily trots along. "Yes, I did see that. My friend gave me the password he used so I could access the site myself. You wanted to meet with me still?"

All right. He's not called me a cheater and stormed off. That's a good sign. "Yeah," I say softly. "We're committed to each other, but we also have an open relationship. I've not really acted on that myself. But when I saw you were doing the Secret Santa…except now I know you weren't…" I trail off, unsure what I'm getting at.

We're taking the main path that curves around with trees to the left and the lake to our right. Evan is looking out over the water, thoughtfully.

"If you already have two boyfriends you love, why did you want to meet up with me so badly?" There isn't anything accusatory in his tone. He just seems curious. And maybe a little cautious.

I bite my lip before speaking. "My Daddy, Sai, always says I've got a lot of love to give. It doesn't mean I'm unhappy with them. Completely the opposite, actually. I just thought you seemed interesting."

He barks out a laugh that gets Bow yapping as well, and for a second we both grin down at her. Then he shakes his head. "I'm an accountant in his mid-forties. That's about as boring as it gets."

I frown. "But you're a Daddy, too, right? And you spend your free time looking after animals who have been forgotten by other people. Those are two big ticks in my book, if you ask me."

I didn't want to come at it head on and blurt out that I was worried he seemed terribly lonely. But the pregnant pause that follows my words confirms some of my suspicions.

Just when I'm tempted to prattle on about anything at all just to fill the silence, he speaks again.

"I haven't been anyone's Daddy in a very long time."

"Oh," I say, unsure how best to respond. "Um, I'm sorry."

A ghost of a smile tweaks his lips. "It's okay. It's my choice."

"Oh," I say again, glancing into the trees, like they might give me some inspiration. "I can see why you'd be so upset that your friend put your name in for the Secret Santa. Do you…I mean, you don't want to be a Daddy again, then?"

He frowns and looks my way before focusing ahead. "'Want' isn't quite the right word," he murmurs. "It's more like…I felt I couldn't. I shouldn't. But someone reminded me last night that by denying myself that, I could be missing out on something amazing."

I nod sagely, feeling like I was starting to understand him better. "Your friend."

"No," he says with a chuckle that goes straight to my heart. Our eyes meet, and his smile seems fractionally brighter this time. "You. Yes, my friend thought he was knocking some sense into me by signing me up to that event. And we had a shocking but good heart-to-heart about it. But it was your text that made me realise I've been punishing myself for something that isn't my fault. That I've not been living my life, just floating through a pale imitation of it. Yet you looked at me and thought I was 'kind'. No one's really seen me in so long…"

He shakes himself and looks away, a blush on his cheeks that's probably because of the wind.

"It's terrifying to contemplate change," he continues. "But I can't keep hiding away. I thought starting with a nice walk in the company of a handsome young man might not be too petrifying, and now here we are."

I won't even pretend that my blush is from the wind. He thinks I'm handsome? *Oh.*

"I have seen you around," I admit. "And I think anyone who makes time for rescued animals like Bow has a good heart."

He scoffs. "I wouldn't go so far as to call me good." There's a playful hint to his voice that makes me smile.

"I'm glad I'm not scary," I say bashfully, and we share a quick but warm glance. I decide to push my luck, not knowing how long he might want to walk. "For what it's worth, I think you'd be a great Daddy. To anyone!" I hastily add. "That wasn't...I didn't mean *me*, or *now*, or..."

Just stop talking, Tian.

He hums, apparently not horrified by how badly I put my foot in my mouth. "I think I've forgotten how to be a Daddy, to be honest. I'm so detached from everyone in my life. I can't imagine I'd be capable of taking care of a boy again, let alone a little. That's a big responsibility."

Apparently, my mouth didn't get the 'no talking' memo. "You probably just need some practice," I say without thinking, but it seems logical to me. If you're rusty at a skill, repetition is the best way to get good at it again.

"Practice?" he repeats.

I nod. "At being a Daddy," I explain.

"You mean date?" he says, the words already heavy with trepidation.

But I shake my head. "No, no. Practice Daddying with

someone who understands the situation. You wouldn't want to use some unsuspecting boy to get back on the horse. You just need a bit of time to remember how easy it is to take care of someone. I bet you're good at it. You've just forgotten. Do you have any little friends? Or Daddy friends that could bring their little and the three of you could have a nice, safe playdate?"

I'm getting so excited by this idea now. If it's his reservations that are holding Evan back, I'm certain this could be the perfect solution.

But he rubs his chin and shakes his head sadly at me. "I'm so out of touch with the lifestyle now, I wouldn't have a clue who to ask that would trust me not to fuck it up. *I* wouldn't trust me not to fuck it up."

I laugh, the words coming out of my mouth before I can stop them. "Well then, *I'll* help you!"

He comes to a halt and blinks at me. I stop and face him. Bow wraps her lead around my legs and wags her tail happily.

"You'd help me?" Evan asks slowly.

I nod, almost a tad annoyed he hasn't realised I'm a genius yet. "Yeah! We could meet at the club and go to the daycare? Or if you'd feel more at home at…well…home, I could come over to your place or something? I can bring some toys and we can…I don't know, make Christmas cookies or something? Snuggle and watch a film or…something."

I clamp my mouth shut before I can repeat myself for a fourth time. But he's staring at me with a sort of bewilderment. "Why would you do that? You don't know me. For all you're aware, I could absolutely deserve being all alone and miserable."

My heart contracts painfully at hearing him admit that he's both all alone and miserable about it. But I'm sure he's wrong about deserving that.

I narrow my eyes at him as Bow unwinds herself from

around my legs. "You said you've been punishing yourself for something that's not your fault," I remind him.

As if agreeing with me, a now free Bow chooses that moment to boop his leg with her snout. When he glances down at her, she wags her tail and smiles the way only corgis can do.

Evan looks back at me in confusion. "I know, but…"

When it becomes clear he doesn't know how to finish that sentence, I decide to help him out. "Genuinely, what's the worst that could happen? You realise you aren't actually any good at being a Daddy anymore, or just don't want to be one again? That's fine. I'll go back to my *two boyfriends,* one of which is actually *my Daddy.* Come on—this is as low stakes as it can get!"

He rubs his chin again, apparently thinking my words over. "I suppose."

Feeling brave, I tap his arm in a friendly way and wriggle on the spot for a moment. "That's the worst-case scenario. *Best*-case scenario is that you get your sea legs back, and you're out fishing for a brand-new boy to adore before the year is out!"

I feel like he really, truly looks at me then. "And you wouldn't feel put out by that or used?"

I shrug. "Part of why my boyfriends and I work—or so they say as they're more experienced than me—is that they don't go looking for anything in particular. They're just open to the possibilities of what might come their way. That's like this. All I wanted was to meet you and to get to know you better, because you intrigued me. We've done that, and now I'm going to help you! It's as easy as that."

"I'm not sure it is," Evan says with a chuckle. "But…the idea of a simple playdate doesn't sound too frightening, I guess. Perhaps you could come over for a few hours after work? Not that I even asked what hours you do. Oh, I'm already getting this wrong."

I wave him off before he can fret over nothing. "Regular nine-to-five, like I assume an accountant would also work?"

"Yes," he confirms.

His smile is so sweet and shy, I want to throw myself into his arms and tell him everything's going to be okay. I want to call him 'Daddy' and see how he reacts. But I manage to catch myself. No sense in rushing ahead and scaring the poor man for real.

"Then it's a date," I say, not wanting to give him a chance to talk himself out of something I'm absolutely certain he's going to love. Something he deserves to have again. I don't know why he's been afraid to rejoin the lifestyle, but it's Christmas, and this feels like a gift only I can give him.

He rubs his chest and looks out over the water. But then he turns back and smiles at me. It's still faint, but it's there, like a promise of better days to come.

"It's a date," Daddy Evan agrees.

CHAPTER 6

Sai

"You know you didn't have to come with me," Tian says with a chuckle.

We're walking around Russell Square—the actual small square park, not just the general area. The grass is a surprisingly lush green underneath the swathes of orange and brown leaves that have fallen from the now bare trees. Through the crooked branches, various buildings the same colour as the leaves loom over us, several stories high.

Night has basically fallen, but the park is illuminated by the usual lampposts and the outdoor lighting incorporated into the architecture. Several Christmas trees have also been set up for the season as well as a charming archway of fairy lights that I'm walking Tian under.

He grins up at me and I'm aware that I'm being overprotective, but I can't help it. I sigh and reach out to squeeze his hand through both our gloves.

"I know I didn't have to come, but you're my baby boy."

"And I love that," he assures me. "However, you didn't have to meet me after work all the way from Clapham. I could have made it to Evan's place by myself."

"It gave me an excuse to leave the house," I insist.

As an architect, I have the luxury of working remotely from home most of the time. Sometimes I only get out to walk Bow, and actually do benefit from having an excuse to put real clothes on instead of jogging bottoms and an old T-shirt. Meeting Tian at Goodge Street station meant I didn't even have to change Tube lines, and now we can enjoy a nice twenty-minute stroll together.

Of course, he immediately calls me on my bullshit.

"I know we like to pretend I'm five years old," he teases. "But I am, in fact, twenty-five."

"And I will fret over you until I'm a hundred and five," I assure him with a wink.

He's quiet for a few moments as we walk along. We're about halfway to the address that Evan gave us, so I don't push him to say what he's thinking as we've still got some time.

"Are you worried about me?" he asks eventually.

I consider my words before speaking. "I know you're perfectly capable of taking care of yourself and making good choices," I say truthfully. "And I know you've been clear with yourself, Jude and I, and Evan about your expectations for this evening."

"But?" Tian prompts playfully, making me smile.

He knows me too well. "But I know you've been doing a lot of thinking about what it means for you to be interested in someone that isn't me or Jude. I wanted to show you that I support you a thousand percent, even if this date is just some innocent Daddy/little time." I glance at him and grin. "Although if things change and you decide you want the very handsome older Daddy to fuck you silly, that's absolutely fine, too. We'll just want to hear all the juicy details afterwards, okay?"

He blushes under his hat and scarf, but he doesn't look uncomfortable. "I know, Daddy," he says softly.

It gives me such a thrill when he says that out in public, even after all this time. Jude has been my everything since the day we met. But Tian and I have a different dynamic, and it brings me so much joy.

Jude was annoyed he couldn't be here to escort Tian as well, but he's on a dayshift so won't get home until around eight o'clock. I do, however, fully intend on finding a way of making it up to him that he had to miss out before we come back and pick Tian up at ten.

My baby boy is right, and there's nothing stopping him making that very simple journey alone. But as this is an evening where he specifically wants to regress, I thought accompanying him would help him get into little headspace before he arrives. Little boys don't get the Tube alone, after all.

But in truth, I know that Jude and I both want to make sure this man who upset our baby last week is actually worth his time and affection now. Plus, looking at his address, I know Jude wants to have a snoop around his house as much as I do. It looks *fancy*.

I sense that Tian is still worrying about things, so I swing our joined arms and smile brightly at him, letting my playful Daddy side come to the surface. "Is my Baby Tee excited to make a new friend?" I ask in a sing-song voice. "Have you packed your favourite toys to show him?"

Tian beams at me and I can practically see the tension fading from his body. He shakes the duffle bag he's got slung over his shoulder. "I didn't know what Daddy Evan would have as he said he's out of practice, so I've brought all sorts!" he declares proudly. "Toys and books and comfy clothes I can change into and even my special plate, and spoon, *and* beaky."

'Beaky' is what he calls the bamboo beaker that's part of his train themed kids set. Evan said he'd make dinner for them both, so I'm glad Tian thought to pack his age-appropriate crockery and cutlery if he wants an evening of being his lovely little self.

Despite all my protests otherwise, I do feel a flash of worry that this man is going to treat Tian properly. I know that he's had some issues, and Tian wants to help him get back into Daddying. But if he makes my boy feel stupid or vulnerable, I won't be impressed. I feel like I'm handing over my most prized possession.

When Jude hooks up with someone else, I never worry unnecessarily, because that cheeky brat can defend himself all day long. But Tian is so sweet and gentle. When Jude and I first met him, I would have even gone so far as to call him fragile. He's come a long way since then, but still, he's mine to protect and this other man better respect what an extraordinary gift he's being given.

We're walking down Evan Zegler's street now. It's long and wide compared to so many other roads in central London. The terraced townhouses are all five stories high including the basement levels hidden behind individual black wrought iron fencing. Every few metres stand trees as tall as the buildings themselves. They're bare like the ones in Russell Square, but in spring and summer they look like they'll give a lot of leafy shade.

It's quiet and I see numerous other people walking purposefully along, possibly heading home after a day at work. I wonder what it might be like to live in an area like this. Would the neighbours be friendly or terrible snobs? In typical London fashion, we don't know another soul in our apartment complex aside from our neighbour, Mrs Havisham, who sometimes looks in on Bow for us. Is it the same here?

A lot of the houses have Christmas decorations and fairy lights outside, but as we near the number Evan told us, it's quickly apparent that his place is dark and a little uninviting. I try not to judge. Some people keep their festivities indoors for various reasons and he might currently be towards the back of the house, leaving the front gloomy.

Still…I do feel Tian slow down next to me. I wouldn't blame him if he was feeling a little trepidation. At first glance, Evan hasn't exactly rolled out the red carpet for my boy. Tian mentioned that Even had said he was out of practice with people. But ultimately, he has invited Tian over, so I think he should make an effort to welcome him.

We walk past the railing, and I glance down to look at the basement window. Ah—that light is on at least, which gives me hope that the house isn't vacant. The black-and-white tiles under our feet are in a cheerful diamond arrangement. The wide front door is a soothing teal colour with a heavy looking brass knocker in its centre.

With an apparent burst of confidence, Tian rushes forward and lifts the bulbous metal, banging twice. Then he scuttles back to wait by my side. I spy a doorbell that might be better to use considering the size of the house. I'm not sure how well sound will travel inside there. But I decide not to undermine Tian and give it a minute before suggesting we try that.

Just as I'm itching to press the button, a light comes on through the semicircle window above the door. Then it's pulled back to reveal a flustered man in his mid-forties. He's white with dark hair that's showing just a touch of silver at the sides, and he's wearing well-fitting light blue jeans and a ribbed navy jumper.

And he's *handsome*. Christ, Tian showed us a couple of photos he found online, but they don't do Evan justice. He's got a strong jaw under his short, dark beard and he greets us with wide, piercing blue eyes. His smile is nervous, but he sighs when he catches sight of Tian.

If he's going to melt at the sight of my boy, that earns a significant amount of favour from me.

"You came," he says, almost sounding surprised.

"Of course!" Tian cries, rocking on the balls of his feet. "I've been excited to see you all day!"

It's obvious to me after all these years that he's allowing himself to slip quickly into his little self, and that means he trusts Evan. So I need to as well. Unfortunately, it's difficult for me in that moment to remember that my boy isn't technically five years old. The urge to shield him surges through me, and I turn to face Evan, ready to challenge him on the spot about his intentions towards my baby.

Except Evan is still looking at Tian like he can't believe he's real. "I've been looking forward to seeing you, too, Tian," he says breathlessly.

He seems like he really means it. Mentally, I stand down, willing to give him some space before I jump down his throat.

He blinks and it's as if he realises I'm there. "Oh, hello."

He thrusts his hand towards me, and I quickly remove my glove before pressing my palm against his. The squeeze he gives me is strong but not in a way that suggests he's trying to prove anything. It simply conveys confidence to me that I wasn't expecting.

"You must be one of Tian's boyfriends."

"Yes, this is Daddy Sai," Tian informs him proudly.

I raise my eyebrows, pleased that Evan hasn't got his knickers in a twist about Tian already being in a relationship. Tian did say he'd explained everything and that Evan had been cool. But I'll be honest I might possibly have had a hidden agenda in surprising him on his doorstep. It's all well and good to say our arrangement doesn't matter to him. But it's a bit harder to ignore when the guy you're about to have a date with is standing next to his current boyfriend who loves him dearly.

Evan just nods at us both, though, before waving his hand. "Come in, come in. It's cold out there. Truth be told, it's a bit cold in here. I don't bother heating the whole house. Downstairs is all cosy, though. That's where I thought we could spend the evening, Tian, if that's all right with you?"

Checking in with my boy is also a green flag. Some Daddy Doms think they can just boss their littles or subs around with no questions asked. If the other person consents to that, I guess it could work for some people. But Tian needs to be cared for, not bullied.

I love the way he beams at Evan, who is already gently taking my boy's coat and hanging it on the wall. "Cosy sounds perfect!" Tian enthuses. "Your house is amazing!"

That smile doesn't reach Evan's eyes. "It was my parents'. I inherited it. I don't even use half the rooms, but…" He shakes himself ever so slightly and puts on a brighter smile for Tian. "Now you're here, it's going to feel a lot less empty." Then he glances at me. "And is Daddy Sai going to stay for the evening?"

Okay, wow. Another green flag. Whatever issues this man has been struggling with, he clearly doesn't have a jealous nature. He almost looks hopeful that I'll agree.

"Oh, I need to get home to meet my husband when he gets back from work," I explain. "I just wanted to drop Tian off." I itch to explain why, but my reasons seem uncharitable in that moment. "Thank you, though," I say instead. "That's very kind of you to extend the invitation. I think Tian's been really looking forward to having you all to himself, however."

"Yes, Daddy," Tian says, looking coy and snuggling up to

me. He looks at Evan through his dark eyelashes. "I'm happy you got to meet each other, though!"

My gaze catches Evan's. "Me, too," I say genuinely.

"Well, would you like to follow us downstairs, at least?" Evan suggests to me. He picks up Tian's duffle that he dropped to the floor when he took his coat off. "Then you can be assured it's a great deal warmer than this old entrance hall."

We share a chuckle, and I nod. "Sure, that would be nice."

The walls are white and the tiles underfoot are brown and cream as well as a little ragged from wear. There are no photos or works of art hanging up and the lights on the brass chandelier above our heads are set low. I can't deny it's chilly and uninviting, but Evan seems aware of that, at least.

Tian has kicked his shoes off and grabs Evan's hand. "Is it this way?" he asks, pointing down the hall to where a staircase bends around to the right. Evan's wide-eyed gaze drops to their connected hands and for a second he just stands there with his mouth open.

"Oh, um, yes," he splutters with a smile. "Why don't you lead the way, Tian?"

Delighted, my baby bounces down the corridor, pulling Evan with him. I follow, giving them some space. We pass by a couple of closed doors, and I wonder what lies beyond them, but there's no real way of knowing. If this used to be Evan's parents' home, perhaps there are rooms where he's just shut their belongings and memories away.

Tian, Jude and I are incredibly lucky that our parents are not only still with us, but we have good relationships with all of them. My dad probably had the hardest time adjusting to a gay son because apparently, I 'just didn't seem like that' when I was growing up. But my mum talked sense into him years ago and she boasts to anyone who'll listen that she has not one but two very handsome sons-in-law.

Looking at the closed doors and glancing up at the rest of the dark, cold house, I wonder what sort of family Evan comes from.

They're still holding hands as Tian drags Evan down the stairs. I could have probably left then feeling satisfied that Tian was going to be okay. But after Evan went out of his way to invite me to check out the basement level, I don't want to be rude. I have a feeling that from one Daddy to another, he wants me to be assured by seeing where my boy is going to be spending his evening.

Green flag.

Going down the stairs is like sinking into warm water. The heating is absolutely cranked up on this level and I almost take my scarf off to appreciate it. But I really do want to leave them to it soon, so I refrain.

"Oh, wow!" Tian cries as I walk past a small bathroom at the foot of the stairs and join them both on the lower floor. My boy has let go of Evan's hand and is slowly spinning around, taking the space in. "You're right, this is cosy!"

Evan looks just the tiniest bit proud. He's got Tian's duffle hanging from his shoulder, and he twists the strap between his hands. "Thank you, sweetheart," he says.

The term of endearment hangs in the air for a second, but not in a bad or awkward way. Just weighted. Important. Tian smiles sweetly at Evan, and my own heart swells at the tenderness of such a simple moment.

My boy is right. This is a lovely space. A reasonably large square supporting pillar stands in the centre of what is otherwise a completely open room. To my left is a kitchen and to my right beyond the stairs we just descended is a rectangular dining table big enough to fit eight people. A large L-shaped sofa separates both those areas to create a living room vibe on the left with a massive TV hanging from the wall. Beyond that are French doors that presumably lead out to a garden that's currently hidden by the darkness of the night.

A delicious scent of roasting chicken fills the air. Instead of utilising the overhead downlights, Evan has lit a few lamps. I see a bookcase full of battered paperbacks with one novel on the coffee table by the sofa, a bookmark slotted in halfway through the pages. The space is still kind of sparse compared to the borderline chaos bursting from mine and Jude's flat. But it's enough that I feel like this is probably where Evan spends most of his time in this enormous house all by himself.

He's not by himself anymore, though. He has my Tian, and I genuinely hope they'll have a lovely time together.

"Okay, baby boy," I say brightly, catching Tian's attention. "I'm going to head home now. Jude and I will see you at ten o'clock unless you message me to tell me otherwise."

He skips over and hugs me. "Yes, Daddy."

I smile and kiss the tip of his nose. "Are you going to be good for Evan?"

It's funny how offended my baby looks at me. "I'm *always* good, Daddy."

Chuckling, I give him another chaste kiss on his cheek. "Of course you are," I mollify him. Then I look over and meet Evan's eyes. He's watching us cautiously. "I'll let myself out," I assure him. "You two have fun."

He slips his hands into the pockets of his jeans. "I'm sure we will," he says.

I sure they will, too.

It's cold as I make my way back upstairs and then even more so out in the night air. But my heart is warm.

Tian isn't just doing this man a favour by reminding him what it's like to have a playdate with a little. I'm confident my baby is going to enjoy himself and realise that he's always free to meet up with someone new with mine and Jude's blessing. That warms my heart up more than enough for the walk back to the Tube.

With one of my boys in safe hands, it's time to think about the other.

I think he deserves a treat as well, and I'm just the Daddy to give it to him.

CHAPTER 7
Evan

I DON'T KNOW HOW LONG IT'S BEEN SINCE I HAD ANYONE VISIT this house. I've been nervous about Tian coming over all day, racing back from the office to make sure the place was in order. I realised too late that yes, it's tidy, but it was as if I could see everything with fresh eyes.

What I saw was a sad and lonely life.

Before I could spiral too deep into melancholy, I forced myself to start cooking. Again, I haven't prepared a meal for anyone else in years. But I always did enjoy puttering around in the kitchen and hosting. This evening, focusing on not burning anything kept my sanity in check until I heard the door knocker.

As soon as I saw Tian I was just so happy that I forgot for a moment to be anxious he'd feel horribly unwelcome in my draughty old house. But then he'd surprised me by bringing his boyfriend—his actual Daddy—Sai along and…well…

During my wild days I slept with a lot of guys, but I have always had a weakness for sweet, joyous younger men. One glance at Sai told me that he's undoubtedly a Dom and his presence at my house was purely meant to remind me that

Tian is his and I had better treat him right. I'd guess he's in his mid-thirties, so younger than me but not *young*, and as a Daddy I'd assume his usual taste ran to sweet subs like Tian, not older men with no interest in being dominated.

Yet I was immediately attracted to him.

It had wrong-footed me for sure, primarily because the only person I want to be thinking about tonight is the beautiful Tian. However, there was something about seeing this Daddy and little together that drew me in.

Physically, they contrast each other nicely. Sai is taller and dark skinned—I'd guess he's of South Asian origin—whereas Tian is small and pale. But there was something I saw in their mannerisms during our brief time together as well. The way Tian moves is light and delicate, whereas Sai radiates strength and calm confidence.

When I shook his hand, I knew from that moment I wanted to impress him.

Not my usual behaviour at all.

I'm probably just keen to explore how they operate as that's what I'm looking for myself. A boy to be a Daddy for. It can be a tricky balance and I'm no doubt looking to study Sai and Tian as a couple. Or a throuple, I guess. Sai said he'd be returning with Jude, their other partner, later on.

I want to know how three people navigate a relationship. Two is difficult enough. I want to talk about everything. But I'm painfully aware that Tian and I have only agreed to this one evening, at least for now, and Sai probably isn't interested in anything with me beyond checking that I'm going to take care of his baby boy properly.

Which I fully intend to do. But as soon as Sai leaves, it suddenly dawns on me that this is really happening and now I'm the one that's supposed to be in charge. But then Tian comes skipping over to me across the room and makes grabby hands for his bag.

"I brought some things with me!" he announces. "Do you want to see?"

That snaps me out of my paralysis. All I have to do is be here for Tian and make sure he's taken care of. I'd quite forgotten what it was like to have someone look at you as if your opinion was the only one in the whole world that matters.

It's mildly terrifying but also breathtakingly beautiful.

Tian just needs to be seen—much like the way he already saw me. He needs to be treated like he's important. That's going to be easy enough, surely. Because I've only known him such a short time, but I can already tell he's an incredibly special boy. So sweet and thoughtful and full of life.

And it's not hard to see him when he's so gorgeous. If I'd been paying any attention at Bootleg recently, I'm sure he would have caught my attention with his dark curls and pretty eyes. He's got such a petite, lithe body, exactly the kind I find so exhilarating underneath me as I take care of my boy in the most intimate way possible.

My thoughts can't go there, though. That's not what tonight is about. But needless to say, I'm effortlessly drawn to Tian and want to tend to his every need.

"I'd love it if you showed me what you've brought with you," I say warmly, handing over the bag. "Shall we sit on the sofa?"

He nods and bounces over to plop down on the cushions, already unzipping the duffle as I join him by his side. "These are my favourite jammies," he announces, pulling out trousers and a long-sleeved T-shirt with cartoon airplanes and happy-faced clouds on. "I brought my slippers as well because I hate cold feet. Can I put them all on?"

"Absolutely," I say without hesitation, wanting him to be as comfortable as possible in my home.

But I'm already kicking myself. I've planned dinner and

found a few films on the streaming platforms I have that we could maybe watch, but I'd kind of forgotten how much *stuff* a little might need to get them in the right headspace or just enjoy themselves.

I got rid of all of those things that used to be in this house. It makes me sad to realise it in that moment, but I can't say I regret it. The pain from seeing anything of Beau's was too much.

However, now I'm worried that I've fucked up my time with Tian before it's even begun. I should have bought some toys, at least a teddy bear or something. And of course he'd want little clothes. Those are harder to get on short notice, but the fact that he's had to bring all his own stuff makes me feel like a failure.

To my horror, I suddenly notice that Tian is staring at me with a tote bag in his hands. I think it has building blocks of some kind in. Did he say something I missed?

"Sorry, sweetheart?" I say, hoping I haven't made things too much worse.

But Tian reaches out and touches my arm, his hold firm through my jumper. "Are you okay, Daddy?" he asks.

The lump appears out of nowhere, so thick in my throat it threatens to choke me. My eyes burn and I make a strangled noise. "Uhh…"

He carefully places the bag down on the couch and steps closer to me.

"Can I hug you?" he asks in a small voice. I don't trust myself to speak, so I simply nod. He slips his arms around me and rests his head on my shoulder, his chest firm against mine.

How many years has it been since I was held like this? I actively avoided it when I was hooking up. The pressure of his body clinging to mine unlocks something in my heart.

I'm shivering from head to toe as I wrap my arms around his back and squeeze him tightly.

"I'm sorry if calling you 'Daddy' made you sad," he mumbles into my clothes.

I shake my head and rub his back. "It was wonderful, sweetheart," I tell him honestly. I give myself a couple of seconds to take some deep breaths. "It's just been a long time since I was anyone's Daddy. That does make me a bit sad, but it's also lovely. You didn't do anything wrong."

I feel him sag against me in what I assume is relief. "Oh, good." He leans back and looks at me. He's so close I can see the flecks of green in his hazel eyes. "Shall I keep calling you 'Daddy', or would something else be better tonight?"

Before I can stop myself, I lift one of my hands and brush back some of his hair by his forehead. I've missed these kinds of intimate, innocent touches far more than I realised.

"You're so thoughtful," I murmur. "Such a kind boy. I'd love to be your Daddy this evening."

He blushes, glancing away as he bites his lip and grins. His obvious delight makes warmth rush through me like hot chocolate. The really good kind with whipped cream and marshmallows.

Now we've got through that first awkward hiccup, I feel a little more reassured. We fumbled, but we didn't fall.

If only for tonight, I am Tian's Daddy. He's entrusted me to do this, and I won't let him down. I can do this. It's in my blood, it's who I am. I need to stop second-guessing everything and just fucking relax.

"How about," I say as I rub his back before letting him go, "you take these super-duper jammies into the small bathroom back there so you can get changed? Then Daddy will get dinner on the table."

He grins and lurches down. I expect him to snatch up his pyjamas, but instead he dives back into the duffle bag and pulls out a relatively large but shallow Tupperware box. I suspect it's designed to hold cupcakes, but when he pulls off the lid, he proudly shows me a children's dining set.

Back in the old days, I would have said it was plastic, but it's probably bamboo. Either way, it's got cartoon trains all over everything, and between that and his pyjamas, I suspect this little has a love of transport. I still feel guilty for not thinking to buy him something like that myself, and the idea flitters through my brain that I can buy him something with cars or space shuttles for next time.

There probably isn't going to be a next time, though, so I quickly shelve that thought.

Tian seems so excited about his trains that I'm not sure he's particularly concerned about my error. If he can ignore my lack of preparation, I can try to as well.

"Am I allowed to have dinner with this?" he asks me.

Bless him for asking permission. I nod and gently take the box from his hands. "Of course you can, Tian. And look! You've even got a bowl we can put your desssert in, too. Isn't that smart."

He beams and swivels on the spot. "Thank you, Daddy." Now he picks up the pyjamas from where he dropped them, but he hugs them to his chest and doesn't move towards the bathroom yet. "Daddy?"

"Yes, Tian," I say, wondering what's got him looking so serious. *Oh, damn it.* I realise suddenly that I never checked with him that he's going to like what I'm cooking. It's just chicken with potatoes (that I still need to mash) and some vegetables. But he could be vegan. A lot of people are these days. What if—

"Daddy, would you like to use my special little name?"

All thoughts of food vanish from my mind. I blink at him, all the air whooshing from my lungs. "Your special name?" I repeat. He nods and looks at me bashfully through his long, beautiful lashes. "I'd be honoured. If that's what you want?"

He nods again and scrunches up the pyjamas. "Tian is my big boy name. But I'm just a baby now, so I think Daddy should call me 'Tee'."

"Tee?" I clarify. "Like the letter?"

"Uh-huh. Baby Tee." He jabs his thumb towards his chest. "That's me!"

"Tee," I say again, like I'm making sure it rolls properly off my tongue. "Thank you for sharing that with me. I think it's a perfect name for a perfect boy."

His blush deepens and he purposefully avoids my gaze. "I'm not perfect, Daddy. But I promise I'll try and be the best little boy I can for you. You can tell Daddy Sai when he comes back that I was a good boy. You'll see."

My heart swells. I've known a lot of guys who like praise —as well as a lot that don't—but I think Tian is one of those special boys who really needs it.

That I can do, no problem.

Feeling emboldened by our cuddle and his confession, I reach out and cup the side of his face with my hand. He sighs, nuzzling against my palm and looking at me once more. "You've already been such a good boy for Daddy," I say, the words making happiness bubble inside me like Champagne. "I bet you can put your jammies on all by yourself *and* wash your hands for dinner, can't you?"

He rises on his tiptoes like he's ready to take flight. "Yes, yes, I can do that, Daddy! Do you want to time me?"

I chuckle as he rocks back on his heels. *God.* When was the last time this house held a fraction of the life that's been breathed into it in the last half an hour?

"There's no rush, sweetheart. I want you to be careful when you change your clothes, and I want you to fold the old ones neatly so you can leave them on the sofa. Then, I want you to make sure you wash all the germs off your hands. That will give Daddy time to mash the potatoes with lots of butter. Um…" My confidence wavers. "Unless you're vegan? I've cooked chicken but if that's not okay…?"

"Is it free range chicken?" he asks tentatively.

"Yes, it is," I say without needing to check. I always buy free range and whatever else they call it when the animals have been treated well.

He exhales in relief. "Then that sounds yummy."

Veering from one extreme to another, my confidence comes back and pushes me just out of my comfort zone enough to tease this sweet boy.

"And are you going to be good for Daddy and eat all your vegetables?"

He wrinkles his nose. "What *kind* of vegetables?" I like that he's getting the details before committing to anything.

"Carrots, peas and sweetcorn," I tell him.

He giggles and nods. "Okay, they're allowed. I'll be good and eat them all."

This time when he stands on his tiptoes, he leans in and presses a quick kiss to my cheek, just like his actual Daddy, Sai, did to him before he left. I'm so stunned that I don't move as he scampers off to the bathroom to get changed.

Slowly, I lift my hand and brush my fingertips against where his lips grazed my skin. The depth of what I've been missing for the last several years threatens to overwhelm me. This time when the lump rises in my throat, I make myself relax.

"You're okay," I murmur to myself. "You're doing okay. Tian is fine. You're taking care of him."

I am. And that starts with feeding him. I've still got the box filled with his dinner set in my hand, so take it over to the sink to give it a quick rinse, just in case it needs it. Once it's all dried, I get the pan where I left the potatoes on the lowest heat so I can now dollop a significant amount of butter all over them and attack them with my masher.

It's only as I start putting Tian's portion on his smaller plate that I have a moment where I realised I've stopped worrying about everything and am just enjoying myself. This evening isn't just for him. In fact, he's doing it *specifically* for me. But until now, I'd just been fretting that I was going to fuck it up and inadvertently hurt him.

What was it he said in the park about best-case scenarios? I've spent so many years hiding myself away, determined to see the worst of the world. I've forgotten what it's like to feel hope blossom in my chest.

Obviously, tonight I'm just borrowing Tian as my little. But for the first time in forever…I wonder if I have it in me to be someone's Daddy again.

CHAPTER 8

Jude

I'M DEAD ON MY FEET AS I TRUDGE UP THE STAIRS AND ONTO the floor of our apartment. Thankfully, I work on the elective surgery ward, so there generally aren't ever any harrowing emergencies. But bloody hell it was still busy as fuck today. I don't think I sat down for the entire twelve hours, and I was lucky to grab half a sandwich for lunch. At least I'm allowed to keep a big reusable water bottle at the nurses' station so I can stay hydrated. But…yeah…

Brain is mush. I'd actually forgotten that Tian was off on his exciting Daddy/little date tonight with the mysterious Evan until I was almost all the way home. Sai said he was going to drop him off like it was his first day at nursery, and I'm not sure who's benefit that was for—Sai or Tian. But I do think it's sweet and I'm looking forward to hearing every detail from my husband any minute now.

After a shower, though. I always do that as soon as I get in. Otherwise, I feel like I'm trailing germs everywhere. And find some food. Ohh, I wonder if there are any leftovers in the fridge. Or anything I can just throw in the microwave and not think about. I doubt Sai had time to cook, so—

I've barely turned my key in the door when it's pulled sharply inwards, taking my bunch of keys with it. Sai fills the gap between the door and its frame, fixing me with a piercing gaze. "You're late," he growls.

My stomach drops. Late for what? Have I forgotten something important? Is Tian's date another night? Have I—

Hold up.

I blink and take in the black leather trousers and dark purple mesh top Sai is wearing, all of which clings to his fit body like a second skin. He's lean rather than muscular, but to me he's absolutely perfect.

Suddenly, I'm not so tired anymore.

"I'm so sorry I'm late, Sir," I whisper, looking up and down the corridor. There's no one there, but it adds to the feeling that this is something illicit, and that gets my blood pumping in an instant. With a shaking hand, I ease the keys out of the lock and clutch them to my chest.

Sai grabs the front of my coat and yanks me inside the flat, slamming the door shut. I drop my keys in the bowl on the little table next to us and let my rucksack fall to the floor. He shoves my back against the door and his tongue down my throat. I whimper, my knees going weak as I surrender to him.

"Filthy," he snarls into my mouth. "Dirty, *dirty* boy. You need a thorough clean."

"Y-yes, Sir," I manage to stammer between rough kisses. Poor Bow has trotted over to me to say 'hello', and I manage to rub her head. "It's okay, girl. Daddy Sai and daddy Jude will be back in a minute."

Sai hauls me off the door and shoves me down the corridor. "Get in that bathroom, now," he snaps, his eyes blazing.

Holy hell, my skin is on fire and my cock is already jumping to attention, trying to escape my scrubs. I shrug off my coat as I stumble down the narrow hallway, desperately shedding the rest of my clothes. Sai follows, casually stepping over the trail I'm leaving, but never taking his heated eyes off me.

"Being slow will only get you punished more," he warns.

I scramble into the bath, going behind the glass screen to turn the water on. It's cold as it hits my skin, making me yelp, but I stand under the spray until it begins to heat up. As it does, Sai closes the door, leans against the wall, and crosses his arms over his chest.

"Clean yourself up, you filthy fucking whore," he hisses darkly. "I'm waiting."

I grab the all-in-one hair and shower gel, squirting it on the loofah before hastily rubbing the suds all over myself. The scent of coconut fills the steamy air as I do, and Sai keeps his gaze locked with mine the entire time. Even though I'm rushing, I make sure to give a moment's extra time to my most intimate areas.

I can't have been under the water more than sixty seconds before I twist the dial and shut off the supply, leaving me shivering as droplets run down my body. Sai smirks and throws me a towel, which I catch clumsily.

"On the bed, now," he says. "Cock down, arse up, legs spread, hands above your head."

I give a cursory swipe of the towel over my body before hopping out of the tub and yanking the door open. He grabs the towel back from me, presumably to hang back up on the heated rail, leaving me to dash to the bedroom naked.

Luckily, Bow is aware that when her daddies play these sorts of games, it's best to go lie down in her bed until they're done. Then they'll give her lots of cuddles and treats afterwards. So I only give a quick check to make sure she's not in our room before throwing myself down on the mattress of our super king-sized bed and display myself the way Sai told me to.

He hums low and dangerous as he stalks into the bedroom, closing that door behind him like the others. It makes me feel trapped.

I love it.

The bed dips as he kneels between my legs and runs a hand down my damp spine. "What are you?" he demands.

"A…a filthy slut," I utter.

He grunts out a laugh. "Not so filthy anymore. Someone had to sort you out. Say 'thank you'."

"Thank you, Sir." I'm panting and my cock is almost painful under me against the mattress, but I know better than to try and relieve myself. Sai is in charge now. All I have to do is submit to him.

"Who do you belong to?" he asks as he pulls my cheeks apart.

"You, Sir, *ohhh…*"

My eyes roll back in my head as he licks a stripe from my balls all the way across my taint and my crack. Then his tongue is plundering my hole, and all I can do is lie there and take it. My hands curl around the bedsheets, flexing and squeezing as I try not to squirm too much as he devours me.

"Squeal all you want, little piggy," he mumbles against my sensitive skin. "You're going to take whatever I give you, aren't you? Whores who can't even show up on time don't get a say in the matter."

"Yes, Sir. Sorry, Sir," I say breathlessly, knowing full well that what he wants is for me to make a considerable amount of noise. He wants to know I'm enjoying myself. He wants to feel how he's in charge and that my body in that moment is nothing more than his plaything.

My trapped cock leaks at the thought of it.

I'm not sure how long he tortures me with his lips, tongue and fingers, but by the time he unzips his trousers, pushes them down his thighs, and slides his rock-hard lubricated cock inside me, my hole is a slick, quivering mess.

"Take it, you fucker, *take it*," he cries as he thrusts hard and fast. I wail and cling onto the bedding as he rides my arse, helpless to his raging lust. I float in my submission, my skin burning as he makes himself feel sublime.

I'm not sure how long he pleasures himself on me for, but then he's bellowing as he comes, filling me up to the brim. Before he's even soft, he yanks himself free, and then he's pulling my cheeks apart again so he can eat my sensitive hole out once more, moaning as he slurps out his own cum.

I'm practically sobbing by the time he flips me over, my red cock bouncing off my belly. "You're allowed to come for me now, whore," he rasps, before swallowing me down to the root and sucking roughly, unconcerned if his teeth scratch along my shaft.

"Yes, Sir! Yes!" I scream, hardly needing any encouragement at all. Within seconds, I'm shooting my load into his mouth where he drinks every drop.

He keeps suckling me until I go limp and begin to whine. Then he lets my cock flop from his lips as he starts pressing kisses along my hip and stomach, caressing my sides until he collapses on the bed beside me. He kicks his trousers off the rest of the way and removes his top so we're both naked, then gathers me up in his arms and hugs me tightly.

"Welcome home, baby," he says as he presses more kisses against my hair.

I groan and cling to him, laughing with what energy I have left. "Hi," I mumble.

"Did you like that?"

Why's he asking stupid questions when I'm in a post-orgasm bliss? Unable to form words, I give him a thumbs-up that makes him belly laugh.

"Good," he says. "Both my boys had to be spoiled tonight.

I've got you some dinner sorted when you feel able to walk. Then we need to go and pick up Tian from his date."

"Love you," I mumble against his chest. After a while, I manage to rouse from my stupor. Blinking, I smile up at him, and he fondly traces his fingers along my jaw. "You dropped Tian off okay?" I ask, my voice croaking from all the sex screams.

Before answering, Sai takes my hand and helps me stand. "Yes, it all went well," he says, opening the door and walking me back to the bathroom. Bow comes running and winds herself around our legs to make sure we're both okay after our 'exercise session'. Her fur tickles my bare skin.

"Good girl," I assure her.

"Yes, you are," Sai agrees. He gets a flannel, runs warm water over it, then gently wipes us both down. Bow supervises with the occasional happy bark.

"You met this Evan guy?" I prompt Sai as he finishes up.

He nods. "Yeah. He was and wasn't what I was expecting at the same time. But I got a good vibe. Tian was excited and Evan looked at him like he was precious, so I felt okay leaving them alone."

That warms my heart to hear. No one should look at Tian any other way as far as I'm concerned. "Good. Tian deserves to have a little crush and a little fun…all the nice *little* things."

Sai laughs at my silly joke as he guides me back into the bedroom where we both dress in jeans and jumpers. I'd prefer joggers right now if I could, but seeing as we have to go outside soon, it's best to go straight for the more structured clothing. Otherwise, I'll crawl into bed and never move again.

Once I'm sat at our small dining table with a big glass of water and some reheated pasta, I'm starting to feel a lot less blurry after my mind-blowing orgasm. "I have a good feeling about this," I say, apropos of nothing.

But Sai smiles at me and nods. "You mean this Evan thing? I agree."

I shrug and swallow another bite of food. "I'm interested to meet him. But it's more that I think it'll do Tian a lot of good. He deserves to be adored. And the more chances he gets to age play I think it actually makes him more confident in the rest of his life. It's like a valve that's good to let off steam. It nourishes him." I wrinkle my nose. "Too many metaphors."

Sai laughs at my rambling, but not in an unkind way. "Yeah, it's good to see our baby boy spread his wings."

I eat a little more, turning my thoughts over. It is a bit strange to know Tian is out there with another man, and I can't help but worry just a bit that he's okay and not being taken advantage of.

This date is probably good for Sai and I as well, come to think of it. As much as we want Tian to have his freedom, we need to make sure he has the space to be free with us in the first place.

There has to be something special about this guy if Tian felt strongly enough to pursue a date now and not before with anyone else. I look my husband up and down as I take a gulp of water and wipe my hand over my mouth to make sure I haven't left any dinner there.

"So you liked him?"

Sai raises his eyebrows. "Evan? Yeah, I did. I wasn't sure at first after the way he made our baby cry." I hum in agreement. "But he's clearly going through something and thinks very highly of Tian now. I think there's more going on than probably meets the eye."

I nod. "Well, I guess the only way I can make up my own opinion on him is to be the last one to meet him."

"You ready?" Sai asks, glancing down at my mostly finished dinner.

Honestly, I'm fifty-fifty on if I want to go out or pass out. But Tian needs me, and if we're going to debrief after his evening, it will help if I know a bit about who he's spent it with.

"Ready," I say firmly, pushing my chair out and getting to my feet. "Let's go see how little Baby Tee and Daddy Evan did with their practice date."

Sai grins as he follows me. "They need a mark out of ten."

I make short work of taking my plate and glass to the kitchen to rinse out and load into the dishwasher. Then I head back into the living room, but before I put my shoes and coat on, I pull Sai to me by the scruff of his jumper and kiss his mouth. "You're ten out of ten, Sir," I tell him, just in case he was unaware.

Sai grins against my mouth. "Good boy."

Why, yes. I *can* be good when I want to be.

CHAPTER 9

Tian

If I'm being totally honest, I've had such a lovely evening here with Evan, but I haven't been able to sink fully into little space.

I can't stop myself from constantly clock watching.

When I arrived, it was just gone five thirty. But knowing that Daddy Sai and Jude were picking me up at ten o'clock has just left me feeling the entire time that it wasn't enough. Rather than letting go and embracing the moment, I've just spent the last few hours trying not to feel like I'm being cheated out of something really good.

But Evan and I specifically said we'd just have one play-date so he could practice being a Daddy again. That way, when he meets a boy he really likes, he won't be so scared of making big mistakes.

The idea of Evan being someone else's Daddy makes me want to throw my toys across the room.

Which is another reason why I don't sink fully into little headspace. If part of me stays big, I can hold on to some logic. If I regress fully, I know I'd just get upset and that wouldn't be fair to Evan if I promised this was okay then got in my feelings about it.

Still, I think I do a pretty good job of being little for him and enjoying our time together. I'm just playing a role, rather than actually letting go and succumbing to the age play.

If Even realises that, he doesn't let on. And I genuinely have so much fun with him when I forget that the clock is ticking. We have the yummy dinner he made then for dessert he's got a dozen cupcakes for us to decorate. It's doing these kinds of activities that I love the most about age play. When all I have to worry about is piping icing and not getting too many sprinkles on the floor, all my adult problems fade away.

He allows me to eat two of the cupcakes, but then he keeps one extra for himself before boxing up the rest for me to take home. I pretend to pout about not being allowed a third helping, but in truth, I think it's super kind that he wants me to take the surplus for Sai and Jude.

If I was staying the night, I would have hoped we could have done bathtime together. But I don't even know if he has a tub in the house, and even though that's never sexual for me, the idea of getting naked in front of him definitely crosses a line.

So instead, Daddy Evan puts a film on about dragons and allows me to spread out my toys on the floor in front of the TV. I mostly brought my blocks that make a castle with a few of my favourite figures so they can have medieval adventures.

There's a rug on the wooden flooring where I've set myself up. But Evan also grabs a big, flat cushion to sit on so he can join me in my game. He seems very hesitant to play at first, but slowly he starts asking about my characters and what they're doing. Even if he's a bit stilted, I can tell that he's enjoying watching me if nothing else.

It makes me a bit self-conscious in a way I wouldn't be if I was properly in little headspace, but it's okay. The whole point of being here is to teach Evan to do some of the things he's forgotten. I bet he'll remember how to play kids' games the more he practices.

All too soon, I catch him looking at the clock as well. It's past nine, so I'll have to get ready to go home shortly. The realisation makes me so sad that I almost drop my little Baby Tee persona completely.

But then Evan visibly rallies, beaming at me. "Okay, Tee. How about you help Daddy tidy up, and then he can read you a bedtime story?"

My interest immediately piques. "Storytime?" He does have a lot of books, but all I can see are big boring grown-up paperbacks, the kind with hundreds of words and no pictures. Still...I don't actually care what the story is. The point of reading with Daddy is *cuddles*.

We had a nice cuddle at the start of the evening, but it was because he was feeling a lot of big emotions. He said he wasn't very sad, but I think he was a bit. If I can get the chance to have a happy cuddle, I'll take it.

Making sure to pick up every single one of my toys, I work with Evan to tidy his living room space. The idea crosses my mind that if I 'accidentally' left something here, I'd have an excuse to come back for it. But...no. I don't want to lie or manipulate him like that.

However, the idea that I won't see him again after tonight makes me want to cry. I manage to hold it in. However, knowing that still makes me sad.

I guess, technically, there's no reason why we couldn't hang out again. The still big part of me knows that wouldn't be fair, though. We're not dating. Sai and Jude are my boyfriends. There's a big difference between having hook-ups and pursuing a new branch to our relationship tree. I'm just doing Evan a favour so that he can go out into the world and find an *actual* boy to date.

So why would we see each other again?

Thankfully, I'm saved from being overwhelmed by too many complicated thoughts as Evan produces a tablet from somewhere. "I'm afraid I don't have any real books, Tee. But I've got some saved on my little computer here. Will that be okay?"

I forget to be sad as my heart melts. He's so thoughtful. Why did he think he wasn't a good Daddy anymore? Sure, he seemed a bit unprepared when I got here. But it's the way he's made me feel that matters, not having a bunch of stuff that I was able to bring with me anyway. The fact that he knows how to get a storybook through the power of the internet just proves he's not just thoughtful but resourceful as well.

"Yes, Daddy!" I cry, leaving my packed bags on the floor to skip over to him and give him a hug around his waist. He stills for a second before relaxing and hugging me back. "What're the books about?"

"Well, there are a couple to choose from," he says. "Do you want to come sit with me on the couch and we can pick the best one together?"

I nod and tug him back to the sofa, eager to snuggle. We sit side by side and we're pretty close. But after a moment of consideration, he takes a small breath that I think makes him feel braver, then he lifts his arm in an invitation for me to tuck under his wing.

Barely holding back my glee, I plaster myself to his side and rest my head on his chest. His arm feels so good around me.

It's slightly awkward as we navigate the tablet, but I don't care. I told him earlier—it's not about being perfect. It's about trying your best to be good, and he's certainly doing that.

He gives me a choice between a story about a rusty car and a penguin. I choose the car, and as he starts to read to me in his dreamy, rumbly voice, I pop my thumb in my mouth and feel my eyelids getting heavy.

It doesn't matter if this is just pretend or for practice. It's lovely.

I must start to doze off at some point, because when we hear the door knocker sound from upstairs, I jerk awake and almost smack the tablet out of Evan's hands.

"Sorry!" I cry.

But he shakes his head and places the tablet safely down on the coffee table. "No harm done, sweetheart. But I need to go answer the door as that'll be your boyfriends."

"Oh, sure," I say, mustering a small smile. We untangle, and he jogs up the stairs. Soon, I hear voices, but not what they're saying. It doesn't matter, anyway. It's home time and I need to get myself together.

That means changing out of my jammies. But even though my big boy clothes are in a neat pile right next to me, I can't make myself move to do it.

I might be in a strange half-and-half head space, but in that moment, I could easily throw a childish tantrum again. I'm not ready to leave. I need more time. If I'm a bad boy, perhaps I'll have to stay so Evan can give me a spanking.

But I don't want to be bad. I want to be good.

I need a Daddy to tell me what to do. Luckily, that's when two of them walk down the stairs along with my Jude.

"Tee!" he cries, nipping past Daddy Sai and Daddy Evan to rush over and hug me on the sofa. "Aww, you look so cute in your jammies. Did you have fun?"

I cling to him and breathe his familiar scent in deeply,

feeling myself centre. "Yes, I did," I say truthfully. I look up at Evan. "I hope you did, too, Daddy Evan?"

His smile is so sweet, and the way he looks at me makes me feel like I'm sparkling. "It was wonderful, Tee. Thank you so much for coming to keep me company this evening."

"Do you remember how to be a Daddy now?" I ask.

He licks his lips and considers me seriously. "I don't actually think I forgot, sweetheart. I think I just needed someone special to give me permission to *be* a Daddy again."

"Am I the someone special?" I ask, being deliberately precocious. It has the desired effect and makes everyone laugh. I feel so surprisingly at ease.

"Yes, absolutely," Daddy Evan confirms, his voice soft and warm. "Thank you, Tee."

For a few seconds, we just hold each other's gazes. I feel Jude squeeze me tighter.

"I guess we'd better get you home, baby," Daddy Sai says, almost sounding sorry.

I don't blame him. It feels wrong for us to walk away from Daddy Evan now. He says I helped, but how is a few hours going to really fix all the things that were making him sad before? We've had our playdate, though, and he did such a good job even if he didn't have any things for age play in the house. Now he'll know what to buy for next time. He probably doesn't need to practice how to be with a little again, he can just do it for real.

Wait a minute.

Yes, he's practiced with me, a little. But...

"I think you need another lesson!" I blurt out. Everyone looks at me.

"I do?" Daddy Evan says, his eyebrows raised.

I nod then look at Jude. "You were a great Daddy for a good little boy. But should you practice with a bratty middle as well? That's got to be more difficult."

I study Jude's eyes to see if I've made a mistake and put him in an awkward position. But his face lights up, and he grins at the two Daddies standing over us. "What do you reckon? Are you up for the challenge?"

Daddy Evan blinks at us, then looks at Daddy Sai, who shrugs. "Don't look at me, they've concocted this all by themselves."

Daddy Evan bites his lip and looks worried. That wasn't my intention, but I know he likes to think things through properly. "Well…that sounds like a lovely idea, boys. But please don't feel you have to. You already have your own Daddy."

Daddy Sai shakes his head gently. "Honestly, it's fine with me. Tian seems determined to help you get back on your feet." He rests his hand on Daddy Evan's shoulder, and he looks away bashfully.

"Uh, thank you," he says gruffly. "But Jude doesn't know me. He shouldn't feel obligated to—"

He's cut off by the rest of us laughing. "Oh, believe me, Daddy Evan," Jude scoffs. "I don't do anything I don't want to, ever. Tee likes you, so that's good enough for me. Besides, I think for the sake of your education you should absolutely practice more than one type of Daddying. And then Tee and I can compare notes and give you a mark out of ten."

"He's already ten out of ten," I mumble as I hug Jude's side, happiness blossoming in my chest.

I might not be able to have another date with Daddy Evan, but Jude can, and that way he won't disappear completely from my life just yet. It'll give me more time to think about how I feel.

Because it's *not* actually against our rules for one of us to see someone multiple times or even date. It's just that before me, Sai and Jude never got serious about anyone else.

I don't know if I'm serious about Daddy Evan at all. I just

know I'm not ready to let him go. I wouldn't blame him if he was wary of getting involved with us three. We are a lot and already in an unconventional relationship.

But I like the way he's looking between the three of us. He doesn't seem put out by the nature of our arrangement. In fact, he seems a little awestruck that I've now dragged my boyfriends into this quest to save him.

"I think," Daddy Sai says using his diplomatic voice, "that it's getting late, and no one has to make any decisions right now. Evan, why don't you sleep on Jude's offer? I'd just ask that you remember that we know ourselves. No one here is cheating or doing anything wrong. If having a date with my naughty boy would help get your confidence up even more, I fully support that."

The two of them share a look that I can't quite read, but it feels deep and meaningful. Then Daddy Evan looks back at Jude and me. "I don't know what I've done to deserve this kindness but thank you. Jude…I'd be honoured to take you out on a date. Would you give me some time to plan something?"

Jude squirms against me. "So long as it's an *amazing* date," he says devilishly.

"Behave," Daddy Sai warns, struggling not to smile at him.

"Shan't," Jude fires back. "That's the whole point of being a brat."

Daddy Sai laughs and rolls his eyes, holding his hand out to us and crooking an eyebrow at Daddy Evan. "Are you sure you want to deal with him?"

However, Daddy Evan just beams at us. "I'm sure," he says quietly.

Relief washes through me. This is probably just prolonging the inevitable. Daddy Evan is going to want his own boy and a 'normal' couple relationship, I'm sure.

But for now, at least, I don't have to say goodbye.

CHAPTER 10
Evan

WHEN MARIAH CAREY STARTS BLARING THROUGH THE seasonal aisle at Waitrose, I join the other customers who look up from the limoncello panettones and the gluten and dairy free mince pies topped with caramelised almonds to give an irritated 'tut'.

Until I realise the noise is coming from my own damned pocket.

Cheeks flaming, I abandon my basket on a shelf filled with boxes of dark chocolate and orange Florentines, muttering something about how all I want for Christmas is to throttle my niece for always managing to sneakily change her ringtone on my phone. I hardly ever bloody see her! How does she do this?

"Hello? Hello?" I splutter, seeking refuge back in the refrigerated aisle beside the bao buns decorated to look like Father Christmas.

"Uncle Evan!" she cries in delight. "I was expecting to get your voicemail."

It's on the tip of my tongue to tell her off for the embarrassing display she just caused me.

When I realise…I don't care.

I literally don't know a single soul in this supermarket. What does it matter if a silly pop song just burst free from my clothing? My only living relative that I know of has called me and said she was glad it didn't go to voicemail.

"Freddie," I say as I rub my forehead sheepishly and let out half a laugh. "It's good to hear from you. How are you? How's Clare?"

The silence lasts so long I take the phone away from my ear to check the call hasn't been disconnected.

"I-it is?" Freddie stammers as I go back to the call. "I mean, of course it is! It's good to hear from you, too. Although, I mean, yeah, I'm the one who called. Um…oh! Yeah, we're fine, fine, fine. You know, in the swing of everything. 'Tis the season, after all!"

I chuckle at her word vomit. She's always been exuberant, so bubbly and striking with her coloured hair and piercings. When she says she's in the swing of Christmas, I have no doubt she means it.

I don't know if it's any kind of reaction to my own poor attitude or just how my niece and her wife are wired, but they're the kind of people who decorate their house for the holidays inside and out a month in advance. And I don't just mean Christmas. They've been doing Halloween for years, but recently they've also added Valentine's Day to their repertoire, as well as St Patrick's Day and, for some reason, International Talk Like a Pirate Day.

That's the nineteenth of September, in case you were wondering.

Deep down, I'm sure that they've become more and more dedicated to these endeavours as a distraction from their true passion. Freddie and Clare have been trying to conceive for years without any luck. So when they decorate their house like Carnaby Street on poppers, they also have it well set up for people going by and admiring to donate to the Great Ormand Street Hospital for Children. Rather than a collection bucket that they'd worry about wrong 'uns pilfering from, they have a QR code for people to use on their phones. It's genius if you ask me.

"Uncle Evan?"

I realise I've been staring at the wheels of baking camembert with sticky plum glaze. "Hmm?"

She laughs, sounding not a little bit exasperated. "I asked how you are? And if you were going to make our Christmas party this year?"

Her voice is flat because she knows I'll say 'maybe' whilst really meaning 'hell no'.

Except what comes out of my mouth in that moment is, "When is it again?"

Another moment of silence. However, this time I'm invested in the answer, so I don't pull the phone away to check whether or not we're still connected.

"Really?" she says softly. "I mean…it's Friday the twentieth. Why? Do you think you'll actually come?"

I'll be honest, the idea of spending an entire evening with her and her noisy millennial friends blasting music I can't stand and drinking terrible corner shop screw-cap wine sounds horrendous to me.

On the other hand…for the first time in forever, I find the notion of having to put up with family a blessing instead of a burden.

"It would be nice to see you and Clare," I admit truthfully.

My niece's wife is a slightly scary barrister whom I have no doubt would ride into battle on a real live horse for my late sister's only child. We've probably only spoken a dozen words in the decade they've been together, but that's probably why I like her so much.

"Well, you don't have to come to the party," Freddie says,

stumbling over her words as I wander back to the pastry aisle. I'm amused to find my basket is exactly where I panic dropped it with everything still inside it. "I know you hate parties," Freddie continues.

I pout even though she can't see me. "I don't hate *parties*," I protest. "I hate strangers."

"Well, yes, that make sense," Freddie concedes. "I know you used to have a big bash every New Year's, but…*anyway!*"

I can practically feel her forced smile down the line. I don't blame her for not wanting to put her foot in anything. In fact, it's kind of sweet that she knows me so well.

"We could just meet for a cup of tea or a mulled wine or something sometime," she suggests. "Are you…how's your schedule? Many plans this month?"

Normally, her awkward way of asking if I'm intending on being a lonely old bastard for the whole of Christmas would irk me. But in this moment, I find it endearing. I always thought she was meddling.

She's just trying to take care of me.

That's a sentiment I can understand wholeheartedly, especially after this past week.

"I…"

My throat clamps up. However, I discover that I really do want to tell another human being about my private life for the first time in several years. My staff at the office always politely ask me how things are going, but no one—not me nor them—expect me to answer with anything of actual substance.

"I've made some new friends," I blurt out.

"Really?" Freddie squeaks back. "How? When? I mean… uh…that's wonderful."

I chuckle and start walking aimlessly down the wine aisle. For the first time in ages, I don't feel the hopeless drive to drink my pain away. I look at some Champagne, wondering if the boys would like it.

I need to stop thinking of them that way, but I can't help it. The boys.

My boys.

Of course, it's all just a bit of fun and games. They see me as a charity case and they're so far from being 'mine' that I should be ashamed of myself for thinking otherwise. Not to mention the fact that Sai most definitely isn't a boy.

But I can't stop thinking about them. All of them.

Just getting to experience a one-time jolly with Tian had seemed to be too good to be true at the time. But then Jude insisted that I needed a date with him to test my chops when it comes to bratty middles. I can't say that's my usual taste, but then again, neither are their strong, confident Daddies. I can still the feel the weight of Sai's hand on my shoulder as if I'm being haunted by a spectre, but in a really hot kind of way.

I realise I've left Freddie hanging again and clear my throat.

"Uhh…some guys at the gentleman's club I go to have decided to adopt me and get me fit for the dating pool again. I think it's a lost cause, but—"

"Oh, Uncle Evan, that's *so* cute! Clare Bear! Evan made some friends! Huh? No, he's not paying them." She cackles then pauses. "You're not paying them, are you? Not that there's anything wrong with that!"

I put her out of her misery before she can launch into her usual rant about legalising and unionising sex work that I already agree with.

"No, they're just being kind to an old man."

"You're not old," she says without any hesitation. "But seriously, Uncle Evan, that's wonderful. I'm so happy for you. Since…well…it's nice to hear you're letting people in again."

"They're a throuple," I say. I don't really know how to follow that up, but I feel like it's important, and I'd like her opinion on the situation.

She doesn't miss a beat. "Oh, cool. How did they meet, do you know?"

I finally decide on a bottle of bubbly and put two in my basket, making it on the verge of being too heavy to continue holding. I take that as a sign to start making my way to a till. "Well, two of them are married and the third guy is their boyfriend. It's him I met and made friends with first."

That's wildly simplifying the situation, but I don't want to go into details over the phone or when I'm about to enter hostile negotiations with the self-checkout machine.

"How very modern of you," Freddie coos, genuinely sounding impressed. "Uncle Evan, are you *dating* this guy? Or all three of them?"

"We're just friends," I insist, signalling to the friendly-looking middle-aged woman manning the self-service lane. She's got to have some mettle doing that all by herself on a Friday night, especially during the festive season. "It's for my alcohol," I mouth as she approaches, not wanting to divert too much from my conversation with Freddie.

The lady grins and winks at me as she jabs the screen, assuring the evil robot that I'm over eighteen. "Ohh, I dunnno. Are you old enough?"

The flirting is harmless and she's entirely barking up the wrong tree, but the flattery does me good anyway.

"Just friends?" Freddie repeats sceptically as the woman moves onto the next customer in need.

"I can have friends," I tell her defensively, tapping my card to the reader before picking up my bag and heading back out into the night.

Even over the phone, I can feel the sympathetic pause. "Of course you can. And you *should* have friends. Lots of them. I was only excited to think that you might…I don't know…be having a little excitement."

Memories of my playdate with Tian wash over me. It was so innocent, but it was also absolutely exciting as well. I felt like maybe he was holding back a bit, but that's understandable. It was only practising, after all, and not for real. I still very much enjoyed it. I just hope he did, too. It seemed like he did from the way he encouraged Jude to also try a date with me.

I exhale, my breath escaping in a cloud of smoke on the cold London Street. "I…it…they're very nice."

"Nice?" Freddie snorts inelegantly. "Is that what the kids are calling it these days?"

"Rude," I grumble, glad she can't see me grinning as I start walking home.

Christ. How long has it been since I had a chat on the phone with someone? Since I felt butterflies in my stomach over a silly crush? It's as if I've been hovering over the grave for the past few years and now I'm finally walking amongst the living again. I feel giddy like a teenager without a care in the world.

Except I have to remind myself somewhat harshly that none of this is real. It's all just training wheels. Once I can ride by myself again, Tian, Jude and Sai will all be gone, back to their happy world, together.

I inhale deeply, the cold air filling my lungs. Well, a taste of something amazing is a hundred times better than the numb existence I've been shuffling through lately. If it's gone by the new year, so be it. The whole point of these practice dates is to get me ship shape for a boy of my own.

But a hypothetical boy is hard to imagine when I already have three already right in front of me.

Again, I firmly tell myself that Sai isn't a boy. And he hasn't agreed to anything with me at all, except to be extremely gracious about sharing his gorgeous boys with me because that's what they want to do.

I think of sweet little Tian and feisty Jude. He's different to Sai and Tian again, stocky with a collection of tattoos peeking out from his clothes and that cheeky grin. He's—

"Uncle Evan?" Freddie laughs, and I clear my throat.

"Hmm?"

"You're clearly *not* daydreaming about the three hot guys that you *don't* want to date."

"I…that's not…uh…"

"It's fine," she assures me playfully. "I need to go anyway. It was so lovely catching up with you. Let's do it in person over the holiday break, yeah? Or in the new year. You don't have to come to our obnoxious party, I promise. But maybe that cup of tea?"

"Sounds wonderful," I say, surprising myself with how sincere I am. "Text me some dates."

"Will do," she enthuses. "Merry Christmas, Uncle Evan."

"Merry Christmas, Freddie," I tell her before hanging up.

For a moment, I stop and stare up at the night sky. I barely see any stars at all, but it doesn't matter. It's what I feel that counts.

And that's hope. Of what, I'm not entirely sure. But for the first time since that fateful night all those years ago, I feel like my life isn't as dark and cloudy as the sky above me.

There's the faintest glimmer of hope, and I intend to follow it like a star guiding me all the way to Bethlehem.

CHAPTER 11

Sai

"BUT WHY DOES IT ALWAYS HAVE TO BE A STAR ON TOP OF THE tree?" Jude whines as I pull tinsel out of a box. "Why can't I ever get what I want?"

"Because we're not putting a sparkly purple dildo on top of the tree, that's why," I say with a crooked eyebrow.

Jude huffs and folds his arms, only succeeding in making me laugh.

"Anyway," Tian chimes in sagely. "That dildo is far too heavy. It would fall off and probably topple the entire tree with it."

Jude's face brightens. "What about that little egg-shaped vibrator you use on my balls, then?"

I throw a stocking at his face, making him splutter indignantly. "Keep that up and you'll be on Father Christmas's naughty list this year," I tell him.

"I'm always on the naughty list," he declares proudly.

Storage is an issue in the flat, so we've only got a couple of boxes of decorations that we keep at the bottom of one of our few cupboards. Then each year we buy a real tree. I can't say I mind that as the scent of pine is lovely, but we've also recently joined this new scheme in London. This tree is technically ours. We bought it last year and when we returned it in January, the company replanted it in a pot, letting it continue growing and then they gave it back to us this year. When it gets too big, they'll plant it for good in a forest, but we should hopefully get several Christmases out of this tree.

I can't say I'm particularly artistic, but I do love decorating day. We've warmed some mulled wine in a pan, there's a Christmas playlist on Tian's laptop, and we bought some mince pies especially. Jude's already had two and is doing a better job of making a mess than putting anything on the tree. Bow is sticking her wet nose in absolutely everything, determined to smell it all.

My job right now is just to get everything out so we can see what we're dealing with. Tian is sat on the floor untangling a string of lights, and Jude has picked up a squeaky toy shaped like a Christmas cracker to distract Bow with as they play tug-o-war, each of them wrestling with a knotted end.

My heart is full. I couldn't wish for anything more than this. Our lives are overflowing with love, and I honestly feel very lucky indeed.

So why can't I get Evan Zegler out of my head?

"Have you heard anything about your date yet?" I ask Jude, unable to sit on my curiosity any longer.

Normally I wouldn't pry if he was arranging to meet up with someone, waiting for him to come to me. He hasn't been out with anyone for a while and usually it's someone he has chemistry with, so it's typically just a night of wild fun for them and then I get to hear all the juicy details of what he got up to when he gets home.

This feels different. I'm invested in what Evan's going to plan for them. I'm not even sure if they're thinking of having sex, so this is completely unlike our usual set up. But I'm excited for my husband. I want him to have a good time.

He beams at me and flops on the sofa, letting Bow run off to maul her toy by herself. "We're meeting up on Sunday as I'm off," he says a little breathlessly. "He's just told me to wear something warm and that the rest will be a surprise."

"That sounds cool," Tian says earnestly.

I study his face for a moment, but there truly doesn't seem to be an ounce of jealously about him. I've been a bit worried about his reasoning for pushing Jude to also go on a date with Evan. But as far as I can tell, he simply thinks that Evan is great and wants Jude to get to know him as well.

We've taken it slowly with Tian when it comes to him seeing anyone else. And to be honest, since the three of us became official, Jude and I have to make quite an effort if we want to connect with an outside party, so we often don't bother. As previously stated, we have such a complete life here together that there hasn't been much of an urge to look for anything else.

Evan has surprised me. He's older, for one thing, and although putting some of his broken pieces back together, everything about him screams Daddy to me. I have only ever played around with other boys and Jude often uses his time outside of our bedroom to Dom himself. Even when he wants to sub with someone different, it's always a Dom. As far as I'm aware, he's not been with another Daddy ever, and that usually only comes out for him when the two of us scene with Tian.

But over the past few days it's been 'Daddy Evan this' and 'Daddy Evan that'. He seems as excited to have a lesson teaching Evan as Tian was.

I'm simply not jealous by nature. I love both my boys and know they are unconditionally mine no matter what. I would have expected to watch their interest in Evan from afar with some amusement, wanting them to have a good time, but that would be about it.

So why does the other Daddy's tentative smile keep floating through my mind? Why do I keep getting butterflies when I think about how he looked at me to make sure all the plans he was making with my boys were okay? I loved the way he spoke to them with respect, but his earnest interest in my opinions made me feel seen in a totally different way than I'm used to.

Being with younger, submissive men has always been the dynamic I gravitate towards. I love being in charge, providing care, and being bossy in the bedroom. It would make sense to me if I was thinking about Evan as a peer—as another Daddy to be a kindred spirit with.

There's nothing comradery about the heat I feel pooling inside me when I picture his large hands and strong jawline. He's not submissive, and even though we're a similar height he's absolutely a bigger build than me.

So why does the thought of him pinning me down turn me on so much?

"What are you thinking about, Daddy?" Tian asks sweetly.

He's almost triumphed in his battle with the fairy lights. Once we've wound those around the tree, we can start the really fun part of placing all the decorations. Some of them Jude and I have had for years, some come from interesting places we've been to, and some just come from supermarkets or DIY stores. I love them all, each of them telling a little story about our journey as a throuple. Last year in particular, Jude and I made a special effort to go ornament shopping with Tian so that he'd have a more equal number to represent his part in the relationship.

I smile warmly at my baby. "I'm just thinking about how rich my life is and all the love in this room."

Jude throws the stocking back at me. "Christmas makes you such a sap," he groans, but from the rosy glow on his cheeks, I think he secretly loves it.

Tian shakes out the last tangle of lights, then crawls up to snuggle next to me. "I love you both," he says in a quiet, thoughtful voice.

I stroke his hair, not saying anything as I suspect he's processing and has something more to say. Sure enough, after a few moments, he takes a breath and looks at me with a tiny frown creasing his brow.

"How did you and Jude know you loved me?"

I blink and look at him for a moment. "Uh...that's a good question, baby boy. But I'm not sure I have a helpful answer. I just knew in my bones very early on that the idea of letting you go and belong to someone else broke my heart."

"I just thought you had a delicious arse, and I don't like sharing my favourite toys," Jude quips with a cheeky grin. Both Tian and I tut and huff, but neither of us can deny the deep look of adoration Jude's currently aiming at our boy.

Tian fiddles with the cuff of my ugly Christmas jumper. "I fell in love with you both so quickly," he says with a bashful laugh. "But I never thought I could butt in on your marriage. I really expected you to get bored of me and move on to someone else."

"Oh, baby boy," I say sadly and wrap my arms around him. "I hope you don't ever worry about that anymore." Jude also slides off the couch and comes to cuddle our boy from the other side, surrounding him with love.

Tian lets out a little giggle and shakes his head. "No, you both spoil me too much."

"You're here to stay," Jude says stubbornly, and I rub his back in appreciation.

"I think..." He fidgets a bit more. "I know you want me to be free and pursue my own desires. But I think I wasn't interested in looking for anyone else when I felt so lucky to have found the both of you. Two seemed too good to be true already. But I think I understand now how exploring things with other people can make *our* relationship stronger."

"Absolutely," I say firmly, feeling proud of my baby boy. "When we learn and grow, we have more that we can give to each other."

He nods against my chest. "I liked my playdate with Daddy Evan a lot," he admits shyly. *Ah.* I was pretty sure that was what this chat was all about, but it's nice to hear him say it out loud.

"Good," I say.

"And I'm excited that Jude has a date now as well. It feels like we're going on an adventure together, holding hands."

Jude chuckles and tickles Tian's side. "I like going on adventures with you."

Tian wriggles out of his grasp then stops Jude's attack by kissing his mouth. But then he turns to me. "I don't want you to be left behind, Daddy Sai," he says sombrely.

It's not escaped my notice that since his date, I've become 'Daddy Sai' instead of just 'Daddy'. And Evan is 'Daddy Evan'. Interesting. I wonder if Tian is even aware of what he's doing. But it tells me that the other man is still holding his interest in some way.

So long as I'm still his Daddy, I don't mind either way.

"Oh, sweetheart," I say in response to his concern for me. My heart melts for him. "I'm not being left behind, I promise. I love seeing my boys have fun."

He peeks up at me through his long, dark lashes. "I was thinking that Daddy Evan might need a lesson from you as well. Just to make sure we've covered all the bases and helped him from every angle."

Laughing, I peck a kiss onto the tip of his nose. "Is that so?"

I try my best to ignore the way my pulse has sped up. Of

course *I* couldn't go on a date with him. I'm not what he's interested in, for one thing.

Jude scoffs. "I saw the way you were eye fucking him the other night," he says slyly.

"You are really begging for a spanking tonight, young man," I say sternly, which only makes him grin more.

I grunt and turn my attention back to Tian, my heart still banging in my chest. I should tell him it's a nice idea but probably not something that Evan's interested in. I should say that *I'm* not interested in *Evan,* because he's another Daddy.

Instead, I say, "I think Evan is very handsome and very nice. If he wanted my help or just to spend some time together, I'd be open to that."

Whoa. Okay then. For a second, I worry that I've made a mistake. My boys need me. I shouldn't be ogling the man they've made into their project.

But Jude snickers. "Told you so."

Tian gives a little contented sigh and rubs his fingers against my chest. "I think he'd like to have a date with you as well," he says.

"If you're nice to me, I'll put a good word in for you when I see him," Jude teases.

I poke his side, making him yelp. "I don't need your help to pull," I grumble.

"You already have a husband *and* a boyfriend," Tian explains helpfully, making me laugh again. "So, yeah, you've probably got options when it comes to getting laid."

"You make a very good argument, baby boy," I tell him.

Jude has a heated look in his eyes. "Hey, Tee?" he says. "Seeing as Daddy Sai doesn't have a date with Daddy Evan to look forward to, shall we take him to bed and give him *lots* of attention?"

Lust flurries through me like a fresh fall of snow. Tian

bites his lip, his expression shy but heated as he looks up at me. "I think Daddy Sai deserves that, yes," he says. "But I'm sure Daddy Evan will also want to see him soon."

I kind of don't want to dwell on how much I'd like that right now. I squeeze him tightly and kiss his lips. "I have absolutely everything I need with my two gorgeous boys, Baby Tee."

He tilts his head and looks at me thoughtfully. "We've never had a foursome."

I blink and glance at Jude, slightly confused by the change of direction in the conversation. "Um, no, we haven't," I agree.

"Did you think I wasn't ready for that?" Tian asks.

For a moment, I consider him, remembering that one of our two sacred rules is clear and honest communication. "That's part of it," I admit." Jude reaches out and takes my hand, showing me his support. "You were very new to polyamory, and I didn't want to overwhelm you. But you were so special—you still are—and I suppose I wanted to enjoy our time together just us three."

He traces his fingers against my cheek. "Is it different now I've been on a date? I know we didn't have sex, but… emotionally, I opened myself up."

"And I'm really proud of you for that," I say. "But it's also okay if you're not interested in having sex with anyone else. I don't want to push anything onto you, Tian. I just want you to be free to follow your heart."

"But if your heart is telling you we should have a foursome," Jude interjects, "I think Daddy Sai and I would both be okay with that."

I poke him *again*, but Tian just giggles at my naughty husband. Then my baby boy nods to himself and licks his lips. "I think I need to know someone before sleeping with them. Not just know them, but like them…quite a lot. If I found someone like that, though, I think it would be incredibly special to share them with you both." He shrugs. "Someday, maybe."

Humming, I kiss his neck. I suspected before that he's probably demisexual, and what he's saying now ties in with that. Jude and I have never had a problem with shagging complete strangers, letting physical attraction do the heavy lifting. But after we met Tian at Bootleg those few years ago, we saw him a few times before bringing him home, building a relationship up first. My gut instinct had told me he needed that, and I'd been right.

I want to ask if he has anybody in particular in mind to invite into our bed. I want to ask why he's been so encouraging of Jude going on a date with Evan but hasn't mentioned anything about himself meeting up with Evan again, even though it's clear to me that he wants to.

Instead, I tuck all this information away for later and keep kissing my baby as my husband and I drag him down to the bedroom. We can finish decorating the tree after all three of us get a reminder of what we mean to each other.

Nonetheless, thoughts of Evan linger in my mind. Who knows if he's interested in sleeping with any of us, let alone more than one at once. All I know is that I'm glad that the chapter of our involvement with him hasn't closed yet.

He's clearly got some ghosts haunting him from his past, but in this present moment he seems determined to change his grumpy ways.

It makes me wonder what could be in his future.

CHAPTER 12

Jude

"I can't believe you've never been here before," I gush as I tug on Evan's hand, pulling us closer to the entranceway to London's Winter Wonderland.

"Are you sure you don't mind going again?" Evan asks. I pause and look at him, realising he seems worried.

"Oh!" I cry, understanding my error. "Of course not! I *love* Winter Wonderland, and I haven't been this year. In fact, I don't think I went last year, either, so I'm overdue." I swing our connected hands between us. "If you've never been, then I'm extra excited to be the one to introduce you. Just because it's not a brand-new experience doesn't mean it can't be amazing and memorable."

He chews his lower lip, apparently thinking my words over. "Yeah, that makes sense," he says slowly. "Just because you've already done something shouldn't mean you can't ever do it again. Especially if you're sharing the moment with someone new."

My heart swells as I catch his double meaning with those words. I bump shoulders with him before continuing to drag him under the illuminated archways that lead up to the ticket booths. Even though he seems so strong and capable in other ways, there's something so delicate about Evan. It makes it feel like a privilege that he's trusting me and my men to be the ones to help him transition into dating again.

"I thought this would be a good place for a middle-type date," Evan says, clearly still mulling things over and wanting to clarify his decision.

"Absolutely," I enthuse. I don't want him second-guessing himself that he should have picked something different. I'm genuinely thrilled to be here. "This place is huge. There are games and rides and food and mulled wine, and *everything* is dazzling with pretty lights. Oh, plus ice skating! Although I don't know if you have to book that in advance."

I frown and go to pull my phone out of my pocket to check, but he squeezes my other hand and smiles bashfully at me. "I already booked us a slot in about an hour. I wanted to wait until we got here to check if that would be something you'd enjoy. Not everyone can skate."

Okay, we've still got, like, all afternoon left of this date. He can't make my heart explode right at the start. "That's so thoughtful," I say softly.

I'm used to simply hooking up with other guys that aren't Sai. So I either go out clubbing with Tian and fool around in a bathroom stall or if I'm by myself I'll pop home with them. If it's something I've arranged via an app, I just got to his place for some fun. Sometimes I stay the night, but it doesn't really matter either way as I haven't ever stuck around and seen anyone more than once. More often than not I feel very satisfied, but it's always related to sex.

Very rarely, the guy will cook us dinner. But seeing as I'm there to get down and dirty, I'm not usually interested in doing that with a full stomach. And that's absolutely fine—

it's what I'm there for and what I want. But it means I'm not used to much romance from anyone other than Sai or Tian.

So for Evan to really take the time to plan something that he thought I'd enjoy is kind of breathtaking. And it's not a grown-up date like dinner at a posh restaurant. He's specifically thought about me as a middle! We're here to have *fun.*

I know it's not the same, as this is an arrangement we've made to give Evan a chance to practice being a Daddy again and build up his confidence. But it does feel like when Sai and I first met and he took care of me in a way that no one ever had before…or since, come to think of it.

We're still walking forwards to the entrance, but I'm so entranced that I hold his gaze for several seconds until we're in danger of bumping into someone. I laugh and look away, sneakily wiping my eyes and hoping he doesn't notice.

"Uh, yes, I can skate," I say, turning the conversation back in a safer, more practical direction. This is just a bit of a lark, after all. "Nothing fancy, but I do enjoy gliding around in a circle for an hour."

"I haven't done it in a *long* time," Evan says with a slightly apprehensive chuckle.

I lift his gloved hand and kiss the back of it. "I'll help you!" I promise.

"Thank you, Jude." He licks his lips and frowns slightly before speaking again. "I haven't done anything Christmassy for a long time, truth be told. Years, in fact."

Something about his tone gives me pause. "This is going to be, like, Christmas times a thousand. Is that okay?"

It's obvious he wanted to pick an activity I'd enjoy. But there has to be a reason he's been avoiding Christmas. Just like he's been avoiding dating. I don't want to do anything if he's not going to enjoy it as well.

He musters and smile and nods at me. "Yes. I've suspected exposure therapy would be a good idea for a while now, but I tried to do it alone, so it only made things worse. I think having an enthusiastic boy by my side might just do the trick."

I search his eyes, but he doesn't seem to be asking me to give him an out. "If it's really okay," I tell him, "I promise no one loves Christmas more than me. We'll have a brilliant time!"

Evan beams at me. "I have a feeling you're right."

We're distracted then as we get to the entrance booths. Evan already bought us tickets, so he shows his phone screen to the lady at the counter, and then we're in.

Winter Wonderland is a huge festival that takes over Hyde Park from the end of November until the start of January. It's got a lot of stalls like a German Christmas market, as well as a whole funfair and the aforementioned ice rink. There's music playing and scents of delicious food wafting through the air. As it's early-afternoon, we've still got an hour or two of daylight left. But then it'll get dark, and all the crazy lights will be so bright you can probably see them from space.

If anything is going to bring out my more childish, care-free side, it's somewhere like here. It's so noisy and shiny with so many things to do, it's easy to feel like a kid and not an adult with an important, high-responsibility job and bills to pay.

"Jude?"

"Yes, Daddy?"

We're walking past the first few stalls and the smell of hot, sweet peanuts makes my mouth water. I grin as I look back at Evan, intending to ask if we can get some. I don't expect him to pay for everything, or anything, in fact. But I do hope he's going to indulge me until I feel a bit sick.

But his expression is pensive, so I stop and give him my attention. "Is it okay that I call you 'Daddy'?" I ask. I really should have checked that before, and I curse myself for being insensitive. Bratting is fun, but not if it hurts anyone else's feelings.

However, he smiles at me, and I feel relieved. "Actually, that's kind of what I was going to ask you. I'd love it if you wanted to call me Daddy today. But is there a special name you'd like me to call you?"

I consider what he means for moment. "Oh, you mean how like when Tian is little, he's Baby Tee?" He nods. "Um, not really. Well, when I'm being naughty and Daddy Sai wants to tell me off, he calls me Judas. But I don't have a name for when I'm a middle. My age play isn't like Tian's. It's not as if I get in a head space and regress. I'm always like this. I just rein it in at work or whatever when it's not appropriate. But I'm generally kind of giddy and playful. Or I don't hold back when I'm sad, either."

"You wear your heart on your sleeve," Evan murmurs. "I used to know someone like that. I think it's lovely. Please feel free to be yourself with me, Jude. You don't have to hide anything or tone it down."

I blush, my heart beating loudly in my chest. He might be rusty, but he has an effortless commanding presence that makes me trust him.

"Thank you, Daddy," I say coyly. "Can we get some nuts?" I ask, pointing at the nearby stall. If he wants me to be authentic, I'm not going to hold back on asking for treats.

He laughs and nods, and soon we have a cone of sweet, sticky goodness to share between us.

"Judas seems a bit harsh for a nickname," he says, wrinkling his nose as he picks up our previous conversation.

I laugh and bob my head, not disagreeing with him. "Out of context, yeah. But it's really just a funny extension of my name that Sai uses to let me know that he's going to fuck me hard and rough in the not-too-distant future."

I smirk at Evan who's watching me with interest. "Is that how you like it, then?"

Oof. That makes blood rush to my cock and my skin tingle, for sure. I clear my throat, reminding myself, yet again, that this is just the start of the date.

"Uh, yeah. Sometimes. I like it all kinds of ways, really. It depends on who I'm with. Tian would never ever be mean to me, and I wouldn't want him to be. If it's just the two of us, I lavish him with praise and he's so good for me. With Sai, we like doing the CNC stuff, but his aftercare is the kindest."

"CNC?" Evan asks.

"Consensual non-consent," I explain without missing a beat. No one should ever be shamed for not knowing a kink. "It's when we pretend that I don't have a choice in the matter and he's just going to pin me down and have his way with me. Some people pretend to fight back in CNC, or you can make it primal play and chase them around. But I like to grovel and apologise and be used like a dirty slut to make up for being a bad boy."

I grin at him. Evan looks a little flushed and wide-eyed as he nods at me. I don't know if he would find that hot to do himself, but he's definitely not horrified by my confession.

"Right, yes, I see," he says, nodding and looking away as we continue to wander around the fair. "I can...yes. That makes sense. And you like that with, um, the other men you see?"

I shrug. "Like I said, I go for different things from different people. Often, seeing someone else is a chance for me to top and Dom in more aggressive ways than Tian might like. But honestly, since the three of us became official, I don't go looking for hook-ups much. Certainly not using apps to find a guy for a specific scene. It's more if I meet someone when I'm out, and I feel a connection, I'll act on it."

Evan is still nodding. "That makes sense. I can see in that

way why you'd want to keep a relationship open—if you've got different dynamics you like experiencing. And Sai's the same?"

That's a good question. When we first met, I'd have said that he just has a lot of love to give and he wanted to look after as many boys as possible, even if that was only for a night. I pop a few more nuts in my mouth and chew for a second.

"He really doesn't seem to feel the need to hook up much these days. Tian and I would be fully supportive if he wanted to, but I think between us we entertain him quite a bit."

I wink at Evan, and he laughs as he rubs the back of his neck. "Honestly? The idea of just dating one guy again seems daunting to me. So I can see why Sai would want to stick with two. But the way you describe getting your different needs met from different people also makes sense."

It's good that he's wrapping his head around the way our particular flavour of polyamory works. However, I realise I also might have put my foot in it slightly.

"Sai might not be going out looking for hook-ups much these days," I explain. "But Tian and I have decided that you still need to go on a date with him, too. For science."

He blinks at me, then chuckles. "Have you, now?"

I nod seriously. "Only if you want to, of course. But he told us he'd be interested if you were. That way, you can go have some sophisticated Daddy date together and get a full spectrum of experience from the three of us."

He drops his head back and laughs before beaming at me. "Oh, you're quite right. That sounds very scientific and logical."

He runs his lower lip through his teeth, looking at me like he'd like to forget the nuts and just eat me instead. If we weren't in the middle of Hyde Park, I would have been a-okay with that plan. In fact, if we could go somewhere warm,

I actually might have considered it. But if either of us got our bits out right now, I'd worry something might drop off.

And…this isn't like my usual hook-up, as I've already realised. The fact that the attraction is there is exciting, but it's not actually my main goal for a change. My job is to help Evan relax into a fun date with a boy who's more of a bratty middle for his Daddy. I'm here to get to know him and let him feel a little vulnerable with me as a safe space.

"You guys didn't need to be this kind to me," Evan murmurs. Apparently, he's having a similar train of thought to me, as it's not just heat behind his eyes now. It's something deeper as well. "I behaved so badly, and not just towards Tian. Although that was bad enough."

I frown. "I thought your friend sent you up for that Secret Santa thing without you knowing?"

"He did," Evan agrees. "But I was so afraid of letting anyone close to me that I immediately let Tian down and hurt his feelings without considering an alternative. If he hadn't sent that follow up message, I'd still be…" He sighs heavily, and I feel the weight of the world on his shoulders in that moment. "Well, needless to say, I'd be having a very different kind of Christmas this year."

"What would it be like?" I prompt gently.

He looks away and I think he might not answer. But he does speak again, keeping his gaze averted. "Lonely. Quiet." He sighs again. "Oh, Jude, I've treated a lot of men poorly over these last few years. I was terrified of getting hurt again, so I told them it was nothing more than sex and I meant it. I don't have much family, but I've still pushed my niece away. I've shut myself off from the world and ignored anyone else's feelings. I'm not sure I deserve to have a merry Christmas."

I pull him closer, so we're walking with our arms pressed together. "Yes, you do. Christmas is for everyone."

I give him some time to respond, but he seems lost in

thought, like a storm cloud is gathering over his head. If he doesn't want to talk about his pain anymore, that's okay. I'll distract him instead.

"Christmas really is for everyone, you know," I announce, my tone purposefully cheery. "For instance, did you know that I'm Jewish and Sai is Hindu?"

By the surprised look on his face as he turns to face me again, I can tell my tactic has worked, and I'm delighted. I want to give him space to process his trauma. Otherwise, judging from what he's said about forgetting how to Daddy and being all alone, he's never going to be able to be close to anyone again. But if now isn't the time, that's okay. My job in relationships is *literally* comic relief. Brats disrupt. That's what we're good at.

"But you still celebrate Christmas?" Evan asks, clearly interested.

"Yeah, it's kind of a case of 'why not?'" I explain with a laugh. "We both grew up in the UK and so did our parents. When the whole country—the whole Western world, actually—revolves around Christmas, it's not hard to embrace it and enjoy it from a secular angle. But my family aren't particularly religious, and neither is Sai's, so it never felt like something was being imposed on us. Realistically, most people in this country don't get particularly religious about it, either, so there you have the 'why not?' argument."

"But?" Evan prompts, and I like that he's interested and paying attention to my story. Because he's right, there is another side to this.

"But," I agree. "When we got together, Sai and I talked about how we do actually have our own cultures and traditions. So we decided that we were going to make an effort to celebrate them with each other in ways we might not have even done at home."

"That sounds lovely," Evan says, sounding like he really means it.

I grin, grateful he isn't looking at me like I'm crazy for doing something non-Christian like some of my work colleagues have in the past. People will swear this country isn't religion orientated then completely ignore how everything shuts down around Easter and especially Christmas and the Christian new year.

"It is lovely," I agree. "It also means that we have a full calendar for the last third of the year. The Jewish high-holiday season is usually around September/October depending on the year, then Diwali—that's the Hindu new year—falls some time at the end of October or start of November. Then it's basically Christmas until the end of December, especially now Tian is in the picture. Despite his name, he's not a practicing, religious Christian at all. But he definitely loves Christmas as much as the next boy. By which, I mean me."

We both chuckle at that, and I look at Evan, loving how easy it is to see he's rolling something over in his mind with careful consideration.

"How do you celebrate the different holidays?"

"Well, Diwali is the festival of lights," I explain, enjoying having a captive audience to share this part of mine and Sai's —and now Tian's—lives. "So you welcome in the new year by cleaning the house from top to bottom and lighting a shit tonne of lights, as you might expect. We try and visit Sai's family when we can. Both his parents are amazing cooks, and I always roll out of their house fit to burst, especial from his mum's onion bhajis and these pistachio sweet cake things that are to die for."

Evan hums. "I think a holiday that is based on good food with the people you love is probably always going to be a winner," he says.

I nod but I'm also waving my hands. "Yes, definitely. However, some of the Jewish ones are about fasting and reflection. Although that first meal after Yom Kippur is always mind blowing. Our new year—Rosh Hashanah—definitely revolves around food. Lots of apples, honey, bread, and fish. Sukkot is actually my favourite. It's the harvest festival and there's obviously food involved in that, too. But a big part of it is building, like, a hut thing called a Sukkah. I never did it as a kid, but Sai, being an architect, really gets involved. It's just a wooden structure with an open front and branches on top, but that can still be quite a challenge."

"You do that in London?" Evan says sceptically.

I laugh. "We tend to go out into somewhere like Dulwich Woods and make it just for a few hours. If we had a place with a garden, we could keep it up for the seven days and actually sleep in there a night like you're supposed to. There was one year where a friend let us do that in the rooftop garden of his apartment building. It was quite an experience."

"I had no idea," he murmurs. "And Hanukkah?"

I try not to laugh or roll my eyes, but I was waiting for that one. It's not his fault that's typically the one non-Jews have heard of and what everyone asks about.

"People have different opinions and celebrate holidays differently," I say diplomatically. "But honestly? It's become more like Christmas to make Christians feel better or Jews feel less left out. And that's *totally* fine. In our house, we light a menorah for the eight days and that's actually really special to me. But as we celebrate Christmas Day, I really don't want Hanukkah presents as well. That's just me personally. I know Jewish families who go all out for the entire week, then go for the traditional Chinese meal on the twenty-fifth."

"That's a thing?" Evan asks.

"Yep," I say with a chuckle. "My family did do that some

years. It can be very cool to go rogue when the rest of the country feels like it's all doing the same thing."

Evan once more takes some time to digest what I've said. For a while, we walk past the stalls and queues for rides as the evening draws in. I get a sense that we're wandering towards the ice rink, but we still have time before our slot, so there's no rush.

"You three have such rich lives together," Evan muses. "It's hard not to feel like I've wasted so much time."

I shake my head. "Healing *needs* time," I say firmly. "I'm a nurse, I know these things. If you try and rush it, it'll just take longer."

He gives me a small smile. "True."

I don't ask him specifically what he's healing from. From what he's said, I assume it was a very bad break-up. If he wants to tell me—or Tian or Sai—he will in his own time. Instead, I want to keep the conversation positive.

"I know you said Christmas hasn't been your thing for a while, but did you used to enjoy it? Or do you have another holiday or time of year you love?"

He seems a bit surprised at being asked about himself. Like it's been a long time since anyone has. Or maybe it's been too long since he allowed anyone close enough to give them a chance to.

But a dreamy look comes over his face. "I've always loved New Year's Eve," he says, his smile growing. "I used to throw a big party every year. I think there's something really powerful about new year and a new beginning. The chance to start fresh or try again."

"Fresh starts are very important," I agree.

We've naturally come to a stop near the Ferris wheel. At some point, he must have crumpled up the paper cone the nuts came in and thrown it in the bin. So his other hand is free to take mine and hold them both. He's a couple of inches taller than me, and I just stare into his piercing blue eyes for a moment.

"I think this is the most important fresh start of my life," he murmurs. "And it wouldn't have happened without you and Tian pushing me. So…thank you."

My heart skips a beat. His face is so close to mine, our smoky breath mingling in the space between. Despite all the ruckus around us, it feels like we're the only two people in the world.

Except we're really not.

"Evan?"

He jerks back suddenly and whips his head around sheepishly. Then his eyes land on someone and he blinks. "Robert?"

Evan lets go of both my hands. I feel bereft in the moment, but I appreciate that if this is just a practice date, he might not want anyone he knows asking awkward questions. Still, I wish he didn't feel he had to.

A man is walking towards us looking surprised but also happy. Beside him is a boy who looks around ten years old, I'd guess, using two crutches to make his way. He's confident on his feet, though, and grinning as he and the man close the distance between us. At a glance, I'd guess his condition to be something like cerebral palsy.

"Good to see you," Robert says, sticking his hand out. Evan, however, looks anxious as he shakes it. "I don't think you've met my son before. This is Timothy. Timothy, this is my boss, Mr Zegler."

My eyebrows raise before I can stop them. Evan said he worked in accounting but not that he was the boss. Although knowing him as I do now, his modesty doesn't really surprise me.

It takes Evan a second to recover, but then he smiles at

Timothy and inclines his head in an almost bow. "It's a pleasure to meet you," he says.

Another stilted pause. But after a couple of seconds, I realise Evan has clamped up and needs rescuing. So I also offer my hand to Robert for a shake. "I'm Jude, a friend of Evan's. It's nice to meet you."

"You must be a good friend if you've convinced Evan to do something Christmassy," Robert says with a laugh. He lets my hand go and places it on his son's back in a sweet, caring gesture. "My boss really hates this time of year and usually hibernates until January."

Evan hums but his expression is pinched. I have no idea what the history is between these men, but Robert seems genuinely friendly at least.

"We were actually just talking about fresh starts and new beginnings," I say lightly, hoping I'm not putting my foot in anything.

Robert's expression becomes more sympathetic. "Fresh starts can be wonderful things," he says earnestly. "Well, I promised Timothy a ride on this definitely safe, very high Ferris wheel, so we'd better get in the queue. It was nice to meet you, Jude. I'll see you tomorrow, Evan."

He nods and musters a small smile. However, then Timothy pauses and lets go of the handle on one of his crutches. The cuff around his wrist keeps it upright, but it means he can wave at us.

"Bye, Mr Zegler! Bye, Mr Jude! It was nice to meet you! Merry Christmas!"

Before I can reply, Evan pipes up. "Merry Christmas," he says back sincerely.

We watch father and son walk away.

I glance at Evan. He seems a bit shell shocked.

"That was nice," I say to break the ice. "How—"

"There are only four of us in the office," Evan interrupts. "It's a small company. My father's before I took it over. I…I haven't thrown them a Christmas party in years. If they do anything, they must organise it themselves out of their own pocket. They haven't had a bonus or a decent pay rise in years because I always worry it'll come back to bite the company later. But what if there isn't a later? No one is guaranteed tomorrow."

He drags his hand over his jaw before looking at me. "Evan," I say firmly. "You said yourself that you've not been well." But he shakes his head.

"It's one thing that I've let myself get swallowed by misery, but I've inflicted it on them, too. I just see them as calculators. Not people with lives and…and families."

He seems stricken and I can't bare it. So before I can overthink it, I throw my arms around his waist and hug him tightly. It only takes a second for him to return the embrace.

"It's never too late to make amends," I tell him. "You can change all that now if you want to."

He nods, our temples pressed together. "I think I do want to change, thoroughly. I don't want to be this man anymore, Jude."

I lean back and cup the side of his face. "You're already changing, Daddy," I say softly. "You're coming back to life. I know you can be whatever kind of man you want to be."

He sniffs then takes a deep, shuddery breath before nodding. "I can certainly try."

"That's the first step," I agree. "I believe in you. So does Tian. So does Sai."

Carefully, like he's not sure if I'll flinch away, he lifts his hand and also cups my face, mirroring what I'm doing to him. Despite the fact that we're both wearing gloves, the touch is still electrifying.

Evan's gaze flickers over my face. "The three of you are like some kind of Christmas miracle," he murmurs. The moment is weighted, and my instinct is to alleviate the tension by making a joke.

I don't.

"We're here for you," is what I say instead.

I'm not sure which one of us inches closer first, but suddenly there's mere millimetres between our lips.

And then there's no distance at all as Daddy Evan kisses me.

CHAPTER 13
Evan

I haven't kissed anyone in almost exactly seven years.

I forgot how wonderful it is.

There are probably differences from before, but it's been so long I'm not really struck by them. What I'm overwhelmed by is not only how soft Jude's lips are but also how confidently he returns my kiss. His arms tighten around my waist, and he moans into my mouth. I taste both sweet and salt from the peanuts we shared, and there's also something warm and spicy that's all Jude.

His tongue explores for mine and I greet him happily. But it's not too long before we naturally pull apart, Jude's eyes searching mine. He seems to understand what a big deal that was for me, and that I appreciate.

"Are you okay?" he asks kindly. For all he's a saucy brat, he's also very thoughtful.

I run my hands up and down his arms. "I'm wonderful," I reply truthfully, even if I am a little shaky from the adrenaline of it all. "You?"

He winks and wriggles in my grip. "Not bad, Daddy, but I think you need more practice."

Brat.

Then I'm struck by the idea of practicing. That means he wants to do it again. And…and *I* want to do it again. I'm not paralysed by guilt like I thought I would be. That's why 'no kissing' was always a strict rule with my hook-ups. This whole time, I assumed it would feel like betrayal. And back then, I'm sure it absolutely would have done.

But this feels like liberation.

The surprise knocks me back somewhat. However, the optimism that comes slowly creeping through my veins is stronger. I'm afraid if I study it too intensely, it'll turn out to be fragile and shatter, so I laugh at Jude's playful banter and let the moment pass.

"Come on, you." I give him a squeeze before spinning him around and grabbing his hand. "Let's go ice skating before you can get into any more trouble."

"I can get into trouble anywhere," he assures me.

That I don't doubt.

We navigate our way to the rink just as the last group is pouring out. The sessions are forty-five minutes with fifteen minutes in between to clean the ice. So it's a bit chaotic trying to pick up skates as everyone is returning them. But eventually we are successful and find a space to sit down and change footwear.

Neither of us are great at skating, but I find that really doesn't matter. We manage to do several slow loops around the space as the sun fades rapidly, the fair lighting up around us as night settles in.

To begin with, we're both mostly just concentrating on our feet. But as we gain confidence, Jude starts chatting at me. I mean, I'm sure he'd like me to join in with him, but I love hearing him babbling on with only occasional input needed from me. I swear he shines as brightly as any of the lights around us.

I hope as time goes by, I can get better at being actively with people in the moment. But I feel like I'm so out of practice, my mind goes blank, and I can't think of a thing to say. Jude talks enough for the both of us, though, and appears to love being listened to. Now that I can do.

Once our time on the ice is done, we spend a few more hours at the park, mostly looking at craft stalls and going on a couple of the rides. But it's just like what happened with Tian. I can feel myself clock watching, dreading when we have to leave here and I have to put him on a Tube home.

"Daddy?" Jude says quietly. It's enough to get my attention, however, and as I blink at him, I realise I was lost in thought.

"Sorry, sweetheart," I say, smiling and forcing myself to be present. We're still doing one last loop of the park, after all. "What were you saying?"

He chuckles. "I didn't say anything, but I was going to ask you if you were okay."

"Oh, I'm fine. Great. Having a splendid time."

Okay, so truthfully, right now I'm quite cross with myself for spoiling what little time we have together with my moping. For both Tian and Jude's dates, I always knew they had a time limit, and there's no point in acting like they're done before they've even finished. Otherwise, there was no point in going on them at all.

Jude looks up at me with big green eyes and I realise I might have missed something.

"Are *you* okay?" I ask.

He nibbles his lip and glances away before looking back and replying, "I don't want this to end yet."

My heart leaps into my throat, not quite able to believe that he's just said what I'm thinking. That's not the arrangement. This is supposed to just be a simple afternoon date to help me get back into the swing of things. As sad as I am, I wasn't prepared to break the rules and ask for more.

But what's the point in lying if that's how we both feel?

I recall what Tian said to me during our walk in Regent's Park. Why not consider the best-case scenario? It's just as likely as the worst. Why not imagine being happy?

Throwing caution to the wind, I take a deep breath. "Me, neither," I tell him. His eyes widen hopefully, making me braver. "Do you...I mean...would you perhaps like to come back to mine? I could make us dinner."

"Really?" he asks breathlessly.

I nod, my heart thumping in my chest. "I'd love to have you over. So long as you're not supposed to be anywhere else?"

He immediately shakes his head. "I just need to send a quick text is all—about the change of plans."

Rather than feeling like we're doing something nefarious, I like the idea of him messaging Sai and probably Tian as well. It's like they're in on our little secret.

Oh, gosh.

I'm bringing someone home.

No, not someone. Jude. The cheeky boy I've been thinking about ever since he came into my house like a whirlwind and hugged his boyfriend protectively to make sure I'd taken care of him properly. This kind, funny, sexy boy wants to come back to my place and let me continue Daddying him.

The voice at the back of my head tells me I still don't deserve this. But I reason with it that really this is just more practice. I'm not actually trying to start a relationship here. Someday I might, it's true. Then I'll have to judge if I've done enough to earn a second chance.

Right now, this is just about me trying to remember how to connect with people again. It's been a while since I quit sleeping my way across London. In those days, I was almost constantly at the end of a bottle, the alcohol making me brave.

The idea of being intimate when sober is more than a little daunting.

But I want it.

If something…more…is going to happen tonight, I feel safer doing it with Jude who's already promised to help me date again. Who's already in a committed open relationship, so won't have any expectations therefore making it very difficult to break his heart. Again, like Tian said in the park, this is about as low stakes as it could get.

Still, I'm a nervous wreck by the time we get on the Tube, unable to think of anything to say. Jude seems content to travel quietly, though, keeping a hold of my hand and smiling at me whenever I look at him. He's safe.

I'm safe.

Thankfully, it's only half a dozen stops from Hyde Park Corner to Russell Square on the Piccadilly Line. As we escape out into the darkness once more, the peace and quiet is almost disorientating after the carnage of Winter Wonderland followed by the packed Underground. It helps calm my nerves, and I pause on the pavement to take a deep breath of cold air.

Jude slips his hand against mine and looks sweetly at me. "Are you okay, Daddy?"

I rub my forehead, trying to dispel some of the tension there. "I'm overthinking," I admit with a rueful chuckle.

"About what?" Jude asks.

"That I'm going to let you down," I reply truthfully before I can dismiss my feelings and tell him—and myself—that I'm fine. "That I'm going to make a mistake and hurt you." Bugger everything. I'm already messing this up. "If you want to change your mind and go home, I'd understand."

"Evan," Jude says, his tone firm but also kind. "I told you already. I don't do anything I don't want to. I'm here because it's my choice and I really, really wasn't ready for our date to be over. I know you're battling some demons, and I want to respect your process and give you all the space you need. If *you* genuinely aren't ready to invite me in, then I'll go home and everything will be totally cool between us, I promise."

We look into each other's eyes for a moment. My heart is hammering in my chest and my whole body is trembling. But I've made it this far and I'd be a fool to let him walk away now. "And if I do want to invite you in?" I ask.

He steps closer to me, angling his face so our lips are centimetres away once more. "Then I *don't* want you to make us dinner, Daddy. At least, not to begin with."

My heart is still thundering, but a good deal of my blood supply rushes south, and suddenly I'm too turned on to be as afraid anymore.

"Can I kiss you again?" I murmur.

"Yes, Daddy," he moans.

His mouth is just as delicious as before, but this time I'm more aware of how cold his lips are. Before things can get too heated out in the open, I break it off and tug his hand. "Let's get you home," I say with about a hundred times more conviction than previously.

"*Yes,* Daddy," this saucy little brat purrs at me.

We make the short journey home without really saying much, the electricity sparking between us doing all the talking. Jude keeps his gloved hand in mine, holding on tightly as we stride purposefully back to mine.

It strikes me as we approach how cold and dark it looks. That hasn't bothered me in so long. I always saw it as a way to save money on the ever-increasing electricity bills. But in that moment, I would have loved it if there was some kind of light to welcome us home or anything festive for the season.

Perhaps that's something to consider. A changed man probably needs a changed home to suit him, after all.

I don't get much of an opportunity to ponder the matter further as we march up my short front path, and I jam my key in the lock without a tremble in sight. This door is all that's standing between me and kissing Jude again, so it needs to get out of my way right now.

We rush inside and the second I close the door behind us, Jude pushes me against it and devours my mouth, his hands fisting around my coat lapels. He moans and rubs himself against my thigh, showing me he's already hard.

At this rate, I'm going to come in my trousers if I'm not careful.

Jude's kicking his shoes off, so I do the same, grateful I went with trainers for warmth and not anything with complicated laces. Then he's pulling off my hat, gloves and scarf, and pawing at my coat zipper. I reciprocate, wanting to do my fair share.

But once our outer layers are off, he grabs my hand and seductively looks at me through his dirty blond eyelashes.

"Is it still warm downstairs?" he asks as he starts tugging me down the hall.

"Yes," I assure him with a dry mouth, knowing the heating will have automatically kicked in by now.

"Good," he says with a wicked grin.

He's already pulling me down the stairs, but my head is ringing. Shouldn't I be in charge? I'm the Daddy. But it feels so right for Jude to be manhandling me like this. Still, my doubts crawl up my throat. Or at least they try to.

"Can…shouldn't I? Uh…"

He slows and turns, pressing his chest to mine as he kisses me. "Shh, Daddy," he mumbles against my lips. "It's okay. Just relax." Then he blinks and looks serious for a second. "Unless something gets too much, and you need a moment. In that case…you say, um…'peanuts'! And we'll stop, okay?"

I chuckle. "Peanuts? Subtle."

My laughter dies in my throat as he suddenly crowds me and steers me towards the couch, his hands slipping under my jumper.

"I want to see you," he growls. The backs of my knees bump against the sofa, making me jump. This boy looks he wants to eat me, and I definitely intend on letting him.

His hands are still hovering by my waist, holding onto the hem of the material. I let out a little gasp and nod, giving him permission to do whatever it is he wants to do. In one swift motion, he's pulled off both the jumper and the T-shirt underneath, leaving my chest exposed.

I won't lie, I'm not buff by any means. I walk a lot and like swimming in the summer, and that's about it. I certainly don't groom like some men do. Not that there's anything wrong with that. Each to their own, after all. But I'm suddenly anxious about what Jude might have been expecting.

The way he runs his hands over my hairy sternum and pecs then dives down to suck one of my nipples tells me that he actually probably pretty fine with what he's seeing.

"Jesus Christ," I hiss as he sucks and nips, making the tender nub harden. I run my fingers through his short dark blond hair as he multi-tasks and fumbles with the button and fly of my trousers. Within seconds, he's shoving everything down, leaving me completely naked.

Before I can panic at how vulnerable I suddenly am, he pushes me onto the sofa and I flop lengthways, my head mercifully landing on a pillow. He bites his lower lip and drags his gaze up and down my body.

"Naughty Daddy," he rasps, yanking his hoodie over his

head and dropping it to the floor. "Keep all this yumminess hidden."

"S-sorry," I stammer, my breaths sawing in and out of my chest as I drink him in. His chest is broad and muscular but not so well defined that I worry he's not eating enough. His pale skin is flushed red on his face and down his chest, and I can see the bulge in his jeans.

I did that.

Whoa.

He continues to strip down and I notice the many tattoos he has, but our eyes are locked together so I can't study the designs in any way. Maybe he'll tell me the stories behind all his ink when we're done.

But for right now, his gaze is piercing into me as he kicks his jeans away and stands completely naked before me. He takes his already hard cock in hand, stroking it slowly, putting on a show for me. It occurs to me that we don't have any supplies down here. But he told me to relax, so until it becomes an issue, I'm not going to ruin the moment by mentioning anything.

Well, anything that's a problem, that is.

"You're gorgeous," I manage to croak, meaning it with my whole heart.

Yes, it's easy to see in the lamplight that he has an amazing body and a nicely put together face. But it's his joy that shines through that's truly breathtaking. His beauty is beyond skin deep.

"Thank you, Daddy," he whispers.

Like a jungle cat stalking its prey, he moves to the sofa and crawls over me, capturing my mouth with his again. His lips are warm now. I like it.

"Is this okay?" he asks between kisses.

I hum in a way I hope conveys that it absolutely is, but I

still have a small gnawing voice at the back of my mind. "I should be taking care of you, though," I protest.

He nips my lower lip and grins. "You are," he says cheekily. "You're being my sexy Daddy toy. You're the one getting back in the saddle, remember? And I'm just the bad little slut who's had *alllll* the practice. You're in safe hands. So just lie back and let me ride you, okay?"

"O-okay," I manage to say with a jerky nod. That seems like the right moment to mention that we don't have condoms or lube. Except he shimmies down the sofa, braces one hand by my hip, then uses the other to grab my cock and guide it right down his throat.

I bellow out some choice expletives as he licks and sucks and swallows with such gusto, I'm worried I'm going to come immediately and spoil all our fun. But he's so good, he knows just how to tease me and drive me wild but still keep me at the edge, never quite toppling over. He fondles my balls and drags his nails down my thighs, but he doesn't touch himself at all. I just look down my body and watch him worshiping my cock like he's got something to prove.

Just when I'm about to lose it, he pops off with wet, swollen lips and shifts quickly back up to kiss my mouth again. Tasting myself gives me a thrill, and I cling to him, digging my fingers into his tattooed sides as if I'm trying to convince myself that he's real.

Meanwhile, he's not slacking off. In fact, he's lined us up and has wrapped his hand around both of our lengths, stroking us together. I have to admit, I've never been one for much precum, relying on lube to help things glide. But goodness me, this boy is *gushing*. His cock feels sublime against mine as he picks up the pace, his hand flying over the both of us.

I think a part of me was holding back, worrying that we didn't have what we need to get us to completion. I should have trusted that with Jude, I already have everything I could possibly want. I'm actually grateful that for this first time we haven't jumped all the way in with full penetration.

It's not like I've been celibate these past several years, not by a long shot.

But this is the first time since Beau that I've been intimate with someone I genuinely care about.

The tears come hand in hand with my orgasm. I come all over myself with a sob, burying my face against Jude's neck as I shake and gasp for air. However, he's already there, hugging me tightly, wrapping me in his arms and making me feel like I just jumped out of an airplane, and he's already caught me.

"It's okay, Daddy," he's murmuring into my ear. "You're okay. I'm here. You're so beautiful. Take your time. You did so well."

He mentioned Tian has a praise kink that he loves indulging. Yeah, I can understand that. For all I've completely fallen apart, his warm words are just as quickly piecing me back together again.

It takes me a minute, but eventually I'm able to take a few deep breaths then wipe my face so I'm not a complete state when I look at him again.

"Hi," he says gently when I do, cupping the side of my face with his hand. But then he shifts ever so slightly, and I realise we've still got a big problem, and it's nudging at my hip.

"You didn't come," I say, distressed.

He shakes his head. "I'm fine," he says brightly, but I'm not having that. I might still be getting back into the swing of all this, but there's no way that any boy of mine is going to go uncared for.

I grab his hip to steady him then wrap my other hand around his hard, red cock. He's still pumping pre-cum like a champion, so it's blissfully easy to start working his shaft, pushing him closer to his climax.

His eyes roll back into his head as he grunts and pants, thrusting into my palm. God, he's so fucking sexy. Seeing him give me everything ignites a spark of confidence within me. Covered in my own seed with a gorgeous boy on the brink of coming undone above me releases something primal and brave within me.

"You like that, you slut?" I ask.

He gasps in shock and whines desperately. *"Yes, Daddy, yes!"* he yells. These houses might be old and terraced, but they are extremely well built and insulated. The urge to make him scream overtakes me.

I don't want to tease him. I want him to lose his shit. But I do the first thing that comes naturally, and bite his neck, sucking and licking as hard as I can.

Part of me knows it's only for tonight. But in this moment, this wonderful boy is *mine.* I'm going to mark him to prove it.

Jude is howling just like I wanted as I bruise his neck and work his cock. Then he's spurting all over my chest, his cum mixing with mine and spilling onto the sofa.

I don't care about the mess. I just care that I've—hopefully—made my boy happy.

He sucks down breaths as his orgasm subsides, then grabs me and hugs me even fiercer than the last time. "Thank you, Daddy, thank you," he gasps.

I'm not sure I did all that much, but I love holding him and stroking his back. I kiss his neck where I've definitely given him a hickey and breathe in his scent.

These boys. These men. They've already given me so much.

I don't know how I can possibly still need more.

But I do.

CHAPTER 14

Tian

I'M OBSESSED WITH JUDE'S HICKEY.

It feels like something personal that I should ignore, but I can't stop thinking about that mark on his neck, imagining how Daddy Evan gave it to him. There are so many scenarios floating around my brain, like clips from a movie on repeat. No one needs to know how many times I've wanked off to the possibilities.

Except when I glance over at Jude *again,* I realise he's watching me and totally catches me in the act. I quickly turn my head back and try and conceal my blush, but now I can feel that he's the one looking at me.

"Is everything okay?" he asks. I can tell he's genuinely concerned, but there's also his usual playful tone as well.

"Yep, fine," I squeak. "What about this?"

We're on Oxford Street attempting to find a Christmas present for Daddy Sai, which is a terrible idea as it's teeming with tourists. But neither of us wanted to sit in front of a computer and do it, especially as that's difficult to do when Daddy Sai's always in the apartment, and my room at my place is so cramped.

Jude came and met me after work, and we're trying to not put too much pressure on ourselves by putting an hour's limit on it before we head home. We've still got time to search elsewhere if we don't have any luck tonight. I'm just trying not to let all the jostling bodies get to me or the Christmas songs being blasted from all sides, competing to be heard.

Outside it's cold and windy, but inside all the shops the heating is blasting, so the staff don't freeze. I've taken my hat and scarf off so many times, I'm worried I'm going to drop one of them, and I've given up on my gloves entirely for the moment, just exposing my hands to the elements.

We're currently looking through the window of a place that specialises in scents. I know aftershave might not be a frightfully original idea, but I love my Daddy smelling nice in something I've bought for him.

"Tian," Jude says patiently, making me look up at him. "Come on. It's me. What's our number one rule?"

"We always come home," I say automatically.

He rolls his eyes. "Don't be a brat. That's my job. What's our *other* number one rule?"

"Communication," I say with a sigh, shoving my tingling hands in my pockets and starting to walk along the busy pavement again.

We're coming up to Regent's Street and I start to steer us that way so we can try looking down Carnaby Street. There are some alternative stores there that might offer us up something more original. Plus, the light displays are stunning. I don't know what the theme is this year, but it's always good.

Unfortunately, Jude isn't letting this go. He loops his arm through mine and jostles me. "Seriously, Tee. Are we okay?"

"Of course we are," I cry in horror, looking at him like he's crazy.

He chuckles and shakes his head. "Then why do you keep looking at my hickey like you want to lick it instead of just licking it?"

I blush again and study my feet as we walk. "Sorry," I mumble.

He squeezes my arm with his. "You don't have anything to be sorry for. But I think we should talk about whatever it is you're thinking. Is my hickey upsetting you?"

"No!" I say honestly. But his gaze catches mine and I realise that he's right. We need to hash this out. "I...it's complicated," I admit.

"Are you jealous?" Jude asks softly.

I give him a one-armed shrug. "Sort of. But not in the way you might be thinking. It's not like I'm feeling possessive over you or Daddy Evan. It's kind of the opposite, actually."

A grin slowly creeps onto his face. "You wish you'd been there."

My blush deepens, and I hope he just thinks it's from the wind. But then I remember that I'm *supposed* to be communicating how I'm feeling, not hiding it away. I rub my forehead, feeling like such a mess. "I *am* sorry," I grumble. "It's like I'm totally fumbling around in the dark with all this. Apparently being in a throuple for three years and spending time with other people are two different kinds of polyamory."

"They are," Jude says. He leans over and kisses my temple, making butterflies in my tummy, even after all this time. "Please stop being so hard on yourself, babe. This is new and complicated, and this is why we have to talk about it. Dating Sai and I and us three being committed to each other is a completely different kettle of fish to me getting off with someone you're interested in."

"No, it's not that," I say hurriedly. "I was just helping Evan out that one time."

Jude arches an eyebrow at me as we walk down the

slightly calmer Great Marlborough Street that will take us to Carnaby Street. The faux Tudor façade of the Liberty department store looms above us.

"You keep saying that," Jude says, "but it's obvious you're carrying a bit of a torch. And it's okay if the fact that me and him were intimate gets you in your feelings." He bumps his shoulder against mine. "So long as you don't bottle said feelings up."

I stop so I can turn and face him, holding both his hands. "They're not bad feelings, not really," I promise him.

He grins and wiggles his eyebrows at me. "Jealousy can be kind of sexy, you know?"

I sigh and smack his arm though his coat. "You're such a dick."

"Noted," he says happily, leaning forwards and pecking a kiss onto the tip on my cold nose. "But you are still sexy."

Taking his hand again, I rub my thumb against his glove, mulling over my thoughts. "I loved my little playdate with Daddy Evan, and I think it really has helped him overcome so much."

"Absolutely," Jude agrees, uncharacteristically sincere. "Honestly, Tee, it's like he's woken up a new man. We had so many breakthroughs during our time together, and I know he's excited to cook dinner for Sai soon so they can keep his progress going."

Pride flutters through my chest. "We've really made a difference in his life, huh?" All because I pushed him with that text I sent. But Jude and Sai helped me write it, so it genuinely has been a team effort.

"We're *making* a difference," Jude says, quirking an eyebrow. "It really doesn't have to be past tense."

But I shake my head and drop one of his hands so we can start walking again. We don't have much longer to shop before we said we'd head home. "I had my date," I say simply.

"Tian," Jude says, sounding exasperated. I can practically hear his eyes roll.

"No, Jude, that wasn't the deal," I say firmly. "He needed help to start dating again. He just wants a boy of his own. We're so much more than that. It wouldn't be fair to start confusing things."

"We're not robots, hun," Jude says in a slightly kinder tone of voice. "These aren't algorithms we're programming. We're human beings with those pesky feelings we keep mentioning. Relationships change and evolve. If you want to see him again, tell him. You don't actually *know* what he's looking for, do you? I don't think even he does."

I nibble on my lip. "He's been so hurt," I whisper, unable to meet Jude's eyes as I feel my own prickling with tears. "I'm not sure how or why, but he's been in so much pain. I couldn't…I'd hate to confuse him or wound him any further. It doesn't really matter what I want. I can't risk that."

Jude stops us again and throws his arms around me fiercely. "Of *course* it matters what you want," he says hotly. I can't help but smile as I sniffle. His protectiveness is adorable. He pulls back and brushes the tears from my cheeks. "And I think you're one hundred percent right. He's been recovering from some sort of terrible heartbreak for a long time. But how do you know that seeing you again won't help to *fix* that?"

I frown, turning his words over. "But we already had our date. He learned so much."

Jude laughs. However, it's not mocking me. "Yeah, you had *one* date. But *my* date unlocked Sexy Daddy Evan. So why can't you go back and help him with *that* as well now?"

My insides bubble nervously. Sex? With someone that isn't Daddy Sai or Jude? That's a big step.

Needing something to do, I fish around in my pocket

until I find a tissue and blow my nose that's running from the cold and wind. "That wouldn't be fair," I protest weakly.

Jude isn't buying it. "Why?"

I shrug. "Because we're all going to have one date and that's it. Surely anything else would be too complicated."

"You're making up what's in his head," Jude says. His words are light and playful, but his eyes are serious. "This is why communication is our number one rule—*one* of them, anyway," he corrects himself before I can do it.

I offer him a little chuckle and sigh. "I feel like I can't reach out to him. That would put too much pressure on him. What if he doesn't feel the same way? I'd be so cross with myself if I put any kind of kibosh on his dinner with Sai."

Jude nods, apparently listening to me for once. "Okay, how about this? We wait until Sai and Evan meet up. Afterwards, Sai can give us an idea of how he thinks Evan was feeling. Then you can decide whether or not you want to message him and ask to see him again. That way, you won't be at risk of complicating things for Sai."

For a minute, I just stare at a nearby display of shooting stars, until the yellow light bulbs are burned into my retina. I blink and look away, still considering Jude's words. "I guess I could do that," I say, feeling guilty for even admitting it out loud.

I don't know how Daddy Sai's evening with Daddy Evan is going to go. For all I know, they're both too Dom to be attracted to each other, so they're just going to swap notes on how best to deal with littles and brats.

But they could have sex. Just like Daddy Evan and Jude had sex. And then I'd be the only one that didn't, and I have a very strong suspicion that I'd spend the rest of my life wondering what I'd missed out on.

If it could have been incredible.

I've never seriously considered having sex with anyone

else once I made things official with Daddy Sai and Jude. Since the first day I met them, in fact. They went to such lengths to capture my heart, and after that, I've had no interest in looking around no matter how objectively hot the guy might be.

But with Daddy Evan…it's like he's a drug and I just need one more hit before I can quit. Or rather, that I need the full experience of a proper hit so I know I didn't miss out on anything.

Inhaling cold air deep into my lungs, I nod and smile at Jude, wiping my face with my gloved hand to get rid of any lingering tears. "I think that's a good plan," I tell him. "I'll see how Daddy Sai does, then maybe text Daddy Evan and ask him up front how he feels and what he wants. I…I'd be sad if he was interested in seeing me again, but I was too afraid to do anything about it."

Jude beams and leans closer to press his lips against mine. "That sounds like a very wise, sensible and logical plan from a brilliant mind," he quips.

I laugh and shove him. "Behave."

"Never."

As we walk the rest of the way to Carnaby Street, I feel lighter. The uncertainty of this whole situation has definitely got me feeling off kilter. Voicing some of my thoughts and concerns hasn't really fixed anything, but Jude was right. Now I've communicated to him what's going on in my mind and, moving forward, he can offer advice and get on the same page as me, or at least appreciate where I'm coming from.

For the first time since I left Daddy Evan's house, hope creeps around the edge of my heart.

Maybe this isn't goodbye forever, after all?

CHAPTER 15

Sai

THE FIRST THING I NOTICE AS I APPROACH EVAN'S HOUSE IS that some of the lights are on in the upper levels. When he opens the door and lets me inside, I then realise that the heating is on in the entrance hall.

It's hard not to think of that as progress, and warm pride fills my chest as I think of what my beautiful boys have been able to do for this man in such a short time.

"Hi," I say a little breathlessly as he closes the door.

"Hi," he says back in his low rumbly voice. Wordlessly, he holds his hands up to take my coat and accessories, so I shrug them off for him.

"Thank you."

He shakes his head. "No, thank *you* for coming. We haven't had much of a chance to get to know one another, and both your boys spoke so highly of you. I didn't want to miss the opportunity."

As we look at each other, something charged passes between us. He's not some shy, sweet boy. The dynamic is so different to what I've been used to for so many years, but that doesn't mean it's unwelcome.

Far from it.

"You didn't even want one date," I joke, breaking the tension and moving down the hall. Seeing as the basement level is where both Tian and Jude spent their time here, I assume that's where we're headed. Sure enough, Evan begins to follow me. "Now you've had three."

"Four." I glance over my shoulder and raise my eyebrows at Evan, who continues to explain. "Four dates if you include meeting Tian in the park, which I do."

I grin and nod, agreeing that I would include that, too. Without that initial meet-up, none of the rest of this would have happened.

And that would be such a shame.

"I hope you don't mind," Evan continues as we reach the bottom of the stairs, "but before he left, Jude gave me some food ideas for us. So I took a gamble and made a chilli. But if that isn't okay, I do also have nibbles and wine."

I laugh in delight. "Yes, I do love a chilli, Jude was right. But this all looks delicious."

On the breakfast bar he's laid out crudités and dip along with a selection of little savoury-looking pastries. There's also a bottle of red with a fancy label and two large glasses standing next to it.

"Wonderful," Evan says as he moves to pick up the wine. "Can I get you a glass?"

"Please." I settle on a stool and watch as he pours us a couple of inches before handing me mine. "What shall we toast to?"

He bites his lower lip and considers a moment. Then he looks up and meets my eyes again. "To fresh starts," he says.

"To fresh starts," I repeat. We tap and the glass chimes delicately through the air.

For a while, I simply watch as he turns the heat up under

the chilli sauce from where it was just warming before and stirs it. He gets white rice going as well, and soon delicious aromas fill the air. Low music plays in the background so it's not awkward. I feel like I should want to babble on so it's not silent between us. But it feels comfortable.

Instead, I help myself to some of the sliced veggies and one of the dips that seems to be some kind of incredible whipped cheese with a hint of spice. It's in a small ceramic bowl rather than plastic from the supermarket. I wonder if that means Evan made it. Even if he just took the time to decant it from the pot it came in into one of his own, it's still thoughtful.

In a moment of clumsiness, though, I miss my mouth, and the carrot slips from my hand onto the floor with a splat.

"Oh, fuck. I'm so sorry," I say with an embarrassed laugh. At least the floor is tiled in this part of the room, so it hasn't left a stain. "Let me—"

"No, I've got it," Evan says, already there with an anti-bacterial wipe to scoop it up.

"Sorry," I mumble again.

He shakes his head, his foot on the bin pedal to lift the lid so he can drop the rubbish inside. "You're my guest. I want to take care of you."

It warms me to see his Daddy instincts coming out. The whole point of this endeavour was to give him back his confidence, so to see that with my own eyes feels like a privilege.

However, I'm surprised how much the sentiment moves me. "I'm usually the one taking care of everyone," I say, keeping my tone light.

Evan turns off both the hob rings and moves to dish up a portion of rice and chilli in two shallow bowls. His got a slight frown on his face as he puts one in front of me, grabs the salt and pepper, then positions himself on a stool oppo-site me. I like that we're here instead of the big dining table. It might be a bit strange with only two of us. This feels more intimate.

However, I'm also a bit nervous. How long is it since I gave up control to anyone else, even if it's just regarding dinner? Why do I like it so much when I never have before?

As if reading my mind, Evan goes to take a bite, but then he puts his fork down and fixes me with a serious look. "Is this okay?" he asks.

Copying him, I rest my cutlery down on the sides of my bowl and fiddle with my wine glass stem instead. "It's lovely," I admit, braving to look up and meet his bright blue eyes. They're tender as they look at me. "It's not like Jude and Tian don't look after me in their own ways. But this is…different."

Without saying anything, Evan reaches his hand out and offers me his palm. For a second, I just look at it. This feels like crossing a line.

But why not? We're not doing anything wrong by any means. It's just…

"It's a long time since anyone made me feel vulnerable," I tell him truthfully as I slip my hand against his.

He grunts, his lips quirking in a small smile. "You and me both."

His skin is warm and dry. I absently trace my fingers along the inside of his wrist, but then it's like we both realise how intimate that is and draw back at the same time. I clear my throat and chuckle as I pick up my fork once more.

"You know, if we drop food at home, we just yell out 'Room service!' If Bow isn't already there with us, she comes flying in to gobble it up."

I grin and see Evan visibly relax, also starting to eat. "It's funny your dog would be called Bow," he says after a while.

"Why's that?" I ask with a flick of my eyebrows.

He licks his lips. "My boyfriend's name was Beau. B-e-a-u."

His tone is sad. However, he looks composed. Like he's got a lot running though his mind, but he's not about to lose it.

"The French for 'beautiful'," I murmur.

As far as I'm aware, this is the first time he's talked about his ex to any of us. Something tells me this is a big deal, and even though my heart rate is picking up, I make myself be still and not fidget, waiting for Evan to open up.

"He was beautiful," he says. His Adam's apple bobs as he swallows thickly. He trades his fork for his wine glass, taking a sip. "God, I miss him."

It's my turn to reach for his hand, relieved when he gives me his free one again. He then puts the glass down and rubs his chin, a shuddery breath rattling his chest.

"You don't have to talk about it if you don't want to," I tell him quickly.

But he shakes his head. "I think I'm long overdue to," he says heavily. "Besides, both of your boys told me that communication is important to you all, and the implication was that I'd better improve at it as well."

His lips twitch with the ghost of a smile, but his eyes are still haunted. I rub my thumb against the back of his hand.

"I'd be honoured if you wanted to tell me about Beau," I say softly.

Evan inhales slowly again, then puffs out his cheeks, shaking his head. "Where to start? He was a little, like Tian. He was more into animals and jungle stuff, though, and he liked ABDL sometimes, too."

"Tian does from time to time," I say. "I like being able to care for his every single need when he's in that state."

Evan gives me a grateful look that I imagine only Daddies of littles can share. "Exactly."

I wonder how long it's been since he's talked to anyone about all this. It feels like he's been bottling a lot up, which is never any good.

"Beau was my world. He was gorgeous and cheeky and sweet. We were together for almost ten years. We'd been living together for the last five. I thought we had forever. I took him for granted, working longer and longer hours, telling him and myself that I was saving for our future, that it would be worth it."

He pauses and takes a big gulp of wine, his eyes shining, his jaw clenched. Apparently fortified, he pushes on.

"I was working late on Christmas Eve seven years ago when he was walking down the street, coming home with the last bits for Christmas dinner. He was struck on the pavement by a drunk driver who'd lost control and killed Beau instantly. He died all alone, out in the cold, because I'd convinced myself that making money was more important that spending time with the love of my life."

"Oh, Evan," I say thickly, my own eyes stinging. I slide off my stool and move around the breakfast bar. When I reach him, he turns to face me, making it easier to push my way between his knees. I wrap my arms around his body and hug him tightly. "I'm so incredibly sorry. That must have been harrowing for you. No wonder you haven't wanted to date or celebrate Christmas for so long, if that's what it reminds you of."

Evan squeezes me back, his head resting on my shoulder. "Beau loved Christmas," he croaks, his voice raw with grief. "He always decorated this whole house from top to bottom. When I resurfaced from my fugue state, sometime in the new year, I ripped it all down and threw every single thing away.

I've never so much had a sprig of mistletoe through the door since."

"I completely understand," I assure him.

But he's shaking his head. "I became such a bastard. Rather than processing my guilt, I acted like the rest world was the problem, inflicting my misery onto everyone else. Beau would be so ashamed of me."

I lean back and cup my hands on either side of his face, feeling his short beard under my palms as I look deep into his eyes. "Beau would want you to survive," I say firmly, knowing my words to be true even though I never met the man. "He would be happy that you're still here. That you clung on long enough to make a fresh start. He'd want you to find joy again."

"I think he sent me Tian," Evan says with a rueful chuckle, wiping his eyes with both hands. "Through a bossy corgi. I think he sent me three Christmas miracles."

My heart aches, but it's not all from sadness. "I know you and Jude talked about religion," I say. "But I'm pretty open in my beliefs. I think there are things out there we don't understand. The universe works in strange ways. I do believe that some things are just meant to happen. That people find themselves in the right place at the right time against the highest of odds. Evan, I'm so happy that you found your way to us."

"I don't deserve any of you," he says automatically.

I scoff. "People get things they don't deserve all the time. Good and bad. Beau didn't deserve to die in a tragic accident, and you didn't deserve to be left with a shattered heart. But I'm certain that you've suffered enough and that you shouldn't spend the rest of your life punishing yourself for something that really wasn't your fault."

Evan pulls a handkerchief from his pocket to blow his nose and wipe his eyes. "That's what Marlon said when he signed me up to the Secret Santa blind dates in the first place."

I give him a lopsided grin. "He sounds like a good friend."

"His heart was in the right place," Evan says. He balls up the hanky and tucks it away again, then places both his hands on my hips. "I never wanted to dishonour Beau's memory. But being with Tian and Jude…it didn't feel like disrespecting him in the way I thought it would."

"He would want you to find happiness again," I repeat, hoping my words sink in. "If something ever happened to me, I would want Jude and Tian to look after each other, and if that meant falling in love with someone else, I would wish that for them with my entire spirit."

"I think…" Evan says, pausing to nibble on his lip before looking up at me, resolution in his eyes. "I think the fact that you're a throuple took the pressure off and helped me to see that love isn't finite. It doesn't have to just be between two people. It can come in different shapes and sizes, and it can still be valid and beautiful."

"That's something I do believe with my whole heart," I say.

"Moving on doesn't mean I'm going to love Beau less," he continues. "I'll always love him. However, I don't think anyone but you three could have saved me." His voice catches, but his shimmering eyes don't look away. "Because you showed me that it's possible to love more than one person at a time. So…thank you."

I take a deep breath and nod, processing the moment as best I can, given its enormity. "I'm so glad the universe brought us together. Maybe Beau put us on this path. Who knows?"

Evan rests his forehead on my chest, and I rub his back for a while, carding my fingers through the short salt-and-pepper hair at the back of his head. I've never had this kind of energy with anyone, but despite the tragedy lingering over us, it's beautiful and powerful. Perhaps by freeing himself of this burden, Evan is finally letting Beau go in all the ways his memory was holding him back, letting himself blossom once again.

When he leans away to look at me, there's only the briefest of pauses before our lips are drawn together naturally for a deep and passionate kiss. I feel so close to him in that moment, there's simply no hesitation. When we pull back for breath, he leans his forehead against mine, his fingers clinging to my clothes.

"Let me take care of you," I murmur.

He shakes his head. "You already have. It's my turn now. Please let me."

Wordlessly, I nod, watching as he rises to his feet. He takes my hand and leads me away from the kitchen and over to the sofa where he starts to kiss me again. I relax into the embrace, feeling the warmth of his body against mine.

Slowly, he starts to peel me out of my clothes. When I reach for his jumper, though, he gently bats my hands away. "I'm taking care of you, remember?" he mumbles into my mouth with a smile.

I can feel his hope and happiness like a living, breathing thing. It fills me with such joy that it's easy to grin and relinquish control where I never normally would.

Once I'm naked, he sinks to his knees, his hands trailing down my thighs as he nuzzles my cock and balls with his nose, trailing kisses along the sensitive skin. His fingers slip around the base of my shaft as his lips glide around my head. He sucks and licks, making me harder. I fondle his soft hair, moaning with my head dropped back as he takes his time to explore my body.

Eventually, he pops off, both of us panting. His lips are swollen and red with my engorged length bobbing in front of his face. He looks up at me through spiky lashes. His pose is submissive but the calm confidence radiating from him now still very much tells me that he's in charge, and I love it.

"I want to bend you over this couch and fuck you," he says hoarsely, as if to prove my point.

My breath hitches. I do occasionally let Jude penetrate me, but I'm still very much topping from the bottom. I can't even remember the last time I let anyone else do it. It's not the act itself I'm averse to, but the giving up my power and control that usually doesn't appeal to me.

However, I've already given myself over to Evan in a way that feels freeing. I know he doesn't see me as a sub or a boy because that's not who I am. He sees me as a lover, and he's going to take care of me.

"Please," I whimper.

Gently, he turns me around and places his hand on my back, encouraging me to lean over the back of the sofa. I automatically spread my legs for him, gasping when he kneels down again and licks straight into my crease, finding my hole to eat me out. I literally can't even remember the last time someone did that for me because I didn't want it.

I very much want it now.

Hugging the sofa, I moan, allowing myself to let go in a way I never usually can during sex. You can't when you're the one calling the shots.

Now I'm at his mercy and it's perfect.

I grind against the couch, but not with enough friction that I'm in danger of coming. In the back of my mind, I worry slightly about ruining the upholstery. But then I reason he wouldn't have told me he was going to fuck me here if he cared about that.

He takes his time, slowly adding his fingers to stretch me out. I guess he knows this is unusual for me and I need a little extra prep, but he seems happy to give it to me. He produces lube from somewhere that he adds to his spit, and by the time I hear him rip a condom open, I'm so well coated it's dripping down my balls and thighs.

"Are you ready?" he asks, nudging his fat head against my entrance.

"Oh, fuck," I mutter, already feeling drunk with lust. "Yes, Evan."

My fingers grip the sofa cushions, keeping my tension there so the most important area can stay open and relaxed for him. We both grunt and gasp as he pushes past my ring of muscle, sliding inside me and filling me up.

"Sweet baby Jesus in the manger," I rasp as he keeps going more than feels possible. He chuckles and runs his hand along my spine.

"You feel phenomenal," he groans.

"I don't just let anyone do this, you know," I tell him, laughing weakly. "You better appreciate it."

He wraps his arm around my chest to make me stand again, then touches my chin with his free hand, encouraging me to look at him. "I know," he says, his voice raw and sincere.

Then he kisses me as he begins to move, dropping his hand from my face to encircle my cock, stroking me in time with his thrusts. I grab the back of the couch to brace myself, gyrating my hips to meet him as he pounds into me. He's found my prostate, and I can't help myself as I let out a low, continuous wail. As much as I love topping, this feels incredible.

"Yes, *yes*," I hiss, gasping for breath as my orgasm comes racing to greet me. "Yes, don't stop, holy fuck."

"Come for me, Sai," he whispers, nipping at my earlobe. I drop my head back onto his shoulder and gnash my teeth, spilling all over his hand and the sofa. "Good boy," he says, sounding pleased. Whether that's with himself or me or both, I'm not sure. But I hope it's both.

"That's normally my line," I protest with a laugh, my body trembling all over with the shock of my climax.

"Not tonight," he says. Then he's grabbing my hips and hammering into me hard, taking his pleasure from me in a way I'm not ever sure I've consented to anyone else in the past.

Evan can have it all, though.

"Yes, Daddy," I whimper, slightly delirious. I've definitely *never* called anyone that. But Evan knows I'm also Daddy, so in my mind it's not only okay, it's hot. He might be topping, but I know he respects me as an equal.

And I want him to come in my arse.

Evan howls and grips me so hard I'm sure I'm going to bruise. Just like Jude. Evan shudders as he pumps his load inside the condom, but I can still feel him throbbing inside me. Eventually, he flops his chest against my back, breathing heavily as he hugs me tight.

"Thank you," he mumbles.

I find his hand and intwine my fingers with his, bringing them up to kiss them. "No, thank you," I say, slightly giddy.

His mouth finds mine once more and he kisses me until he goes soft inside me, and we get too cold and sticky to stay there any longer. But before I can think about what to do, he's the one going to the small bathroom, bringing back two washcloths so we can carefully wipe each other down. Perhaps he thought we might just clean ourselves, but we both naturally reach for the other.

I kiss his lips again, unable to contain my grin. "Thank you," I tell him once more, wanting him to understand what a gift he's given me. And hope that he's given himself.

I also hope he knows now that change isn't inherently

bad. Different can be amazing. And that he absolutely deserves happiness in his life after all this time.

Before we can find our clothes and reheat dinner, I pick up my wine glass. Holding it up until he mirrors me, we toast a second time. "To a fresh start," I repeat.

"To a fresh start," he agrees with a nod before we both take a sip. "Thank you."

I don't fight him. He can have the last one.

For now.

CHAPTER 16
Evan

Going back to Bootleg seemed like a good idea at the time. After completing my three different kinds of dates with Tian, Jude, and Sai, it made sense to put myself back out there and see how I felt about the scene with renewed enthusiasm.

Except I'm sitting here looking at the pretty boys, and all I can think about is what my three Christmas miracles are up to.

It's not like I haven't made any progress. When I first arrived, I actually went to the daycare to sit awhile with the littles playing with their toys. But I became too preoccupied worrying what I would do if one of them actually approached me, because that might mean they'd want more. They'd want to play or fuck, and I just can't give that to anyone else right now.

So I removed myself before any of them could come ask me how I was doing or if I was interested in joining their fun. I'd only disappoint them or hurt their feelings, which is definitely not what I want.

Which begs the question: what *do* I want?

I'm nursing a glass of merlot as usual, letting the loud music and swirling lights in the darkness consume me. I know I *don't* want to fall back into old habits, so perhaps I should get myself out of here before I do something I'll regret. But realistically, I'm not sure I'm in danger of catching someone's eye for a no strings quickie. The thought doesn't appeal to me in the slightest, with a little or anyone else.

I wonder what the trio are doing right now as I idly thumb through my messages from all of them. Unsurprisingly, Jude is the chattiest. He doesn't seem to need replies from me, happy to send updates almost daily on what he and the others are up to. I treasure the words I've received from each of them equally, but I appreciate that he's making me feel like I'm still connected to all of them.

Whether or not that's his intention, I really couldn't say.

Our arrangement was only ever supposed to boost my confidence and remind me not just how to be a Daddy but that I still love this lifestyle even after everything. In that regard, it's been a huge success. So much so that now I'm finally moving on from my soul-deep grief, I'm not interested in any more meaningless hook-ups. I want to try and build a life with someone again.

Sai, Jude and Tian already have a life together. We had fun and it meant a lot to me—I hope it wasn't superficial to them. But they were never looking for anyone to date.

How would that even work, anyhow? Seeing them each as a one-off was fun, but where would we go from there?

I'm lingering on Sai's last message, sent after he went home that evening after our dinner date. Just thinking about the way he let me fuck him gets me throbbing in my trousers. But it's more than that. Confessing to him about Beau felt cathartic in ways I'd never dared to imagine. It was as if my boy was there, giving me his permission to open up my heart again.

I reread the simple message for the hundredth time.

SAI: Don't be a stranger

I rub the side of the phone, rolling those four words over in my mind. He specifically said to me that he was glad I'd come into his and his boys' lives. He said that he wanted me to be happy and that I mattered.

But does that mean I could text back and…what? Ask if I could see him and the others again? Would that be the right way to go about it or should I message them all individually? That immediately feels too daunting to consider. Perhaps I could just message Tian? He was the one that started all this, after all. But what would I say?

"Evan!"

I look up to see Miller beaming at me. I'm propped up at the bar and he's behind, serving. I'm sure I didn't notice him before, but it's pretty busy tonight, so maybe he came out from his office to help the guys on shift. Either way, I realise I'm genuinely pleased to see him.

"Miller," I say, reaching out to shake his hand. "How're things?"

"Good," he says, looking proudly around the club. "We're having a great month. The Secret Santa event was a huge success." He suddenly winces and peeks at me. "Sorry, I didn't mean to bring that up."

But I shake my head and smile. "It actually turned out really well," I confess, feeling warmth blossom in my chest. "I reached out to Tian and ended up going on a few dates, not just with him, but his two boyfriends as well."

Miller's eyebrows shoot up. "Wow. Congrats, mate. I didn't think you were interested in that, though?"

"Neither did I," I admit with a chuckle. "But Tian is special. They all are."

Miller beams. I know he's supposed to be serving customers, but his staff don't seem too swamped at the moment. So if he's okay chatting with me for a bit, I appreciate having someone to voice my thoughts to. Perhaps he might be able to give me some advice.

Right on cue, he nods at me. "So are you going to see them again?"

I sigh and swirl the wine in my glass. "I'm not sure. It's complicated. I didn't think I was ready to date anyone a couple of weeks ago. There are *three* of them."

Miller hums and rubs his chin. Then his eyes light up. He holds a finger up to me as if to tell me, 'wait there' and dashes down the bar to say something into his kitty boyfriend's ear. Charlie nods as Miller speaks, then he ducks out into the throng of the club. Miller gives me a thumbs up and points after Charlie before turning to serve another customer.

I'm not sure what they're up to, but I've got nothing better to do than wait. My wine keeps me company for a few minutes until Charlie returns with a handsome man beside him. The kitty struts back to work, but the newcomer has obviously been told by him to come see me. He looks to be in his mid-thirties and if I know anything about tailoring, I'd say his suit costs more than my whole wardrobe. I never was a clothes horse, but this man makes me reconsider whether I should be making more of an effort.

From one Daddy Dom to another, I immediately sense the vibe, but his smile is warm as he approaches.

"Jacob!" Miller cries over the music and chatter. "Thanks for coming over. This is my friend, Evan. I thought you might be able to offer him some advice."

I blink and automatically offer him my hand, which he shakes. "Nice to meet you," I say politely.

"Likewise," Jacob says. He sounds genuine, which is a relief. I feel a bit awkward that Miller has bothered someone with my problems. However, Jacob doesn't appear put out as he leans against the bar, smiling between Miller and me. "How can I help?"

Miller smirks knowingly but not in an unkind way. "Evan here has accidentally found himself involved with a throuple and he's not sure how to go about taking things further."

Jacob blinks, then slowly turns his gaze to me. "No, shit?" he asks with a laugh.

"Um, yeah," I say, feeling like I'm missing something. "That's the very abridged version of the novel."

Jacob laughs again and claps his hand on my shoulder, giving it a squeeze. "I accidentally found myself taking three best friends on individual dates. The abridged version of *that* novel is now we all sleep in the same bed."

It's my turn to stare and then eventually blink slowly. "Are you fucking with me?" I ask genuinely.

"See?" Miller says gleefully as he slices up lime wedges. "I told you he'd probably have advice."

Jacob turns and looks out over the dance floor. "Ah! There they are. You see those three guys grinding against each other by the speaker?"

I follow where he's pointing and make out three young men. The smallest looks a little shy and the tallest like he's a lot of trouble. The chubbier one has a protective air about him with his hands on both the others as he looks adoringly at them.

"You're all in a relationship together?" I say, hardly daring to believe it.

Jacob nods. "It's unconventional, I know. Sometimes people don't understand it, but that's their problem. It's one of the reasons we like coming here. We know polyamory isn't just accepted, it's pretty tame compared to some of the other shenanigans that go on. Plus, we've been encouraging Luke to explore age play more in the daycare."

My heart flip-flops in my chest as I think of Tian. "He's a little?" I ask faintly.

Jacob nods. "They're all my boys, and they enjoy different things. Luke has overcome the most, though. Age play helps him let go. Sometimes he struggles to accept that he deserves love."

The admiration is clear in Jacob's words, and I feel that old familiar lump rise in my throat. "How do you help him do that?" I hope my tone is casual and not a desperate plea for help. It's not really a mystery to me that even after my groundbreaking talk with Sai, I'm still having difficulty believing that I'd be worthy of love from just one man, let alone three.

Jacob's still watching his boys like they're the most precious things in his whole world. I imagine that's exactly what they are. "Sometimes one-on-one time with Daddy," he replies, "so I can love him slowly and tell him over and over that he's perfect and beautiful and mine." He flicks his gaze back to me and winks. "Sometimes my big boy and my naughty boy help as well, and we gang up on our pretty boy. It's hard to argue you're not adored when it's three against one."

"That's wonderful," I murmur.

My thoughts are buzzing and I'm still feeling over-whelmed. But seeing a real-life foursome in front of my eyes makes some of my doubts a little quieter. Jude oh-so-casually mentioned to me a couple of times that there's an adult entertainment four-piece polycule that he's mildly obsessed with, but that's different. People control what they release on social media.

I'm seeing this for myself firsthand. It's hard to deny the way that Jacob is looking at his three boys or the erotic way they're dancing with each other.

I know I had an arrangement with Tian that has morphed

into something with Jude and Sai as well. But if I take a step back and look at the big picture—like I have been with rereading all our messages—there's really nothing to suggest that any of them are keen to be rid of me now that my Daddy lessons are over.

"How did you decide that you wanted to make it work with all of you? Did you know from the start?"

Jacob scoffs and shakes his head, rubbing the back of his neck. "No. We had to cut through far too much bullshit and stop getting in our own way. There might have been a break-down involving a pile of kittens."

"But?" Miller prompts with a grin. He's still hovering doing prep work, apparently wanting to oversee our heart-to-heart. I'm not sure I can be trusted not to be a moron and completely self-sabotage myself, so I don't mind him getting involved.

"But," Jacob repeats with his own grin. "We got there in the end by taking some big, scary baby steps. I'd been with them all individually, and that gave them to confidence to try moving beyond friendship with each other. The chemistry was all there, so we slowly tried more as a group. Once we got over the fact that western society is still so hung up on monogamous couples being the only way to achieve true happiness and played by our own rules, it all came surprisingly naturally."

I exhale and sip my wine, thinking over everything he's said. "My situation is slightly different. They're already together. Sai and Jude are married and have been dating Tian for a few years. It's me who's the outsider, and I guess I'm worried about messing things up."

Jacob gives me a serious look and squeezes my shoulder again. "Life's too short."

I grunt and shake my head. "Don't I know it."

And I do. But although the sadness is still there when I

think of Beau—I imagine it always will be—it doesn't wreck me.

That's kind of incredible.

"What do you really have to lose?" Jacob asks. "If the three of them are stable, then it's just you putting yourself out there. It'll either work out or it won't, but you'll never know if you don't try."

Humming, I look back over at the three dancing boys. They're trading kisses and shaking their backsides to the perky Christmas song currently pumping over the sound system. A woman with an incredible voice appears to be counting down the days till Christmas, and the tall boy in particular is losing his shit in the sweetest way. Like his life depends on this songstress making it to December twenty-fifth with her secret love.

His larger-than-life energy reminds me of a certain tattooed nurse who always seems to be searching for a spanking.

I've lived with remorse like it's a physical weight these past several years, letting it drag me down and hold me back. I don't want to regret letting my three Christmas miracles go without finding out if we could be something more.

"Baby steps?" I ask with a crocked eyebrow, looking back at Jacob.

"Big, scary lurching ones," he says, flashing me a knowing smile.

He's right. I don't have to arrive on their doorstep and ask them all to be my boyfriends. We're not there yet. But just realising that could be what I *do* want sounds like one of those scary steps.

And thinking about it, there is something I can do to even up what we've shared so far between the four of us.

I pick my phone up from the table. But before I unlock it, I clasp Jacob's arm and catch Miller's gaze.

"Thank you," I tell them both sincerely.

Miller salutes at me. "Us Daddies have got to stick together."

I think of Sai and warmth blossoms in my chest. "Yeah," I agree.

With a final nod, Jacob goes back to his boys and Miller starts serving customers again, leaving me alone with my phone and my wine. I want to choose my words carefully, but before too long I'm happy enough and press send.

There. I've tried. It's a great lurching baby step, and all I can do is hope that it's in the right direction.

CHAPTER 17

Jude

It was my turn to pick a Christmas movie that evening. Obviously, I went with *Elf* because it's the best, and I too take every opportunity to scream *"SANTA!"* during the month of December. Sai's more of an *It's a Wonderful Life* kind of guy, and Tian likes to rewatch all the Disney classics at this time of year, which is fine by me. But they always both humour me with my slightly wackier choices. Honestly, they're lucky I'm not bullying them into watching Die Hard…yet. I've still got time.

In my opinion, it's not officially Christmas until Hans Gruber falls off the Nakatomi Plaza.

But as I glance around the living room, I can sense something is a little off. Both Sai and Tian keep absently scrolling through their phones beside me on the couch. Even Bow is subdued at our feet, like she's sensing a vibe.

It doesn't take a genius to guess what's probably on their minds.

One Mr Evan Zegler.

From what I can tell, Sai had an excellent time with him the other night. The bruises on his hips certainly suggest so.

The hickey on my neck is mostly faded now, which is probably a good thing for work as my uniform collar only covers so much. But I do miss it and I'm enjoying living vicariously through my husband.

But despite all his cheery smiles, I can tell there's a sadness lurking there just like there was with Tian. When I pressed Sai on how he was feeling about the whole Evan situation, he just said, 'I've left the ball in his court' and that was it. To make things worse, Tian took that as a sign that the time wasn't right yet to reach back out to Evan himself.

Honestly, I love both these men with my whole heart. But right now, they certainly are being twats.

Can't they see how we all have such amazing chemistry? I know they're aware that Evan has improved in leaps and bounds since we started this little project of ours. But why are they so convinced that there's a limit to how far it can all go?

Perhaps it's time I taught them some brat lessons in how to go after what you want and not stop until you get it.

"Okay," I say in exasperation, reaching for the remote and pressing pause. It doesn't matter that I've seen this movie twenty times already, I'm not missing any of it because the men I love need their heads smacking together.

"Is everything all right?" Sai asks, immediately on alert.

"No," I say simply. I move the big bowl of half-eaten popcorn to the coffee table and rearrange myself under our shared blanket. As usual, Tian is in the middle of us, so I can turn and rest my back on the sofa arm whilst I berate my lovers. "You're being idiots. Both of you."

Tian's eyes go wide, and I immediately regret going in hard. "I am?" he squeaks.

I find his knee under the blanket and give it a squeeze. "Loveable idiots," I assure him.

"Any reason in particular?" Sai asks with an unimpressed arched eyebrow.

Blimey, I thought I was the brat. He's *definitely* aware of what I'm banging on about and is being deliberately obtuse.

I huff and arch my own eyebrow back at him. "Oh, I don't know. A certain salt-and-pepper haired Daddy who's currently all alone in Russell Square because for some reason you two are walking on eggshells about seeing him again."

"Jude," Sai says firmly with a frown. "It's a delicate situation and you know it. Evan has to move at his own pace. That's why we've left it with him to reach out to us."

I tsk. "The man who thinks he's unworthy of love and who's about as confident at Bambi on ice right now when it comes to dating? You want him to be even braver than he already has been?"

"He's the Daddy," Tian says quietly but with conviction. Then he glances at Sai, and it looks like they hold hands under the blanket. "I mean, he's *a* Daddy. The whole point of this was to remind him that he's in charge. If we overwhelm him, he might shut down again."

"It's going to take time for him to remember what this power dynamic can do for him," Sai agrees. "You can't just brat your way into his life and demand that he lets you through the front door."

I pout, not wanting to acknowledge that he might have a point.

That being said, I'm not done.

"Can we all at least admit how we're feeling, though?" I whine.

Bow's ears flick up, and I make an effort to bring my pitch down. There's no point in bitching if she's going to be the only one who can hear me.

"About Evan. Tian, you promised you'd message him and let him know how much you'd been thinking about him and ask if he wanted to see you again. I think we should all feel free to meet up with him again!"

"Have *you* messaged him, then?" Tian asks curiously.

I sigh and roll my eyes. "No, I have not," I grumble. "I'm trying to be respectful of both your wishes and all that, aren't I? We have to be on the same page, right?"

"Right," Tian agrees warmly.

"Which is why I want to talk it through now," I insist. "I can't help but feel like we're all scared to admit that we really like this man, which is wild since we're *literally* polyamorous. No one is doing anything wrong here!"

Sai sighs and reaches forwards to squeeze my leg through the blanket. His expression is one of deep affection. "You've always worn your heart on your sleeve, baby. I don't know why I'm surprised this time isn't any different. I think… honestly, I think that the reason I'm so hesitant is precisely because this seems so important. I do have strong feelings for Evan, and I want to make sure we're doing this right." He rubs my leg and smiles. "I love that you want to rush in, though, my gorgeous boy."

I cross my arms and roll my eyes, but I'm also smiling. "I hate being patient," I grumble.

"Good things come to those who wait, though," Tian counters sweetly.

"Good things come to those who work their arses off," I fire back.

I've always been very resistant to the idea of sitting around hoping the things I want will fall into my lap. The urge to be proactive is strong.

But I'm also incredibly sympathetic to the fact that Evan is recovering from a big trauma. He gave Sai permission to relay to me and Tian what he disclosed about his previous boyfriend, Beau. It broke my fucking heart, if I'm being honest, and explained a great deal of Evan's behaviour up until this point. I'm really glad he felt like he could open up and tell us that. I feel closer to him because of it.

Sai and Tian are just trying to respect his healing process. I want to do that, too. But I also can't help but think that I know what's best for everyone, and they're not listening to me.

"Hun, I know you feel strongly about this," Sai says in that annoyingly soothing tone that works too well. I huff, but my heart rate calms all the same. "We do, too. Just because we're not shouting it from the rooftops doesn't mean we're not passionate."

"Daddy Sai is right," Tian chimes in with a nod.

I sigh and rub his knee, liking how we're all touching each other in this moment. That feels significant. Because we're doing this together. I've only felt like this once before, and that was when Sai and I were falling in love with Tian.

And, yeah, when I frame it like that, I get that this is actually kind of important, and a bit frightening because it's so big, and maybe I shouldn't go charging in like a bull in a china shop.

"Sorry," I mumble.

Sai reaches out for my hand, which I give him. "You have nothing to be sorry about, hun. Thank you for pushing us into talking. But I hope you can see why we have to let Evan set the pace and respect his boundaries. If he—"

Tian's phone pings and he lunges for it like it's a grenade that will go off if he doesn't get to it in time. I can't lie, though. I hold my breath in excitement. It's probably just one of his friends, but—

"It's from Daddy Evan," he whispers reverently, his eyes darting back and forth across the screen as he reads. I'm still holding my breath, dying to know what he's said. "Oh my god," Tian utters.

"What?" I cry, unable to take it any longer.

Tian looks up at Sai and I with shining eyes. "He wants to invite me over again," he says, his voice trembling. "He says he's learned so much from all our dates and thinks he can do much better than our first one. If I'm up for that, he's told me not to bring anything this time. He says…" His voice catches and he places his hand on his chest as he hiccups down a little sob. "He says that Daddy Evan will take care of everything."

"YES!" I bellow, punching my fist in the air, making Bow jump up and bark. "I told you! I *told* you!"

Tian sniffles but he's grinning. Sai reaches over and brushes the tears from Tian's cheeks with his thumb. "This is all because of you, baby boy," Sai says proudly. "You've helped Evan so much. I'm so happy he wants to see you again."

But Tian's face drops. "What about you two, though?" he asks anxiously. He looks down at his phone with guilt, then back at us. "Why does he just want to see me?"

"Because you're amazing," I say. "Duh. Don't worry about us. Evan knows he was very wobbly when he first met you. I bet he wants to see you again so he can bring his A game." I tickle Tian's side and make him yelp. "Besides, I bet he wants to have a chance to mark you like he did with me and Sai."

I waggle my eyebrows as Tian blushes. "Oh, I don't know about that. He doesn't say anything like that in the message about…you know…."

Sai brushes a lock of Tian's hair back from his face. "It wouldn't surprise me if Evan felt confident enough now to get to know you more intimately. Whether that's with a proper age play date or in bed. How would you feel about that, Baby Tee?"

He's still blushing as he squirms to snuggle up to Sai. "I like Daddy Evan a *lot*, Daddy Sai."

My heart feels like it could burst with pride. It's not lost on me how monumental it is for Tian to admit his physical attraction to someone else like that. It shows he's secure in his relationship with me and Sai enough to follow his heart and open up to the possibility of something with Evan.

"What are you going to reply?" I ask excitedly.

Tian bites his lower lip and can't quite contain his shy smile. "I don't know. Can you both help me?"

"Of course," Sai says as I nod enthusiastically.

"I think this requires fresh popcorn!" I declare, grabbing the bowl and jumping up. Bow barks and runs in a couple of circles before following me to the kitchen.

As I get another bag popping in the microwave, I take a moment to just be in the moment and grip the counter, sitting with my feelings. I meant what I said. This is Tian's opportunity to get the quality time with Evan that Sai and I had. He's almost a different man now. Tian deserves to experience Daddy Evan at his very best.

And after that, who knows? But I think it's safe to say that there are so many possibilities, I can't stop myself from being hopeful.

The four of us have so much more to discover together.

CHAPTER 18

Tian

NERVES FLUTTER IN MY TUMMY AS I RING DADDY EVAN'S doorbell, but this time I insisted on coming to his house alone. I'm sure Sai and Jude would have both loved to drop me off, but this is something I need to do on my own. Besides, they know Evan now. It's not that they're worried about me. Far from it.

I think if I'd let them tag along, they'd be unable to stop themselves barging in and joining us.

But this is special. When I first came here, both Daddy Evan and I were filled with such trepidation. I was trying to be there for him whilst he fumbled his way back into Daddy-ing. But since then, he's had such wonderful dates with Jude and Sai.

I'm excited to think I might get to see the real Daddy Evan tonight.

He was very insistent that I didn't need to bring a bag of goodies like last time, but I am still wearing a silly Christmas jumper under my coat and a pair of my favourite undies that have racing cars on. My heart is thumping as I wait under the awning, noticing how more of the lights are on inside the house. It's as if Daddy Evan is slowly waking up from hibernation.

When the front door flies open, I can't help but gasp in surprise. Daddy Evan is also wearing a Christmas jumper. It has a gingerbread man playing an electric guitar on it.

A laugh bubbles out of my chest before I can help it. "Daddy Evan, you look so good!" I cry.

He beams and holds out his arms, displaying the jumper in all its glory. "You like it?"

"I love it!" I declare as I skip inside the house. He closes the door and immediately wraps his arms around me. It's a good job he's strong, because my knees have gone weak and I'm in danger of folding to the floor. "Thank you for inviting me over again."

He squeezes me tighter and rests his head against mine. "Thank you for accepting, Baby Tee. Here, let me take your things."

As we remove my coat and other outer accessories, he cries out in delight at my jumper with Father Christmas riding a skateboard on. I also proudly show off my socks that are patterned with mince pies.

"I hope you don't mind, but I did bring my slippers," I tell him, pointing to the tote bag that's resting by my shoes.

"Of course that's fine," he says, fishing them out for me. "We don't want your toesies getting chilly."

I giggle, but then he's crouching down and slipping them on my feet for me, and suddenly my heart is at a high risk of melting like a snowman in summer.

"Thank you, Daddy Evan," I whisper.

He stands up and takes my hand. For a second we stare into each other's eyes, and I want to kiss him so badly. But I also need to let him set the pace, so I smile instead and swing our arms.

"What did you want to do this evening?" I ask, genuinely curious.

Daddy Evan's returning smile is bashful, but he also looks excited. "I've got us an easy dinner. It's just chips and chicken nuggets shaped like Christmas trees that we can put in the oven, and baked beans we can microwave. The nuggies are organic and free range, I checked."

I beam, so pleased he remembered that's important to me. "That sounds yummy for our tummies!"

"That's what I thought," he agrees. "Nice and warm for a cold winter's night. But the reason we have an easy tea is because we're also going to be baking gingerbread. Some to eat now and some…to make a gingerbread house!"

I gasp and dance on my toes. "Really?"

He nods. "You enjoyed decorating the cupcakes last time, so I figured this was like the next level up."

"Can we go start now?" I cry, genuinely eager. This is already such a good little date!

Daddy Evan takes a deep breath and squeezes my hand. "If it's okay with you, Tee, I'd love to show you something first. It's very special to me, a bit like a secret. I want to share it with you."

My heart starts thumping again, so loud I'm sure he can hear it. A special secret just for me?

"I'd love that, Daddy Evan," I whisper.

He nods and takes another breath before turning…and leading me up the stairs. I try not to tremble with excitement but also pride. It's a big deal for him to share something of the rest of the house with me. I know from Sai and Jude that all of us have only been down to the basement level before.

Quietly, I keep hold of his hand and follow him up to the second floor where we stop in front of a closed door. "This room used to belong to someone extremely important to me, Tee," Daddy Evan says, his low voice a soft rasp. "He's not here anymore, and that made me so incredibly sad. I didn't go in here for a very long time. But I thought you might like it, so I gave it a good clean. I think he would want you to enjoy it. We've got lots of time for baking, so if you wanted to stay here for a while, that would be okay." He takes another deep breath. "Or if you don't like it, that's okay, too. No pressure."

I bite my lip, trying not to feel overwhelmed. This is absolutely incredible. I feel so privileged to be here in this moment. "I'm sure it's wonderful, Daddy Evan," I tell him sincerely.

He swallows and looks like he steadies his nerves. Then he reaches out and opens the door, letting it swing inwards.

I can't help it. I gasp again, my eyes brimming with tears.

This is Beau's playroom. I just know it. The bedspread has animals all over it and one of the walls is papered to look like big, jungle leaves. A hammock hangs in the corner from the ceiling, filled with animal cuddly toys. As I step inside, the rug under my slippers is shaped like a lake with fish and octopi peeking out to say hello. Butterflies hang from the lampshade above my head, and there's colourful flower-patterned bunting all around the tops of the walls.

The room smells fresh and lemony. Daddy Evan did say he'd given it a good clean. But there's also a big candle in a glass jar on the dresser, recently lit and filling the air with sweet and spicy scents of Christmas. The lightbulb is dimmed low, making the space feel cosy.

It takes me a moment to trust myself enough to speak. "It's amazing," I say, sincerity in every syllable. I could imagine losing myself in here for hours, my imagination running wild.

"I bought you some presents," Evan murmurs, moving beyond me to where a few items are laid out on the bed. "I know you like vehicles and travel themed things, so this is a game where you have to sail your hot air balloon around the world."

I try not to let my hands shake as I take the box and look at the beautiful illustration on the front. It's an old-fashioned map of the globe, and like Daddy Evan said, each player gets a different coloured hot air balloon piece to play with, just like my bedside lamp in my playroom back over at Daddy Sai and Jude' place.

At a glance, the game rules look like a version of Snakes and Ladders, and I can't wait to play it. "Can we open it when the gingerbread is cooling?" I ask excitedly.

He nods with a hint of a smile. "That's what I was thinking, too." Then he reaches back to the bed and picks up a neatly folded pile of clothes. "I had to guess your size, so I hope they're not too big. But good boys deserve special Christmas pyjamas, don't you think?"

Carefully, I place the game on the dresser away from the candle and accept the bundle. The material is thick and soft under my fingers, and when I shake it out, I discover a long-sleeved top with a single big design of reindeers flying Santa's sleigh, then full-length bottoms with lots of little sleighs and reindeers.

"I love them!" I squeak, clutching them to my chest.

"If they fit, they're yours to keep, baby boy," Daddy Evan says warmly.

I jiggle on the spot before thrusting the clothes back into his hands and yanking my jumper over my head. "Help me put them on, Daddy Evan!"

It's only when I drop the top on the floor that I realise my T-shirt came off with it, leaving my torso naked. Daddy Evan's eyes have gone wide, and I giggle. Rather than feeling shy, I'm playful.

"Dah-dee," I whine with a pout, really leaning into my

regression. "I only little. Baby Tee need Daddy help." I lift my foot and waggle it in front of him. "Pull! Pull!"

Swallowing, Daddy Evan places my pyjamas back on the bed. Then he gently touches my ankle, easing the first sock off.

By the time both socks are off and he's unzipping my jeans, I'm no longer giggling. My breaths are ragged and I'm clasping my hands in front of my chest, watching the way his big hands move so delicately to take care of me. As he slides the jeans down my legs, he looks up at me, his eyes filled with wonder.

"Daddy Evan," I whisper, touching the side of his face lightly. I'm only wearing my undies now, and my pee-pee is feeling all stiff and tingly inside them.

"You're so beautiful, Baby Tee," he croaks. His fingers are resting on my shins, and even just that little bit of contact is electric. "Thank you for coming back to see me again. Thank you for rescuing my broken heart."

I'm definitely trembling now, even though it's nice and warm in the playroom. I brush my thumb against his cheek, looking into his bright blue eyes. I'm a bit bigger again now.

Sexier.

"Baby Tee would do anything for Daddy Evan," I say, realising in that moment that I mean it. I trust him like I do Daddy Sai and naughty Jude.

"I'd do anything for you, too, baby boy," he says, still kneeling at my feet with his hands pressed against my skin. "Tell Daddy Evan what you want, what you need."

My chest rises and falls rapidly as I look down at him, and I'm almost getting dizzy from the shallow breaths. It's a rush. I like it. "Daddy play with Tee?" I ask in hushed tones. "Play a special grown-up game?"

He groans and closes his eyes for a second before looking back at me. "Do you want Daddy to touch you, Tee?" I nod, bunching my hands in front of my face to try and hide my grin.

"Daddy. Daddy, Daddy, *Daddy.*"

There's only me and him in this moment. I know I have another Daddy who loves me, but right now, I don't need to use *this* amazing Daddy's full name. We both know who we're talking about.

"Do you want Daddy to make you feel good?" he asks, and I nod again. He takes a breath. "Do you want Daddy to take his clothes off as well?"

"Yes, please," I hiss urgently. "And we can play on the nice bed with all the animals. I'll be *soooo* good for you, Daddy. I promise."

Daddy makes a keening noise and pulls me into a hug with his head against my hip. I run my fingers through his soft hair, scratching his head with my nails. He shudders. "You're already so good for me, baby boy. Better than any Christmas present. You're so beautiful."

My cheeks flush and I almost lose the battle with my unstable knees. "Thank you, Daddy," I whisper, my throat thick with emotion. I want to show him that he's such an amazing Daddy and that I can be absolutely perfect for him. "I'll do anything you want me to. Just tell me and I'll be good."

He's breathing heavily as he rises to his feet, his hands cupping on either side of my face. "Can you kiss me, sweet boy?"

I don't even bother answering. I just rise on my tiptoes and press my lips to his, tasting his warm mouth. He moans and immediately kisses me back as he holds my sides tightly, his mouth connecting with mine over and over. Then his tongue starts sneaking through, licking past my lips, and I giggle, copying him.

My pee-pee is *very* tingly now.

"Can Daddy kiss me on my special private places, too?" I ask against his lips, squirming in his grip. I'm clinging to his jumper with both fists, otherwise I think I might have collapsed like a puppet whose strings have been cut. I'm completely boneless and quivering, my skin hot and my breaths fluttery like the butterflies above our heads.

Daddy hums and runs his hands up and down my flanks. "Where are the special places you want Daddy to kiss, Baby Tee?" He wraps one of his hands over mine, covering it completely. "Show Daddy."

Giggling, I guide his hand, making a map like the one for the hot air balloons.

"Here," I say, starting by brushing his fingers over one budded nipple, then the other. Then I push it down to where I'm hard and wet in my undies. "H-here," I say again, feeling lightheaded as he strokes me through the soft cotton. "A-and here." I turn around and slide his middle finger along my crack over the undies, my hole puckering at just the thought of it.

Daddy moans as he fondles my botty. Then he starts kissing the side of my neck, his other hand reaching around and rubbing my pee-pee. "If you lie very still and be such a good boy," he mumbles against my skin, "Daddy will kiss you in all those places for as long as you want."

I gasp, leaning my back against his chest for support. "Until my pee-pee is happy?" I ask.

He squeezes it and I yelp and shiver. "Is this your pee-pee?" he asks.

"Uh-huh," I say with a nod.

"I bet it's so pretty, just like Baby Tee," he murmurs between kisses along my jaw. He's massaging my pee-pee firmly, making it throb. "I bet it tastes like candy canes. If Daddy plays with his baby boy's pee-pee, will it be happy enough to drip yummy cream for Daddy to lick?"

"Y-yes," I practically sob. "I promise, Daddy. I'll be so good for you. You can play with my pee-pee and my botty and anything you like."

He growls and hooks his thumbs over the top of my undies. "You're so sweet, Tee. So good for Daddy. Please lie on the bed with your botty in the air and your head on the pillows."

He slides my last scrap of clothing down my legs, leaving me totally naked. My pee-pee is pointing upwards and shiny. I want Daddy to make it so happy, I'll do whatever he asks.

I scramble onto the bed and hug the pillows, resting on my knees so my botty is up high. I spread my legs so Daddy can see my hole. I feel so naughty but in a good, tingly way. Twisting my head, I see that Daddy has already pulled his jumper off so I can see his solid, hairy chest. His eyes meet mine as he undoes his trousers and pulls everything else off together so he's naked as well.

"You're gorgeous, Daddy," I say breathlessly. I love that he looks different to both Daddy Sai and Jude. I'm such a lucky boy with all these beautiful men in my life.

His pee-pee also looks excited as he walks towards me, smiling at me and making me feel adorable. "Not as gorgeous as Baby Tee," he insists, running his hand along my spine and cupping my botty. "Thank you for doing exactly as Daddy asked. Now, can you be a good boy and stay still whilst Daddy gives you all his kisses? You can talk as much as you like. In fact, Daddy wants to hear all your pretty noises. But you have to be good and stay still unless Daddy tells you otherwise, okay?"

"Yes, Daddy, yes," I say over my shoulder. "I promise I'll be good. You'll see."

He leans forward and holds the side of my face, looking at me with such warmth I feel like melting all over again. "I know you will, sweet baby. Now you just relax and let Daddy make you feel so good. If your pee-pee gets very happy, you have to tell Daddy. You only have permission to make Christmas cream when Daddy says it's okay. Do you understand, baby boy?"

I nod, having hung onto every word. "Yes, Daddy."

"Good boy," he says softly.

The bed dips as he kneels behind me. Then his strong hands pull my botty wide, and he starts to kiss my secret hole.

I wail. I cry. I call his name and say all the bad words baby boys are allowed to say. I grip the pillow and tears run down my face, but I never move, not even when my legs are trembling like crazy.

He buries his face between my cheeks as he licks and sucks and kisses me silly. His hands tickle up and down my thighs, around my bee-bees, and along my pee-pee. It feels so amazing, my cream wants to spit out, but Daddy said I can't until he says it's okay. So I hold on, because I'm going to be the best boy ever for him.

"So perfect," he mutters as he kisses up my spine and squeezes my peachy cheeks. "So good, Baby Tee. You're being absolutely perfect for Daddy. Can you roll on your back now?"

I shift under him, my chest heaving and my limbs all shaky like jelly. My skin is sweaty but so is Daddy's, and that means we're playing the special grown-up game right. I can smell it in the air along with the nice Christmas candle, and I like the way it tastes on my tongue.

Not as much as I like the taste of Daddy kissing me when I can taste Baby Tee on his lips as well. I giggle and squirm against him.

"I'm having so much fun, Daddy."

He grins and brushes my hair off my sticky forehead. "So is Daddy, baby boy. Now, can you lie still whilst Daddy kisses you some more? Remember, Daddy is allowed to play with Baby Tee's pee-pee for as long as he wants. Baby Tee has to be a good boy and stay still and he's not going to make Christmas cream until Daddy says so, is he?"

"No, Daddy," I say breathlessly, but then I'm not sure. "I mean…yes, Daddy? I'll be good, is what I mean."

He chuckles and kisses my mouth gently. "Of course you will, sweet boy. Because you're the best Christmas present a Daddy could hope for. Now, you just relax. Daddy will take care of everything."

My hands flop on either side of my head as he slowly trails kisses down my tummy before swallowing my pee-pee all the way down, so it hits the back of his throat.

"Yes, Daddy, yes! Don't stop! Like that! I love it!" I just babble and squeal and gnash my teeth, desperate to spit out lots of sticky cream, but I dig my fingernails into my palms and hold on, even when Daddy is being so wicked. "I'm a good boy," I chant. "I'm a good boy for my Daddy. I'm good, I'm good, *I'm good.*"

Eventually, Daddy pops up and kisses his way back up to rub his nose against mine. I'm gasping for air and danger-ously close to shaking apart. He snuggles up next to me on his side and wraps his big hand around my pee-pee, caressing it.

"So perfect and pretty, Baby Tee," he murmurs against my lips. "So gorgeous and good. You stayed so still, just like Daddy asked. He knew you could do it. Now Daddy wants to watch you spill your cream. Do you want to give it to him?"

"Yes, yes, yes," I sob.

"Tell Daddy what you are," he says, his hand speeding up. *Oh, oh, oh!* My cream is almost coming!

"I'm a good boy," I say, my face burning. I feel so shy I have to close my eyes rather than look at him. My hands fist the animal duvet cover.

"What else?" Daddy asks. "Remember, Baby Tee can't come until Daddy says so."

He's stroking my pee-pee so fast, and where it got shiny it's made it slippery, so it feels especially good. I moan and try and make my brain tell my mouth what words to use. "Uh…uh…I'm perfect."

"What else?" Daddy Evan demands.

"I'm…I'm good and perfect and pretty and gorgeous," I whine, the tears leaking down the sides of my face.

Daddy kisses my cheek. "Daddy loves watching Baby Tee and touching his pee-pee. Tell Daddy one more thing, and then you're allowed to come, baby boy. What are you?"

It's like my mind has a bluescreen computer error. I just need to say one more thing, just one…

"I'm…I'm…I'm *yours!*"

As I let go, the cream explodes all over my tummy and I scream, burying my face against Daddy's shoulder. Sobs wrack through my chest as the cream keeps coming and coming, making a big mess all over me and Daddy's hand. When I can, I take a really big breath in, then relax back on the pillow.

Daddy's face is shocked at he looks at me, and suddenly all the lovely floaty feelings are in danger of disappearing as I get worried.

"Was I bad, Daddy Evan?" I whisper in horror.

He blinks and shakes his head. "Oh, goodness, no, baby boy! Tee, you were even better than perfect. Daddy was just surprised because, well, I didn't know you could be so good. That's Daddy's fault for underestimating his amazing boy."

His.

His boy. I said I was his, just before I spilled my cream.

And he liked it.

Even though a lump rises in my throat and my eyes sting, I ignore that and smile. Because even if I'm having a lot of big boy emotions, they're happy ones. It might just be for right now, but I *am* his.

"Thank you, Daddy," I say hoarsely. Then I reach down and gently stroke his big, hard pee-pee. "Can Tee help you make cream, too?"

He shakes his head before kissing me, pushing me on my back again and straddling my hips, sitting up on his knees. "You're helping by being so good and doing everything Daddy says. You look so pretty covered in all your cream. Daddy is going to paint you with his as well. You just lie there for him."

He starts pumping his hand, and I watch his shiny red pee-pee disappearing again and again inside his fist. He looks so strong and powerful as he looms over me. His thick, hairy legs are trembling like mine did and his heavy bee-bees swing and bounce between them.

My hands are by my head again as I lie underneath him. "Can I still talk?" I ask, and he nods.

I take a deep breath, knowing what I say right now is very important, even if I'm just a baby.

"I want my Daddy's cream all over my body," I say, deliberately switching from third person to first. I don't want to detach myself from this experience at all. "My Daddy Evan is so sexy, and he takes such good care of me. I don't have to worry about anything when I'm with Daddy Evan because he's perfect, too. I want to watch him touch himself and spill his cream all over me because I'm his baby boy. I do whatever he tells me to because I'm his."

He snarls and drops his head back, close to the edge. "Baby boy," he rasps. "Baby boy, sweet baby."

"Come all over me, Daddy. I'm yours."

Thick ropes shoot out, streaking along my chest. Some of them even hit my chin as he keeps pumping it out. I drink in the sight of him as his whole body shudders until his bee-

bees are finally empty, and he collapses on top of me, squishing our mess between our chests.

"Mine," he croaks, hugging me tight.

It might not be something I can take home and show Daddy Sai and Jude, but I know I've still been marked all the same.

We stay like that for a while. He shifts so he's not crushing me, but he keeps me wrapped in his arms as he strokes my sides and kisses my damp hair. My big boy thoughts come drifting back, but not in an intrusive way. I'm ready to mull over certain things.

Like how I don't think these are dating lessons anymore. Like how Daddy Evan might need some help to understand that he's ready to take the next step and how we all want him to do that together.

And about baking.

"Daddy Evan?"

"Yes, baby?" he answers sleepily, kissing my temple.

"You know how it's a Friday?"

"I do, yes."

"Did you also know that you have to let gingerbread houses set for several hours before you can decorate them?"

He blinks and lifts his head to look at me. "Really?" I giggle and nod, and he crinkles his brow for a second. Then he smirks at me. "And because it's a Friday, you want to stay overnight and decorate it in the morning?"

I wriggle gleefully in his arms. "I *do* have new Christmas jammies I can wear," I say wisely. "And Daddy Sai packed my toothbrush, just in case."

"Did he now?" Daddy Evan says warmly. He traces his fingers over my face for a bit, touching my cheeks and lips and nose, like he's memorising a map. "I'd love nothing more than for you to stay over, Baby Tee," he murmurs.

Happiness rushes through my entire body and I can't stop myself leaning up and kissing his mouth.

I think we're so close to something monumental happening not only between us two but Daddy Sai and Jude as well. This is such a huge step forward.

But if he's going to jump off the cliff with both feet, I have a feeling he's going to need a gentle push.

Luckily, I don't just have an idea of how to do that. I know two men who are going to be *very* eager to give me a hand doing it.

CHAPTER 19
Evan

I LOOK AROUND AT ALL THE BOXES AND BAGS OF STUFF I JUST rather impulsively bought and wonder where on earth to start. It's not that I'm trying to distract myself from thinking about three absolutely gorgeous men and what the hell to do with them next. Nope. I'm a grown man, a Daddy Dom no less. I know what the fuck I'm doing.

Yeah, right.

Logically, I know that making love with Tian and having him stay the night was one of those big, scary lurching baby steps that Jacob told me about. I cleaned him up after we had some of the best sex of my life, dressed him in his new pyjamas (which fit perfectly, thank the lord) and spent the evening baking. We had our dinner and watched a movie, then went to bed at a reasonable time.

The only time I faltered was whether or not we should sleep in my bed on the top floor. But my gut instinct told me that it wasn't quite the right time. Luckily, the playroom bed is a double and we hadn't messed it up at all, so we slept there.

And I do mean sleep. As wonderful as it had been earlier

to share that intimacy with him, he seemed to sense that sharing a bed with someone who wasn't Beau and relaxing enough to fall asleep was enough in and of itself. But we snuggled up together and I was surprised just how fast I nodded off. It was strange, and I kept waking up disorientated, but it was also wonderful.

On Saturday morning I made us breakfast and we decorated the gingerbread house as planned, and then Tian went back to Sai and Jude's place. My heart definitely ached as I waved him off, but he'd left with a cheerful, "See you soon!" like it was inevitable.

Is it?

I feel like after I'd made such huge progress in sorting out my feelings and what to do with them, I'm back to square one again, worrying how to now move forward. If it was just Tian, I'd text him and make plans to do something next week. But I feel paralyzed with indecision. Do I invite all three of them over? What kind of dynamic would that be? Would they even want that? Should I just message Sai and Jude and make individual plans?

Rather than sort through all those questions like an adult, I've spent my whole Sunday shopping. But now I'm home again and just as intimidated by the sheer volume of stuff I've bought as I am my love life. There are even more bits being delivered over the next few days.

"Fuck," I say with a rueful chuckle, rubbing my tense forehead. It seems like I've just replaced one problem with another and am nervous about tackling either of them.

When my phone pings with a text notification, it's a welcome distraction from my other distraction. Especially when I realise it's a message from Tian. My heart leaps in my chest like I'm a teenager with a crush. We didn't have mobile phones when I was at school, though.

We certainly didn't have video messages.

Glad I'm at home on the Wi-Fi, I tap to download it. The accompanying text simply reads "Get comfy, Daddy" with a winky face. Deciding to abandon my shopping altogether, I jog all the way upstairs and flop on my bed, eager to see what my baby boy has been up to.

No, not mine. He was for that day, and it was wonderful, but I can't make that claim on him just yet. However, the idea that maybe it could be a possibility makes excitement bubble inside me like Champagne.

As soon as I snuggle down amongst the pillows, I press play. Tian's face fills the screen, then he crawls back with an adorable smile and sits up on his knees, waving at the camera. I notice several things at once, and it causes quite a physical reaction within me.

Tian is dressed in a sparkly top and a white thong. His cock is clearly full where it's trapped under the thin material. He also has glittery feathered angel wings strapped to his back with elastic around his shoulders. Nestled in his hair is a headband with a feathery white halo attached to it.

"Hi, Daddy Evan," he says breathlessly. He stops waving and touches his chest with both his hands, his fingertips grazing over his nipples through the sequined material. "This is your Christmas present. We want you to unwrap us. Because you've been such a good Daddy, you get a sneak peek of what's waiting for you under the tree!"

My heart is already thumping and my cock thickening when onto the bed crawls Sai and Jude from either side. I can't help but bark out a laugh when I see that Jude is wearing a green and red elf hat, complete with jingling bells, and Sai has on a Santa hat to match. They're both wearing black harnesses as well…and that's it. Their free cocks are fully erect and leaking as they crowd Tian from in front and behind.

"Dear God," I croak into the otherwise quiet of my bedroom as I watch Jude kiss Tian's mouth and Sai his neck.

They run their hands over him as Tian reaches out, slipping his hands around both their lengths. He's mostly just fondling them than actually trying to wank them off, but it's still hot as all fuck.

"Baby boy," I moan, my own dick already rock-hard. I palm myself through my trousers but stop there, wanting to give all my attention to what's happening on the screen.

"Who are you thinking about, baby boy?" Sai asks Tian.

"Daddy Evan," he pants in response, turning and looking into the camera. I gasp as if he can see and hear me back. "I hope he's enjoying this. I'm being *so* good."

"Yes, you are, Tee," Jude says affectionately with a big grin. "I know he's loving watching you right now. I bet he's so hard and calling you his good, perfect boy."

"You are, Tee," I utter.

Sai also looks into the camera. "Shall we give him more?"

"Yes, Daddy," Tian begs.

Jude and Sai shuffle backwards a little, still on the knees. Tian drops to all fours, and that's when I realise he's not wearing a thong.

It's a jockstrap.

Jude and Sai waste no time in lining themselves up. Jude rubs his fat cockhead against Tian's open, eager mouth and slaps his cheeks and chin noisily with his length. Tian moans as Sai pushes his cock inside Tian's hole. I guess that they already stretched him before they started filming, just like Jude and Sai got themselves hard before, and *fuck* the realisation that they did that for me is both incredibly touching as well as scorching hot.

It doesn't take Sai long to bottom out, and then he and Jude start fucking gorgeous Tian from both ends, grunting and groaning as they gaze into each other's eyes. Sai grips

Tian's hips and Jude has his fingers thrust into Tian's luscious hair. Tian's eyes are closed, looking like the filthiest, most beautiful angel as his boyfriends spit roast him.

"Good boy, Tee," Sai says, his voice raw. "You feel so good. So perfect for Daddy Sai's cock. So good letting my slutty Jude fuck your pretty mouth. Do you like that, baby boy? Do you like being stuffed with two big cocks like a Christmas turkey?"

Tian practically screams, making the most noise he can with Jude sliding his dick in and out of his throat. Drool drips from his chin and he trembles as these two stunning men use him for their pleasure. He's so still for them, just like he was for me.

I drink in every detail as Sai and Jude rock back and forth, their beautiful bodies slick with perspiration. "Can I come, Daddy Sai?" Jude begs, his breathing ragged. "Please, can I come? Baby Tee's mouth is *so* good. Please, *please.*"

Sai nods, pounding Tian's arse even harder. "Come now. Our good baby boy is going to drink it all down while I fill his tight hole."

Jude looks down as Tian looks up. It's difficult to see in the small video, but Tian seems to be crying as he takes everything they're giving him so perfectly.

"I love you," Jude says as Tian hungrily sucks his cock. "You're amazing, Tee. I love fucking you like this. You look so stunning with Daddy Sai's cock fucking you raw. You were made for us. You're so perfect. God, oh, *god!* Take it, baby. Take it all, just like that!"

He bellows as Tian whines, visibly swallowing as Jude empties his load. Tian splutters and gasps, cum and spit spilling down his chin. Sai roars, snapping his hips and gashing his teeth as he also climaxes. I remember the way his hole clenched around my own dick when I was buried inside him, and I moan desperately.

For a few moments, Sai and Jude simply pant and look at each other as they come down from their highs, letting their cocks soften inside Tian. When Sai nods, they slide out at the same time, flopping back against the pillows, dragging a trembling Tian in between them. The camera is at such an angle that I still have a good view of their bodies and not just the soles of their feet.

Jude and Sai work to pull down Tian's jock strap, discarding it as Tian's gorgeous cock springs free. He's hard and leaking and I can still practically taste him on my tongue.

"Daddy Evan," Sai says, making me jump slightly. He's looking directly at the camera as he wraps his hand around Tian's neglected cock. "We're going to make this sweet, good, obedient boy come all over himself now. If you'd like to wank off with him, I suggest you get your cock out now." He smirks. "If you haven't already."

Unable to hold out any longer, I don't need telling twice to do as he says. I drop the phone on the bed and crane my neck to keep watching as I unzip and yank my trousers down. Feeling ridiculously glad I came up to the bedroom initially, I pull open my bedside drawer and grab the bottle of lube that lives there, hastily squirting some on my hand and wrapping my slippery hand around my member, picking up the phone again with my free hand.

Whilst I was doing that, Tian drew his heels up to his bottom and Jude slipped two fingers inside Tian's stretched, glistening hole, pulsing the digits in and out. Tian is shaking and panting as Sai strokes his cock, speeding up.

"Do you want to come for Daddy Evan?" Sai asks. Still with his eyes screwed shut, Tian nods frantically, but that just makes Sai laugh. "Are you going to be a good boy for him and look at the phone so he can see how badly you want him?"

"Yes, Daddy Sai," he gasps. He lifts his head and stares

directly into the camera, making me feel like he's watching me as my hand flies over my aching cock. "I'm yours, Daddy Evan. We all are. P-please. *Please!* Come unwrap your presents. Don't make us wait any longer. I've been so good for you."

He's writhing as Sai and Jude mercilessly use their hands to drive him wild. He's a sweaty, tearful angel, even if his wings are getting crushed as he fights to hold back his climax, and his halo has slipped.

He's perfect.

"Do you want to come now for Daddy Evan?" Sai teases. He and Jude are both watching their boy intensely, but Tian's gaze is still locked with the camera.

"Yes, yes, yes!" he screeches.

"Such a good boy, waiting for permission," Sai praises. "We're all watching you, sweetheart. Daddy Sai and Daddy Evan and naughty Jude. Come for all of us. Show us you're our good, sweet boy."

His cock erupts, spurting everywhere as he jerks and flails, his orgasm ripping through him. I speed my hand up, tipping over the edge only moments later, spilling all over my hand as I gasp and tremble.

When Tian finally flops down, Sai and Jude gently withdraw their hands and hug him tightly between them. Tian blinks his eyes open and smiles sleepily at the camera. "Merry Christmas, Daddy Evan," he whispers.

The video ends. The screen goes black.

I suck air into my lungs, sagging against the mattress and flinging the arm without the sticky hand over my forehead, staring at the ceiling in shock. My limp cock rests on my hip, my trousers pulling awkwardly at my thighs. I don't move for the moment, though. My mind is racing too fast to coordinate my body anyway.

That was one of the most incredible things I've ever experienced in my life. And I don't just mean the video that I'm sure I'm going to treasure forever. It's like all the weight that had been lingering on my shoulders has been lifted.

They all want me. Together. I don't have to choose. I can stop dithering. They couldn't have said it any clearer that they're inviting me into their lives. No, I don't know what that ultimately might look like, but it's time to seize today and stop letting the past hold me back. The future will bring what it does regardless.

We've been playing this game all month. It's my move, and I have a feeling it's time to overturn the board and throw out the rulebook.

I have three presents that need unwrapping.

CHAPTER 20

Sai

ONCE MORE, I FIND MYSELF STANDING OUTSIDE EVAN Zegler's front door. Except this time, I'm there with both Tian and Jude for the first time.

And there's a wreath hanging in front of us.

"Oh my god, I'm so excited," Jude hisses as Tian presses the doorbell. "I can't believe this is *finally* happening."

"I can," Tian says with a shy smile at us over his shoulder.

I hug Jude to me affectionately. "We've only known him a month. Don't act like we've all been unreasonably dragging our heels."

I don't think anything is going to spoil my husband's mood, though. He just grins and bounces next to me. "I'm still excited."

"Me, too," Tian says, joining our hug.

That's how Evan discovers us a few moments later when he opens the door. We all turn to look at him, and I catch my boys beaming at him as much as I am.

"Hi," he says breathlessly. He's wearing a Christmas jumper with singing carrots and Brussels sprouts all over it. I'm obsessed.

Tian's the first to move, throwing himself into Evan's arms and snuggling in close. Jude also launches over the door's threshold to join in, leaving me to bring up the rear. I close the door and wrap the three men in my embrace, squeezing them tightly.

"Hi," I echo Evan, meeting his eyes with a smile I can't seem to turn down let alone off.

I do understand where Jude is coming from, even if it's my job to rein him in. There were plenty of times where I never would have thought we'd reach this moment. But here we are, the four of us together.

All falling in love.

Evan leans over and kisses me with such ease it melts my heart. Then he greets Jude and Tian the same way before he blinks and laughs. "I can't believe I just got to do that."

"You can do that any time you like," Jude chirps. I subtly tap his shin with my boot. We agreed we would ease into this conversation, not jump in when we're still in the entrance hall bundled up in our winter wear.

"Coats and bags off," I announce, and Evan helps me divest the boys of everything they no long need and hang it up. The coat rail suddenly looks very full, as does the shoe rack underneath it, and my heart swells.

Tian and Jude both bought their slippers along with them in their backpacks, whereas I've got the bag of groceries. Evan said he wanted to cook us all dinner, but I insisted on bringing the wine and some dessert.

"Shall we head downstairs?" I suggest.

Evan gestures down the hall. "Lead the way." I love how bright his eyes are and how strong his voice is. He's not nervous anymore. He's the Daddy he was always meant to be.

Before the boys can barrel in front of me and knock the bag full of bottles out of my hand, I march down the corridor and trot down the stairs.

When I turn the corner and head past the small bath-room, I stop abruptly.

If I thought the wreath was good on the front door, that's nothing compared to the seven-foot real tree that's been erected in the corner by the dining table. It has lights and baubles and tinsel and everything. There's even a star on the top.

"Oh, Evan," I say, my voice thick as Jude and Tian join me by my side, mouths hanging open. I turn to look at my fellow Daddy as he stands beside us, bashful but proud. "You did this for us?"

"And myself," he says firmly. "It took a long time, but I finally discovered the true meaning of Christmas again."

"Presents?" Jude asks, waggling his eyebrows.

Evan laughs and reaches for his and Tian's hands. They reciprocate eagerly. "Love," Evan says softly. "And family."

I place the shopping bag on the counter before moving in for another hug between all four of us. "You're not alone anymore," I promise him.

Eventually, he's the one to pull back and break it up, snif-fling and laughing like the rest of us. "Thank you so much for coming over. I didn't think you'd all be free on Christmas Eve."

"I did work today," Jude says with a tired chuckle. "That's why we had to make dinner a bit later. But I'm off tomorrow *and* New Year's Day."

"He's working New Year's Eve," I explain. "That's okay, though, as he finishes at eight and the important stuff will happen at midnight."

Evan beams at us. "That's lucky it worked out like that."

"Or fate," Tian suggests, clinging to Evan's side.

My heart flip-flops in my chest. I have a feeling it'll be doing that a lot this evening. "Right," I say before I can get too emotional too early on. We still have to have The Chat, after all. "Prosecco?"

Tian and Jude cheer, so Evan fetches long glasses from the cupboard. I open one of the bottles we brought with us, still cold from being in our fridge all day.

"Shall we toast?" I ask when we're all topped up.

"Actually," Evan says. Now he sounds a little nervous, so I reach over and give his arm a reassuring squeeze. The look he gives me in return is grateful, and he visibly puffs himself up a bit. "I'd like to show you something and propose a toast there. If that's all right?"

"Absolutely," I say.

"Yes, please," Tian chirps as Jude nods, half his prosecco gone already. I roll my eyes but top him up anyway.

"Wait this time," I warn him firmly as we follow Evan and Tian back up the stairs.

He gives me a cheeky grin but doesn't take a sip. "Yes, Daddy," he hisses playfully. Ooh, he's asking for a spanking later.

I look forward to it.

Evan is waiting by one of the closed doors as we join him and Tian. He glances at my—*our*—baby boy, then turns the handle, opening the door and inviting us inside.

It's a living room with wooden floorboards, a fireplace and an honest-to-god gold chandelier hanging from the high ceiling. The leather sofa and armchairs look vintage but well cared for. The sideboard is made from dark wood and exquisitely crafted, as is the drinks cabinet filled with top shelf liquor.

What catches my attention more than all of that, however, is that the room looks and smells freshly cleaned. There's another large Christmas tree standing proudly in the corner with very similar decorations to downstairs. If Evan has gone out and bought everything new, it makes sense that he'd get big packs of generic ornaments.

The thought crosses my mind that for next year, we can get him more personal ones. I love that doesn't seem so crazy anymore to be planning ahead.

Perhaps the most important detail I notice about this space is that there has to be a dozen photos on display of Evan with another man. In them, they're both smiling so much it brings a lump to my throat. It's easy to see how in love they are.

Evan takes a breath and reaches out to pick up one of the frames off a sideboard. "This is Beau," he says, his voice only catching a little. He shows us the selfie proudly before turning it back to look again himself. "Losing him almost meant I lost myself. But you three found me, and I know he'd be grateful for that." He looks around at us with shining eyes. "You saved me. My Christmas miracles. Not only did you make me see that Beau would want me to be happy, you showed me that I never have to stop loving him, even if I make room in my heart for someone else."

"Or three someone elses?" Tian asks hopefully.

Evan laughs and puts the frame back down so he can hug Tian to his side. "Exactly. I won't deny this has been a big and fast learning curve for me. I've been very apprehensive about finding the best way to go about it all. But then I realised that the only way out is through, so here goes." He huffs and meets my eyes before looking at Jude then Tian. "If you want me in your life, I want you back just as much, possibly even more. If you'll be patient with me, I'd really like to try dating you all. I know I have room in my heart for you."

Poor Tian bursts into tears and buries his face into Evan's jumper. A sob tries to escape my throat as I reach out and grip Evan's arm again, this time keeping a hold of him. Jude punches the air and whoops.

"It was the sex tape that did it, huh?" he says cheekily.

Evan laughs and shakes his head. "I mean, who could resist that? But…seriously, yes. It really hammered home that this could be a really beautiful constellation of stars. That I'd already seen glimpses of all your souls and knew I wanted more. That you already loved each other, and you wanted to make space for me. And…and maybe a little room for Beau."

His voice trembles as he mentions his lover's name. I rub his arm, Tian rubs his chest, and Jude picks up the same frame from before, studying the image. "If you tell us all about him, we can love him as well," he says thoughtfully.

Sometimes, my naughty boy has the biggest heart of all of us. I watch as he carefully touches his fingers against the photographed face of a man we'll never meet, but hopefully we can get to know over time.

Tears spill down Evan's face, but he's smiling. "I'd like that," he says softly. He looks around the room. "I shut him away for so long. I threw away all the Christmas decorations he adored and locked this room as well as his playroom. But I want them to be open now. I want to share them with you. I'm done living in a mausoleum like a ghost."

I lean in and press my forehead to his, and we both close our eyes for a moment. "I'm so proud of you," I tell him earnestly.

"So, does this mean I have *three* boyfriends?" Tian asks, making us all chuckle. I pull away and look Evan in the eyes.

"Is that what we all want?" I ask.

Evan looks at each of us in turn. "I'm sure it's going to be carnage, but…yes. That's what I want more than anything."

I laugh at myself. "We had this whole big Chat planned about making things official that I thought would take us hours. And we just tripped and fell into it within about ten minutes."

"That's because when things are meant to be, they *can* be that easy," Jude proclaims smugly.

"Yeah, yeah, you were right all along," I say, rolling my eyes and yanking him over so I can kiss the top of his head. "Brat."

"But you love me anyway," he says, knowing full well he's right.

Tian pulls us all into another four-way hug, which we manage without spilling too much prosecco. "So it's official, then?" I say, unable to stop myself from Daddying and ensuring that we're all communicating on the same page. "The four of us are a polycule?"

Evan laughs and shakes his head. "I can't wait to go from the commitment-phobe to the guy with three handsome boyfriends. Yes, I want to make it official. If that's what you all want?"

"Yes!" Tian cries.

"I thought we'd moved past that," Jude says in exasperation. "Can we toast already so I can get a refill?" He shakes his empty glass at us, and I cuff the back of his head.

But then Evan holds up his glass and we all copy him. He thinks for a moment before nodding once. "To love. Past, present, and yet to come."

"To love," we all agree. I give Jude some of my prosecco so he can properly toast with the rest of us.

It might be too early to say it out loud, but I'm sure in my heart that what we have with Evan is already love, and it's only going to get stronger.

And that's the best Christmas present I think any of us could hope for.

CHAPTER 21
Tian

"WE HAVEN'T FINISHED THE TOUR YET," DADDY EVAN announces once our glasses have been refreshed back down in the basement. The bubbly is helping me feel light and happy, but I think that's probably mostly to do with the fact that we're all *dating* now.

I have two Daddies. Officially.

I knew it, I just knew. When I used to see Daddy Evan at Bootleg when Jude and I would go dancing, I knew he was sad and that I could help him. I've never been interested in anyone else since I got together with Daddy Sai and Jude, so I was sure such a strong pull had to mean something important.

Honestly, I didn't think it would change the course of all our lives, but I'm not mad about that in the slightest.

My heart is bursting with joy as Daddy Evan shows us proudly around the rest of his house. Some rooms are still in need of some TLC to bring them back to life, but that's to be expected. In fact, I love the idea of us all helping him with that.

Like he said, he's not alone anymore.

Daddy Sai and Jude love the playroom. I'm hesitant to call it mine even though it's for me, as I want to share it with Beau. It will always be his. When the time is right, I'll talk to Daddy Evan about keeping things like the jungle wallpaper. I think it still works really well with my travel themed things. We can blend both concepts together.

There are almost too many rooms to know what to do with. But when we look around the office where his father used to work, Daddy Evan casually says that Daddy Sai can come and work there any time he wants. And there's a bedroom that he says he'd been thinking about putting a TV in, to which Jude asks if he could play video games on it.

Daddy Evan is already making room for us in his life.

"And this," he says as we climb the stairs to the top of the house, "is the primary bedroom, where I sleep." I see there's also a bathroom on this smaller floor, but I don't pay much attention to that because hanging from the doorframe leading into Daddy Evan's bedroom is a large sprig of mistletoe.

"What's this?" Daddy Sai asks slyly as he points to it.

Daddy Evan blushes. "Well, um, my last decoration," he says sheepishly. "And maybe an invitation. Only if you want. I'd understand if that was moving way too fast. But, um, I've watched your video about ten times already and the way you talked to me in it, I just...um..."

Daddy Sai takes pity on him, leaning in for a kiss to stop him stammering. "If you thought we didn't have a game plan before we arrived on how best to fuck you senseless, you've still got a lot to learn about us."

"Oh," Daddy Evan utters, his face flaming but sounding incredibly pleased.

Jude sneaks in for a kiss as well. "Tian and I are *prepared*," he says, waggling his eyebrows suggestively.

Daddy Evan darts his gaze to me, his eyes suddenly lustful. "Really?" he asks.

It's my turn to blush, but I nod. "Jude convinced me to join him in trying on a not so little accessory."

"They've been wearing them this whole time," Daddy Sai says, shaking his head, but when he looks between us, I also know he's proud of his good boys.

"Come on, come on!" Jude cries, pulling Daddy Evan into his own bedroom. It's nice but a bit plain. That's okay, though. I'm sure that'll change soon enough with us chaos demons in his life. Besides, what really matters is that the bed with the navy covers is a super king.

Lots of room.

Daddy Sai guides me by placing his hand on the small of my back and takes our Champagne glasses, putting them safely on the dresser. I love that Daddy Evan does the same with Jude, who spins around to me as soon as his hands are free, tugging at my jumper.

"You first, Baby Tee!" he announces.

But I push his hands away and shake my head. That's how we usually do things between us three, but not tonight.

We're not three anymore.

"Daddy Evan first," I insist.

"I agree," says Daddy Sai, slipping his arm around Daddy Evan's back and smiling at him. They share a tender kiss. "I'm sure there are going to be plenty of opportunities in the future for him to boss us all around. Tonight, let us look after you, Evan."

He looks around at all of us, then nods. "I trust you."

Those words could warm me through the coldest winter night.

It doesn't take long for the three of us to strip him out of his clothes and get him lying on the bed on his back. Then Daddy Sai and Jude make a show of undressing me for him.

Apparently, Daddy Evan can't help himself, as he's retrieved a bottle of lube and is already stroking his shaft. I giggle, loving everything that's happening right now.

"Is this better than the video yet?" I ask as Jude pulls off my last sock.

"By a million times," Daddy Evan says, his voice even lower than usual. "Come here, baby boy."

I happily crawl up the bed and straddle him, kissing his lips and running my hands over his gorgeous body. I know Daddy Sai and Jude will be undressing each other behind me.

Speaking of my behind…

I take Daddy Evan's hand and guide it to my bottom. "See?"

As his fingers brush over the rather large butt plug, his eyes go wide and I moan, feeling it bump my prostate.

"Such a good boy," Daddy Evan murmurs. "All ready to go for his Daddies."

"And me!" Jude cries, scrambling onto the bed to join us. He flashes his bum as well so Daddy Evan can see he's also been stretched out with a plug.

Daddy Sai sits beside Daddy Evan on the other side and threads their fingers together. "Evan, we've all been tested recently and everything's clear. Depending on your status—"

"Yes," Daddy Evan interrupts. He brings their hands up to kiss Daddy Sai's fingers. "I got tested this week just to be sure, and I'm fine. I don't want anything between us."

Daddy Sai hums as he leans down to kiss Daddy Evan's mouth. "Perfect. Do you want to know what we have in mind, or would you like to be surprised?"

"Surprise me," Daddy Evan says without hesitation.

"Fuck yeah," Jude cries, wiggling his bottom. "Daddy Sai, I don't think we need these anymore!"

Daddy Sai rolls his eyes and slaps Jude's bottom with a loud crack that makes him moan wantonly. But then Daddy Sai moves around the bed and starts carefully pulling it out. As he does, he looks to me. "Baby Tee? Do you think you could be our good boy and get some of that lube on naughty Judas's cock?"

"Absolutely!" I say, eager for a job to do right.

"Thank you, sweetheart," Daddy Evan says, running his hand along my flank. He watches as I apply the lube, and Jude makes a spectacle of writhing in pleasure as I touch his cock and Daddy Sai removes the plug.

"Yes, Daddy, I need it," he whines.

"Such a slut," Daddy Sai grumbles. He gets the plug off with a slurpy pop, then spanks Jude's bottom again. "I bet Baby Tee is going to be much better behaved for his Daddy, aren't you?"

"I will," I say, anxiously grabbing Jude's hand. "But Jude doesn't mean to be bad. I'll help him be good for you and Daddy Evan."

"Nah," Daddy Evan says with a grin, reaching for Jude's other hand. "We love him *because* he's naughty."

My breath hitches. I know Daddy Sai didn't miss that Daddy Evan said 'love' either. It might have been in a general sense, but it doesn't feel wrong.

In fact, it feels so right.

"Your turn, baby boy," Daddy Sai murmurs into my ear. He caresses my bum and gives the plug a little wiggle. "Are you ready?"

"Yes, Daddy Sai," I say earnestly, leaning forward so my bottom is sticking out more for him to remove the plug. It's the biggest one I've ever worn, and we only play with it for certain occasions.

Like tonight.

Daddy Sai does a good job getting it out swiftly without causing me too much discomfort. As soon as it's free, I crawl back over to Daddy Evan and line myself up. "Ready?"

He bites his lip as he runs his hands up my thighs and wraps them around my sides. "I can't wait another second, baby boy. Let Daddy have that sweet little botty of yours."

I whimper as I don't waste any more time, and impale myself on his length. As he enters me, I'm overwhelmed knowing that we're now connected as intimately as possible. I'm so happy he wants us in his life. I'm so happy we're all here together.

"Shh, it's okay, sweetheart," he says as I sink down. He reaches up and wipes my tears with his thumb. Jude and Daddy Sai hug me from behind. "You feel amazing. Are you okay?"

"I'm just so happy," I admit with a half-laugh, half-sob. "And you feel amazing, too."

Jude peeks over my shoulder. "And we're just getting started. Are you ready for me, Tee?"

I nod, pleased that the plug did its work, and allowed me to take Daddy Even inside me without too much trouble at all.

But then Jude slides his finger into my hole as well. Not only do I feel that, but Daddy Evan's eyes go wide.

"Oh. Oh, right," he says, nodding with understanding. "I see."

Daddy Sai offers him his hand again, squeezing it reassuringly. "Is this okay?"

Daddy Evan scoffs. "This is *incredible*. I want to feel our naughty boy whilst we both fuck our good boy."

"And that's exactly what you're going to get," Jude crows as he adds a second finger. "Christ, Tee. You're so tight, it's so hot. Does that feel all right?"

It's burning a little, but I know that will fade, so I nod. "Are you still hard? Do you want to try and fit as well?"

He giggles and nips my shoulder. "I don't think I've ever

been harder in my life, baby boy. Let's make a sexy man sandwich with us as the fillings."

I snort inelegantly but then groan as he pulls his fingers out and starts nudging his cock head at the rim of my fluttering hole. Daddy Evan makes some amazingly filthy noises as Jude forces his way inside, their cocks rubbing together as he does.

Daddy Evan is still tracing his hands all over my body like I'm a work of art. I lean down and give him a kiss. "Still having fun?"

"The best," he assures me. "You're so beautiful, baby boy. So good, taking everything we're giving you so prettily."

I shiver in pleasure, and he only intensifies it by rolling my nipples between his thumbs and fingers. But there's one last piece that still needs adding to this puzzle. Looking over my shoulder, I see that Daddy Sai has lubed up, and now he's behind Jude, pushing his way inside his stretched-out hole.

"Yes, yes!" Jude howls.

"Holy fuck," Daddy Evan rasps.

Daddy Sai grunts and presses against Jude, which moves him against me. Then he reaches around and gives my hip a squeeze before linking hands with Daddy Evan for a moment.

"Are you ready to fuck these beautiful boys, Daddy?" he asks.

Daddy Evan nods reverently. "Together, Daddy," he says.

Then they both start to thrust.

Jude and I cry out together. I feel like driftwood in a storm, being tossed helplessly by the waves. Except my Daddies are actually my safe harbour, and Jude is clinging to me fiercely like he's my life raft.

I don't speak much other than repeating "Yes!" and "Daddy!" a lot. My fingers dig into Daddy Evan's chest to keep me steady. His and Jude's cocks pound into me and I've never felt so full in my life, even when Daddy Sai and Jude have done this to me before.

Behind us, Daddy Sai is in charge, his every movement through Jude giving us all so much ecstasy.

I don't know how much more I can take. But Daddy Sai always knows what I need. "Make our baby boy come, Evan," he shouts out.

Then Daddy Evan's big hand is pumping my cock and within seconds I'm coming all over him. I lose track of who's also throbbing inside me, but all around me are the sounds of my lovers as they smash headlong into their orgasms. The room stinks of sweat and cum, and then all I can hear are panting breaths mingling together.

It's utterly glorious.

Slowly we all still, clinging to each other for support. Then I sense Daddy Sai withdrawing from Jude before he helps him ease out of my tender hole. I whimper and wince, feeling a little sore despite all the pleasure.

But Daddy Evan hugs me until I'm able to shift and let him slide out of me. Daddy Sai is already there, ready with warm flannels to gently wipe us all down. Daddy Evan doesn't move, pulling me to lie beside him. Jude bounces onto his other side with far too much energy, in my opinion. Then Daddy Sai is back, spooning up behind me.

"Was that good?" Jude asks Daddy Evan.

He snorts and shakes his head. "I'm worried you've set the bar too high. I don't know how you'll ever possibly top that."

Daddy Sai hums and links their hands again over me. Seeing them like that is becoming my new favourite thing. "That sounds like a challenge."

We all laugh sleepily before Daddy Evan groans. "I've still got to make dinner."

"We'll order Chinese," Daddy Sai counters.

"It is basically Christmas Day," Jude comments thoughtfully.

"Hmm," Daddy Evan says, not sounding like he's putting up a fight. "I know tomorrow *is* Christmas but…would you consider staying the night? The thought of you all going back out into the cold is breaking my heart."

I giggle and touch his face. "We already packed everything for tomorrow, hoping you'd say that."

"Our neighbour is watching Bow," Jude assures him.

"We packed everything we need," Daddy Sai says confidently.

Daddy Evan groans and hugs us all to him as best he can. "If I get my way, you'll never leave," he warns.

That sounds pretty good to me.

CHAPTER 22

Jude

"I'M I TOO LATE?"

Tian laughs happily down the phone. "No, no, they're not here yet. Are you far away?"

I'd called him as soon as I'd emerged from the Underground, guessing he'd be the most likely of the three to pick up. My manager at work had taken pity on us and sped through the fastest handover ever so we could all get on our way for New Year's Eve. I'd nipped into the twenty-four-hour gym near the hospital for a record-breaking shower and then made my way into central.

"I should be there in a few minutes," I say, jogging down a side street that's still busy because this is London and it's New Year's Eve. But Evan's office is pretty close, located between Bank and Liverpool Street. "I'll see you soon. Did everything go okay?"

"It's brilliant," Tian gushes. "You wait until you see it."

"Okay. I'll be there before you know it!"

I hang up and pocket my phone, dodging around a group of people all wearing star-shaped party boppers who are singing loudly as they stumble down the street. I chuckle and shake my head. There are still a few hours to go until midnight. I hope they make it.

I'm tempted to break into an actual sprint, but that would ruin the shower I just had. So I take a breath and slow down a touch. Tian said I was doing all right for time, and I'd rather not stink when I arrive.

Instead, I take the few minutes I have by myself to marvel at what a week it's been. We eventually left Evan's house on Boxing Day, but only so we could go to both our homes to pick up more clothes and fetch Bow. Our neighbour, Mrs Havisham, took her in on Christmas Day, but we didn't want to leave her any longer.

Besides, Evan was delighted to have her at his place, along with the rest of us.

Seeing as the three of them were off work for the festive break, we decided why not all spend some quality time together before January fourth? I mean, what happened was I bitched a lot every time I had to go in for a shift, but other than that…it's been magic.

Like, I knew we had chemistry with Evan, and I was determined that everyone saw that so we could move forward. But the way the four of us have slipped into a routine is kind of unreal. Considering how frightened he was of commitment and getting hurt again, Evan hasn't had any issues at all in making us feel individually special as well as adapting to group sexy times with gusto.

Which is a good job, because there has been a lot of those. A *lot*.

But there's also been jigsaw puzzles, and baking, and long walks with Bow, and snuggles watching movies. It feels like we've been in our very own snow globe.

I expected at least one of them to have a wobble and stress about how this was going to work when we all got back to 'real life' after the holidays. However, it seems that they're all on my wavelength that it's going so well now and we'll just see what happens when our regular routines kick back in.

I suppose it helps that I've the one who's had to keep working. But I'm also the one that knows everything and is a genius…so…

The fact is that Tian, Sai and I already have a few bits and bobs in drawers in the spare room where Evan said he might put in a TV for gaming. Evan's started buying the kind of wine we drink, and the sugary cereal Tian likes. He's even got food pouches and bags of treats for Bow.

The house in Russell Square has gone from cold and lifeless to a real home in a matter of weeks. Evan was right. He has so much love to give, he just needed us to come along and show him the way.

But he knows that he hasn't been a saint and hurt some people along the way. He's told us about how he's meeting up with his niece, Freddie, and her wife in January to reconnect. It was adorable how cute he got when he asked us if it would be okay for him to tell them that the four of us are a thing.

I know it's all new and exciting right now and we want to do everything together as a polycule. However, it's easy for me to see how we'll all be able to spend time with each other exploring our different interests. Evan has so many different sides that come out depending on who he's around. I've only seen glimpses of it with Tian and Sai, but I've heard a lot more from them. Even with just me and him, though, I can see that sometimes he wants to fuss and Daddy me, but he's starting to enjoy my brattiness, I can tell. I bet I can get him and Sai to Dom me soon enough.

The thought almost makes me hard walking down the bloody street, so I pull my scarf off and let a blast of cold air hit some of my skin to try and help me cool down. I am one lucky little shit. It's as if I have a sex buffet waiting for me whenever I walk through the front door now. It doesn't have to be Christmas. I can have naughty or nice any time I like.

It's glorious.

Tonight isn't about sex, though. At least not yet. Maybe in the morning to start off the new year right. *Anyway!* Tonight is about something arguably more important.

Family.

Because it's not just who you're related to. Families can take on so many different shapes and sizes. Unfortunately, Evan knows there's some other people he's been letting down. But hopefully, that's all about to change.

This is the first time I'm visiting Evan's workplace. Not that I would have had any reason to until now, but it's interesting to see the accounting firm that once belonged to his father is tucked away in one of those streets where every building looks like it could have been erected in a different decade.

I double check the number and am glad when I walk past the grim-looking postmodern sixties structure to a sturdy, dignified Victorian construction. As I glance at the coms panel by the front door, it looks like each floor hosts a different company, with the accounting firm at the top. That makes sense, given what I know Evan and Sai were planning.

Pressing the buzzer, I wait a few moments in the covered entranceway, grateful that the weather is quite mild this year. I've had a couple of miserable New Year's in the pissing rain or howling wind. I don't even want to watch the fireworks on telly when it's like that as everyone in the crowd looks like they'd much rather be home in bed.

But not tonight. Not this year. Because Evan is rediscovering the power of a fresh start, and when the clock strikes midnight, he's going to step into next year as the new man he's already becoming.

"Hello?"

Tian's voice is unsure through the intercom, and I chuckle. "It's me, baby," I tell him. Hopefully he'll get the hang of using it before the evening is through. Or perhaps I'll take over as the welcome committee.

"Oh! Come up!" he cries. The door buzzes, telling me I'm good to pull it open, and I hurry inside.

Surprisingly, given the age of the building, there's an elevator. It can only probably fit four people at a push, but I'm thankful for it as I'm heading to the top floor. I'm also pleased that the heating has been cranked up. But that does mean that by the time I step out into the short corridor, I've already yanked my hat and gloves off and am in the process of stripping my coat when Evan opens the door to his workplace with a big grin for me.

"You made it," he says, drawing me into a hug before taking all my extra crap. "Did you find the address okay? You look gorgeous. How was work?"

Before he can spiral, I grab his shirt lapels and pull him in for a kiss. He's nervous, but I really don't think he needs to be. "Of course I made it," I say, still holding him close and nuzzling my nose against his. "I found it just fine, thank you, and work was blissfully not crazy. Now, where's the prosecco?"

He laughs and kisses me in a more relaxed manner. "I'm so glad you're here," he says, brushing his thumb against my cheekbone. "Now I have all my miracles. I feel complete."

My heart melts in my chest, wondering if I'll ever get bored of his earnest affection. I very much doubt it. Especially when his favourite nickname for the three of us is his 'Christmas miracles'. Like…wow. Get you a boyfriend who looks at you like Evan Zegler does.

I give him a tender hug. "Everything's going to be fine, Daddy," I say. It's funny how natural it feels to call him that. I don't do it all the time like Tian does, but I enjoy it in these kinds of sweet moments. "Show me what you guys have done."

Evan scoffs and shakes his head as he leads me inside. "I feel bad I let Sai do this all for free. I should have paid him."

I waggle my eyebrows at him. "I'm sure you'll find a way to say thank you," I say suggestively, making Evan laugh and blush. But dear god, they let Tian and I watch as they fucked the other night, and I don't think I'm ever going to need porn again with all these hot as sin men in my bed.

"Anyway, uh, yes," Evan says, rubbing the back of his neck. "This is where I work. That's my office." We're walking through a general area with three desks set up. He points to a closed door with his name on it and frosted glass, then to another room with a glass wall partitioning it off. "That's the client meeting room. I thought about doing this in there, but Sai had other ideas."

I chuckle, having heard all about his other ideas. Sai's love language is doing projects for people, like making Tian his playroom. So when Evan first floated the idea of hosting a New Year's party for the first time in seven years, Sai jumped at the chance to 'help'.

What that actually meant was take over, but Evan has been so bowled over by Sai's enthusiasm, I know he hasn't minded at all. In fact, I think he's been deeply touched.

And I don't just mean that other night. Lols.

The three of them have been here since this morning, setting everything up. It's a shame it's only going to be appreciated for one night, but so long as the guests of honour actually come, it'll be worth it.

Knowing my husband, my expectations are reasonably high, but still. When Evan ushers me into the staff break room, my jaw drops.

Tian sent me some photos of what they had to work with when they arrived several hours ago. It's a reasonably sized room with a few velvet green armchairs, old, mismatching side tables, and a little kitchen area with a microwave and kettle on the countertop.

Pretty sad and bleak, and Evan knew it.

Those things are all still here, but the armchairs and tables have been pushed to the sides to leave an open space in the middle. The kettle looks to have been hidden away in a cupboard, but the microwave is still in the same place. However, every inch of the kitchen is sparkling, and the carpet might still be threadbare, but it's clearly been hoovered.

Then there are all the things that they've added.

I knew they were getting an Uber here from Evan's place, and I'm very glad they didn't attempt to navigate the Tube with all this. It's a mixture of things Evan used to bring out for his parties, new decorations Sai insisted on, and a big grocery delivery that I know came directly here so they didn't have to try and travel with all that as well, thank goodness.

My favourite feature is on the floor by the kitchen—the small vintage bathtub filled to the brim with ice and bottles of prosecco, beer, wine, a couple of spirits, and a few soft drink options. Around the rim, Sai has done a very convincing job of making it look frosted, with icicles hanging from the edges.

Every surface of the room is decorated. The backs of the armchairs, bookcases, the walls, ceiling, kitchen counter, everything. I see frosted pinecones, dried cranberries and orange slices, flameless white pillar candles, sprigs of holly, white baubles, and strings of red beads. It's all interspersed with warm white fairy lights and long, fresh smelling pine tree boughs that connect it all together.

It makes it seem like the building is in the process of being reclaimed by a forest. I half expect woodland creatures to poke their heads out and give a tentative sniff. Also, the velvet green armchairs don't seem so tired anymore as they fit the natural, vintage vibe of the décor.

Then there's the table.

I know it's just a basic function folding table that Evan pulled out of storage at his house. But with a purply-red velvet cover it now looks luxurious. At one end they've arranged the glassware and plates. The rest of the space is bursting with party food, displayed expertly in white ceramic dishes, glass jam jars, and wooden cake stands. There isn't a scrap of cheap plastic in sight, and more of the natural decorations fill up the space in between the refreshments.

It looks like a medieval banquet. I know Evan wanted to cook, and we didn't have time for that. But even though the party food is store bought, it still looks delicious.

That's the moment I remember I'm starving.

"Can I sneak some nibbles, or do I have to wait?" I ask Evan excitedly.

Sai laughs as he comes through the other door with Tian and alongside a blast of cold air. "Of course you arrive and immediately need feeding."

"Jude!" Tian cries, running over to hug me. "You look hot."

I give him a kiss and affectionately brush his hair from his forehead. "So do you," I say with a grin.

As I was coming from work, I just opted for a black singlet vest under an open shirt and jeans. This kind of outfit shows off my muscles and tats, which steal the show if I'm honest, so it's best to keep the clothing plain.

Tian, on the other hand, is gorgeous in a sheer purple blouse and tight black trousers that show off his cute arse. Sai looks sophisticated in his red kurta tunic with gold braid trim. Evan has gone for a classic white shirt and navy slacks.

He's got just the right number of buttons undone at the top to show off the edge of his collarbone.

My men are so fucking handsome, I can't even.

I open up my arms and draw them in for a big hug. "Happy new year," I tell them.

"Not until midnight," Sai points out.

"Shh," Tian says with a giggle. "You know what he means. So—what do you think?"

"Of this place?" I spin around and tsk. "You could have made an effort."

"Brat," Sai says, digging a finger in my ribs.

"Okay! Okay!" I hold up my hands in defeat. "It's stunning. I think they're going to be blown away."

"And check this out!" Tian grabs my hand and hauls me through the door he and Sai just emerged from. "Isn't it cool?"

Despite being told that Evan's office had a balcony they hadn't opened up in years, I'm still gobsmacked by how amazing the view is. I can see the London Eye and so many other famous landmarks that you can take for granted when this is your home.

It's quite long and narrow, but I reckon we'll be able to get everyone standing out here when the clock strikes midnight to watch the official city fireworks display. The best part is that Sai has wound god knows how many fairy lights around the railings. Apparently, in the daylight, it's all a little rusty and grubby. But currently in the dark you can't see that at all. It just looks Instagramable.

"You absolutely need to fix this up for the summer," I tell Evan as Tian and I head back inside. The weather might be mild, but it's still nippy out there without a coat.

Evan gives me a small smile. "There are lots of things I need to fix," he says with just a hint of sadness. "But I'm working on it."

I stride over and grab his hands, looking him in the eye. "You are," I agree. "And it's not going to happen overnight, but you've already come *so* far. Please remember that."

"Hear, hear," Sai agrees as he and Tian come and join us for another hug.

Of course, that's when the buzzer goes on the intercom.

Evan immediately stiffens, but Sai grips his shoulder. "You've got this," he says firmly.

"We believe in you, Daddy Evan!" Tian cries.

I give his hands one last squeeze. "We're right here with you. Now go answer that so I can finally start eating and drinking."

"*Judas*," both my Daddies growl in unison as a warning, but I just grin, knowing my work here is done.

Sai, Tian and I step back, letting Evan go first to the receiver where he greets whoever is downstairs, then out the front door into the short corridor.

As we wait, I nudge Tian, and he gets his phone out to start the party playlist we've been working on for the past couple of days. This is the main thing I've been able to contribute to this endeavour as I had to work through all the set-up, and I'm proud of how it turned out, with lots of favourite party tunes to help everyone relax and have fun.

To begin with, we have it on low volume through the Bluetooth speakers the guys brought from home. We can crank it up later for dancing. But right now I just don't want there to be any awkward silence.

Soon, we hear voices. I'd guess some people took the lift and then the rest walked up the stairs. Hopefully, that means they'll have worked up an appetite.

Despite all my bravado and everything I've said to Evan, I'm suddenly nervous. I really want this to go well for him.

"Yes, we all just sort of arrived at the same time," someone is saying as Evan opens the door, ushering people inside. The man sounds quite cheerful, but my instinct tells me that he and whoever else he's with absolutely planned on getting here as one group.

Safety in numbers and all that.

They're probably wondering what the hell Evan is doing, and I can't say I blame them after his behaviour over the past several years. But fingers crossed this little stunt pays off.

Robert—the man I met at Winter Wonderland—was apparently the speaker. He's the first to enter the break room with his son, Timothy, by his side on his crutches. As the door swings inwards, I catch a glimpse of Evan's anxious face, and I do my best to send him positive vibes through the air.

Robert's jaw drops as he looks around the formerly very drab room where he's no doubt eaten countless lunches. Timothy laughs and cranes his neck. "Bloody hell!"

"Language, hun," a woman whispers as she follows them inside the room. By the way she's touching their shoulders, I assume she's Robert's wife and Timothy's mum. She's curvy underneath a faux fur white coat, with cherry red glossy lips and wavy blonde hair styled with sparkly pins. She blinks at the room she's found herself in. "Oh, bloody hell."

I like her immediately.

Evan nips around them as four more people come in after him. From their body language, I'd guess they were two couples, and that seems to be the extent of the group. They all stare in shock at what my men have done in such a short space of time.

"Welcome, welcome," Evan says, his hands clasped together, displaying his nerves. But his smile is authentic. "Thank you so much for coming. It means the world to me. Can we get you something to drink? Perhaps bubbly to start?" He nods and catches Timothy's eye. "We've also got lots of juice and fizzy pop."

"Yes, please!" Timothy says cheerfully, which is good, because everyone else seems to be rendered mute for the moment.

Luckily, Evan and Sai must have discussed this plan in advance, because whilst Tian and I set up the music, Sai had gone ahead and poured several glasses of prosecco and a few sparkling apple juices as well.

There's something about holding a drink, though, that feels like wearing armour. I feel the tension ease in the room as people pile their coats on one of the armchairs and then stand in a huddle, plied with refreshments. It's a little bit us vs them for now, but hopefully things will relax soon enough.

"Thank you, again, for indulging me by being here," Evan says, holding his glass out.

Robert laughs nervously. "We were just going to stay in, so this is quite exciting." The other adults nod in agreement.

Evan seems to need a second to remember what he was saying, and I just want to jump in and rescue him. But even I understand this is something really important he has to do by himself. We're only here as support. So I send more of those good vibes through the air instead.

"Before I begin, some introductions," Evan continues, only tripping a little on his words. "Guys, these are my coworkers. Robert, his wife Em, and their son, Timothy." Evan then indicates a bearded man and a person with an undercut and tattoos who's giving off a lot of gender, and I immediately want to make friends with them. "Jim and his partner, Hen. And finally, Oz, and his boyfriend, Fran." There has to be at least a twenty-year age gap between the last couple, but the way Oz has his arm protectively around his man tells me that doesn't matter.

Evan takes a deep breath, then looks at us. "Everyone, this is Sai, Jude and Tian, my..." he licks his lips before something resolute flashes over his face. "My boyfriends," he finishes confidently.

Sai stiffens next to me as Tian gives a little gasp and my eyebrows shoot up my face. *Well, fuck.* We agreed he should just introduce us as his friends to keep things simple.

My whole body zings that Daddy Evan threw that plan out of the window and decided to publicly claim us all instead.

"What? All three of them?" Em splutters, her gaze raking over us.

"Yes," Evan says with a nod. "It's all quite new, but we're very happy together."

Em whistles and clicks her fingers. "I don't doubt it. You *get* it, Mr Zegler."

I can't help but laugh and wink at her as she grins and elbows her husband's side. He looks a bit shocked, but then he laughs and shakes his head my way. "I said it would take a miracle to get my boss to like Christmas again. Didn't I, mate?"

I nod in agreement. "Three miracles, actually."

"That's why we're all here, in fact," Evan says, his tone serious. "Robert, Jim, Oz—I owe you an enormous apology. I've been a terrible boss to you all and an even worse friend. But now," he smiles at us three, "I've been shown the error of my ways. These remarkable men helped me to stop living in the past by dragging me into the present, and I can finally be excited about the future again."

"We know you've had a rough time of it, Evan," Robert says quickly, his words filled with sympathy. He indicates the break room. "This party is wonderful. Thank you."

Evan blinks. "Oh, this? This is just...no, no, no. This is just...I always used to love celebrating New Year's, so I resurrected the tradition. This isn't my apology. These are."

He fishes three envelopes out of his back pocket and

hands them to their respective owners. "What's this, then?" Robert asks, his brow knitted as he and the others open them up and slide out slips of paper.

"Well, I wanted to write you cheques for your holiday bonuses," Evan says sheepishly, rubbing the back of his neck. "But apparently a lot of banks don't even accept them anymore. So those are simply decorative. However, that amount is already winging its way to you, ready for January second when trading starts again."

When Em sees the number on her husband's not-cheque, she gasps and covers her bright red lips with a manicured hand. "Mr Zegler!" she squeals, her eyes wide. "You can't be serious?"

I don't know what's written on any of the slips of paper, but my chest fills with pride at my Daddy's obvious generosity. All his employees have been left speechless.

Evan is shaking his head, though. "It was the least I could do," he insists. "You all work so hard, going above and beyond. It's about time I recognised that. You'll also be receiving a ten percent pay increase at the start of the new financial year in April."

Robert's eyes have gone glassy as he looks between his wife and son, then to Evan. "That's incredibly generous of you, Evan. I don't know what to say."

Jim and Oz both murmur in agreement, but Evan waves his hands. "You don't have to say anything. Just eat, drink, be merry, and join me and my loved ones to usher in the new year."

Loved ones. *Ha.* None of the three of us have directly said it to Evan yet and he hasn't admitted it to us. But I know. We all know. This is love, baby, plain and simple. I'm sure it'll slip out any day now, so I'm not worried.

As usual, I'm way ahead of the curve with regards to what's actually going on around here.

Timothy breaks free from his parents and launches himself at Evan, wrapping his arms around his waist. "Thank you, Mr Zegler. You made my dad happy." He peeks around Evan and grins at us. "And thank you Mr Zegler's boyfriends for making Mr Zegler happy again!"

His heartfelt words make everybody laugh, breaking any lingering tension. "I say it's party time!" I declare. "Cheers, everyone!"

"Cheers!" they shout back, raising their glasses before taking a drink. Tian turns up the music. Sai congratulates Evan then makes a point of talking with Timothy.

I look around, eager to get to know everyone. But first, I catch Evan's eye, then dash over for a hug before anyone else can nab him.

"I'm so fucking proud of you," I whisper so young ears don't hear.

"I can't believe I got through that speech," he whispers back, shaking his head.

I laugh and boop his nose with my finger. "Not the speech, silly. Although that was good, yes. I mean everything else. Everything you've accomplished in only a few weeks. You're like a completely different person."

He smiles and kisses my cheek. "I kept thinking I was feeling like my old self again, but you're right. I'm not going backwards. I'm going forwards. I'm making amends and rejoining the world with more life in me than ever." He glances as Tian, who's already chatting animatedly with Jim's partner. "All I needed was a little push."

"Or a push from a little!" I joke. Evan stops me from clowning with a kiss. "I mean it," I say once he releases me. "Well done. Here's to an amazing year." I lift my glass and tap it against his.

Evan looks around the room and sighs in contentment. "I think it *is* going to be an amazing year."

I lean in close to his ear. "With a *ridiculous* amount of hot sex."

Evan almost chokes on his prosecco. "Bad boy," he splutters.

I hum and pretend to think. "I'm pretty sure bad boys should get punished, Daddy."

"Just wait until I get you home, you little slut," he whispers in my ear, making me shiver.

Yeah. I'm pretty confident that this is going to be the best year ever, ever, *ever.*

Epilogue

Evan – One Year Later

My house is filled with ghosts.

And a crap ton of truly excellent living people as well, especially tonight.

But, seriously. I spent so many years trying to shut my memories away in a box, hoping to forget them. But all that did was make me bitter.

Now I see my beautiful Beau in every room of this house, because it was his house, too. He belongs here. I have photos of his smiling face everywhere to remind me to never forget him again. That I still love him and always will love him, and that's a *good* thing.

There are three men here that love him as well, in their own ways.

At their insistence, I started opening up about Beau, telling them stories of our time together on this earth, no matter how mundane, not shying away from the happy or the sad. Jude asks a lot of questions. Sai is an excellent listener, always giving me space to open up. And Tian...well, more than once I've overheard him in his playroom, chatting away with his new imaginary best friend.

I don't care if it was too fast. It was absolutely ridiculous to keep living in three different homes, particularly when Sai confessed to me one night that the only thing that had stopped Tian moving out of his awful house share into their apartment was space.

I've had far too much space for far too long.

Of course I was afraid to ask outright because I still get frozen every now and again. But when I realised Jude was spearheading a campaign to just sneakily move more and more of their stuff in here anyway, it hit me that I was worrying about nothing as usual.

We haven't looked back since.

Over the summer, we did so much renovating and decorating. Some rooms we were dragging into the twenty-first century. In those spaces, I found the ghosts of my parents and my sister and set them free as well. Our family wasn't perfect, but we loved each other the best way we knew how. Now my father's books are displayed proudly in the living room, my mother's thimble collection has been arranged in a custom-made glass case, and my sister's map of the world—complete with colourful pins to show all the places she visited—is hanging in the playroom with all the other travel-themed paraphernalia.

With their spirits set free, I'm able to celebrate their lives and share their legacy with the men I love now with all my heart.

Some of our renovations were simply to incorporate their tastes into their new home. Sai oversaw the construction of a new conservatory that connects the basement level to the garden. Tian spent most of August weeding and then planning new flowerbeds for the summer. And Jude upgraded my Wi-Fi and installed a smart doorbell that we can hear throughout the whole house—handy now that it's actually all being used.

Being in our bubble of four never concerned me. But branching out into the rest of the world was a little frightening. Like coming out all over again. Except this time, I had three amazing men by my side and, ultimately, there was nothing to be scared of. Sai, Jude and Tian's parents already knew about their relationship, so introducing me wasn't as shocking as I might have expected.

In fact, Jude's dad has already been in touch about me helping him with his tax returns next year, and Sai's mum texts with me weekly. We're always swapping recipes, and she's been my biggest cheerleader as I've rediscovered my passion for cooking.

Telling Freddie was probably the most stressful, as our relationship was already so strained thanks to me evaporating from her life. But if anything, it's made us closer than we've ever been before. We met for a cup of tea as planned at her place in the new year, and after about fifteen minutes I lost my nerve and just blurted out that I was in a polycule with three wonderful men.

Once she stopped screaming in joy, we switched from tea to wine. After about a bottle of that, I confessed that I'm actually Daddy Evan to them, and she genuinely cried.

I love that she and Clare are here tonight.

I love that *everybody* is here tonight.

Unsurprisingly, it was Jude who insisted that I invite all and sundry to my first New Year's party at the house in a very long time. He argued that the worst that could happen would be that they all already had plans, and we'd have a fine time with just the four of us. Oh, and Bow, of course. And our new bulldog, Brussels, and the cats, Noel and Holly. All rescued from Battersea, naturally. It was Tian who thought to keep the themed names going, so we could 'keep the spirit of Christmas all year round'.

Anyway, if it had just been the four humans and the four animals, I would have still been happy. It's not about the size of the party. It's the sentiment behind it. I never want to get stuck in the past again.

Good job then that practically every bastard we invited said yes. Some of them have even brought friends along. Freddie is proudly showing a throng of lesbians around the house, highlighting all the DIY work we've been doing recently. I think they got a bit excited looking at the power tools.

Clare is resting in the living room, listening to someone tinker with the old piano Sai got for free off the internet because 'someone will play it at some point'. I guess he was right. I'm trying not to hover over Clare because she scares me enough regularly.

But her pregnancy hormones are making her extra formidable.

Every time I think about the fact they've finally achieved their dream and are having a baby, I get emotional. Not least because they succeed in no small part thanks to me. Well, one of my boyfriends, anyway.

Sai is allowed to fuss over Clare because in the end, Sai was the sperm donor and saved Freddie and Clare so much red tape with their conception. But he also uses his Daddy voice on Clare when she won't sit down and put her feet up. She'll still glare at him like she knows where the nuclear codes are (I wouldn't be surprised if she did) and isn't afraid to aim one of those suckers at him. But usually, she'll just give in to his demands.

It's the best of both worlds. Sai doesn't want to raise a child himself because, as he puts it, he already has his hands full with two boys and a whole zoo under the roof. But he'd been sad at the idea of not continuing on his genes in some way or another. Part of the deal for him to get involved was that he could be Uncle Sai and—perhaps more importantly—his mum could be an auntie to the baby. The girls not only agreed enthusiastically to those requests, they hoped that we'd *all* be uncles when the little nugget came along.

And they've already been to stay the weekend with Auntie, firmly establishing that relationship.

So I do my best to avoid the living room, lest I annoy any terrifying pregnant ladies. Instead, I mostly stick downstairs in the kitchen, doing what I love most at parties: keeping everyone extremely well fed and watered.

This year, I *did* manage to have enough time to cook, which is what I've been doing almost since Christmas Day when I made a feast for our little family of four. It worked out nicely that we saw Tian's family then on Boxing Day, where I got a day off, but since then it's been nonstop baking vol-au-vents, blending baba ganoush dip by the vat, slow roasting meats, and chopping veggies to make a metric ton of crudités.

Sai's mum popped around yesterday with two big Tupperware boxes full of handmade bhajis and samosas that I'm pretty sure have already been devoured. Tian's mum dropped off an enormous lasagne this morning that recently came out of being reheated in the oven and has made the whole house smell amazing. And Jude's mum somehow managed to *post* a giant apple cake that I cut up into as many pieces as possible for our guests to enjoy now or take home later.

I'm not saying they're all trying to outdo each other, but I will admit that our refrigerator is never empty and I've never had so many compliments at any of my parties before.

As I serve up the latest batch of handmade halloumi fries

from the oven and get another plate of pre-made devilled eggs out of the fridge, I stop and sip some prosecco, looking out over the ridiculous number of people crammed into my basement, knowing that there are so many more in the living room and probably hanging out in some of the other areas we've opened to our guests. Some rooms have big 'OFF LIMITS' signs taped to them. We've locked what doors we can and are just hoping people will respect the rest.

Because…y'know. Let's just say that we've reclaimed one of the many spare bedrooms and Sai is turning it into a very different kind of playroom.

Mind you, there are plenty of people here that wouldn't be shocked to see that. In fact, they'd probably be very interested to have a poke about when it's finished. Perhaps we'll have a special, smaller party soon, just for them.

Thanks to my newly reclaimed social skills, I'm very happy that I stayed in touch with Jacob, and he's become a good friend not just to me but Sai as well. Like Miller said, us Daddies have to stick together. They're both here: Jacob with his harem of boys, and Miller with Charlie, who's still dressed in some of his finest kitty wear tonight—just no butt plugs. I'm pretty sure I saw Tian sneak off with Luke earlier so he could show him his playroom. Sorry—his and *Beau's* playroom.

But that's not the only familiar face I see from Bootleg, although the newest addition to the party is someone who never RSVP'd and wasn't anyone I was expecting to actually see.

"Marlon?" I say in disbelief as I venture out of the kitchen to give my old friend a hug. I'd extended an invitation, but with no reply, I never, ever thought he'd show. "It's so good to see you. You look fantastic!"

I mean it. His face has lost the broken ruddy blemish across his nose and cheeks, his hair is clean, his clothes fit, he's got new, stylish glasses, and he's lost several pounds at least.

"Evan," he says earnestly, slapping my back and squeezing me tightly before letting me go. "I wanted to surprise you. Plus, I'm doing this thing where I take one day at a time, so I didn't want to commit to anything just in case."

I look him up and down, catching his drift and feeling incredibly proud. "Can I get you a fruit punch? I made it myself. Or there's lemonade, cola, squash, a bunch of zero percent wines and ciders that actually don't taste like arse, tea, *iced* tea—"

He laughs and waves me down. "The punch sounds great, but I can get it myself in a minute. Evan, I'd like you to meet Dickie. Dickie, this is my old pal, Evan Zegler."

A young man I hadn't noticed before steps forward. He's tall and slim, with a mop of brown hair and black framed glasses, which he pushes up his nose before offering his hand to me.

"Nice to meet you, Mr Zegler. Daddy says the way you turned your life around inspired him so much that he came back to me to be the best Daddy I always knew he could be. So, thank you—about a million times."

He's got a serious air about him which contrasts really sweetly as his little surfaces. That lump in my throat—my old friend I haven't seen in a long while now—rises briefly. "You found him," I whisper, glancing between Marlon and Dickie. My old drinking buddy's physical transformation makes even more sense now.

It's remarkable what we can do in the name of love.

"We found each other," Marlon says firmly. "And I'm never letting him go again."

Dickie blushes and holds out his left hand, proudly showing me a ring.

"Oh, fuck," I say with a laugh, losing the battle I'd been

having with the tears in my eyes. I throw my arms around Marlon, then sensing it was welcome, I gently hug Dickie as well. "I'm beyond happy for you both. Congratulations! Mazel tov!"

"Thank you, thank you," Marlon says bashfully, ducking his head but grinning like a fool. "Still a long way to go yet. I'll probably be fighting the good fight forevermore. But this beautiful boy is worth it. I'll spend every day of my life proving that to him if I have to."

Dickie bites his lip before sneaking a kiss on his Daddy's cheek. "Love you," he says, joining their hands. "Shall we go get some food? It looks delicious, Mr Zegler."

"Thank you," I say sincerely. "Please help yourselves as much as you like, and Marlon? When you've got a moment, there are some friends of mine I'd love you to meet."

Of course I want to introduce him and Dickie to Sai, Jude and Tian. But I'd also like to make sure that Marlon doesn't leave without Jacob and Miller's phone numbers.

Us Daddies have to stick together, after all. And having several like-minded friends to reach out to could make all the difference with both Marlon's relationship and his sobriety.

I watch them disappear into the crowd, feeling the urge to escape myself for just a moment. It's getting close to midnight, and before all the madness, I need to re-centre myself.

As I make my way upstairs, several people catch me to say hello as I pass, including Robert and Em. Timothy is apparently playing some kind of racing car game against several adults and kicking their arses, which makes me laugh. Jim and Oz are also here somewhere with their other halves. I love that the company has made its most profit in years because my people are so much happier.

Every aspect of my life is brighter, and I couldn't be more

grateful. But as we're about to enter the new year, I want to make sure I'm not forgetting the past, even if I'm not dwelling in it anymore.

It's quiet in the master bedroom at the top of the house. This whole floor has an off-limits sign at the bottom of the stairs, and it looks like everyone has respected that so far. Gratefully, I pick a photo frame off the dresser and sit on the edge of the bed.

"Hi, Beau," I say to my favourite selfie of him. I didn't know if it was weird to have this in our bedroom. Sai thought it was important that I not hide Beau away anymore. Tian said it was like he's always watching over us.

Jude said it was kinky, and he was into it.

I love how he jokes about Beau. It normalises it, rather than letting me tread on eggshells all the time. I trace my fingers over the glass and sigh happily, but with that echo of grief that I'm sure will always be with me.

"Happy new year, baby. It's been a really great one, but I think things are only going to keep getting better. I...I wish you were here with all my heart. But I'm sure you know that my heart isn't empty anymore. I'm not alone. You don't have to worry about me. I have Tian and Jude and Sai, and I love them all so much it's hard to breathe sometimes. But I do love them, passionately, every day. I think you'd love them, too. So I love them for the both of us."

I inhale shakily, but I'm still smiling.

"I'll always think of you at Christmas, sweetheart. Not just because that's when you left me. But because you bloody loved it. I'm glad I've found that joy again, and not just at Christmas! We have so many holidays now between us. I feel like I'm absolutely privileged and making up for all those years I let pass me by. We stayed with Jude's family for Rosh Hashanah and Sai's for Diwali. They're all such welcoming people and *holy shit* the food was so good. Jude loves Sukkot, so we were able to build a proper Sukkah for him in the garden this year and sleep in it, just like he's always wanted to."

I take another breath, caressing his image but also remembering how lively he was and how enthusiastically he moved. It's not really possible to display videos, but it's pretty easy to recall how he would skip and leap and spin through life.

"It's almost midnight, baby. So I need to go back down and host everyone who's come tonight. You wouldn't believe how many friends I have now! I don't sometimes. Anyway. They do these low noise fireworks now that are so much better for wildlife and people with PTSD and all that. I'm sure most people will still be doing the bangs and whistles, but it makes me feel good to be doing my part by using those. Jude has designed a playlist to match the display we're doing in the garden, which should be fun. I better go find him and Tian and Sai. I want them by my side as we enter the new year. I always want them by my side. I'm thinking I might ask Tian to marry me someday, then the four of us would be linked legally as best we can. But also…I just want to stand up and tell the world how much I love all of them. We never got to do that, you and I. But if it ever happens for the four of us, please know you'd be with me, like you always are. So—"

There's a thump outside the door and someone hisses "SHH!"

My heart lurches and I drop the photo frame on the bed, darting across the room to yank the door open, horrified to think some guest has stumbled up here looking for a bathroom and might have heard something deeply personal.

Instead, I find a naughty boy and a good, sweet boy sitting on the landing. Jude has an open magnum of prosecco in hand, his eyes wide in excitement, and Tian looks like he's just seen a ghost.

"Uhh…" I say, already feeling extremely raw from the heart-to-heart I was just having. I have no idea what to say.

Luckily, Jude is there to bulldoze through all of that. "Are you going to *propose* to Baby Tee?!" he screeches, his eyes shimmering with happiness. Tian still looks frozen, though, so it's him I sit beside and take his hands.

"I'm sorry if you heard something that upset you, sweetheart. Daddy thought he was alone." I shoot Jude a look, feeling like he should have known better. But he's too hyper to care, or so it seems.

"Yes," Tian whispers, and my heart drops into my shoes.

"Yes, I upset you?" I try and clarify.

He blinks his pretty hazel eyes at me, a hint of a smile tweaking his lips.

"No, Daddy Evan. I would say 'yes' if you asked me to marry you. I'd marry Jude and Daddy Sai, too, except the law says I can't do that. But we could, couldn't we? Legally. And then I'd marry Daddy Sai and Jude in my heart, just like you'd marry Baby Beau in your heart."

This time when the lump rises in my throat, I can't fight it. My eyes blur and I try and regain some composure to respond to the beautiful words he's just said.

However, we're interrupted again before I can.

"Is everything okay here?" Sai asks, and honestly, there isn't anyone else I'd rather see in that moment. He climbs the stairs, and I reach for his hand, which he gives without knowing why. I go to speak, but then Bow chases Brussels past us in a whirlwind of fur and excitable barks.

It rattles the shock out of me somewhat. I shake my head and blink, looking between him, Jude, and Tian. *Oh.* My baby boy is watching me anxiously.

"Evan just *proposed* to Tee," Jude says in a stage whisper. "Well, sort of. But then Tee *definitely* proposed to Evan, and then you stomped all over it."

Sai raises his eyebrows then sits down next to us on the edge of the stairs, his hand still firm and soothing against mine. "Is that right?" he asks. His tone is kind but there's also just a hint of excitement there as well.

It makes me realise that he'd want this. Jude wants this. Tian just told me flat out he'd say yes.

"I told Beau that someday I'd love to ask Tian to be my husband," I explain, keeping my gaze on my sweet boy. "That bit would be legal, but I'd want to claim all three of you as my own forever. But I was talking about *someday*, Jude, to a *photo*, and—"

"Tomorrow isn't guaranteed," Tian interrupts me. His face is blotchy, he's trembling, and his eyes are red. But he's smiling.

Oh, how he's smiling.

"Daddy Evan, if you're sure, then I'm sure. I promise I mean it."

I huff and look to Sai for help. He shrugs and squeezes my hand. "This is on you, gorgeous," he says gently. "If you're not sure—"

"I've been sure for a whole year," I blurt out. "As far as I'm concerned, when you all moved in, that was it. I'm in this forever. I just..." I roll my eyes and scowl at Jude. "I wanted to plan something romantic and have a ring and—"

"Take my ring," Jude says. He manages to put the bottle down without spilling it and starts pulling at the band on his left hand. "We all belong to each other, right? If you want to buy something different, whatever. But for right now—take mine."

"And mine." I look as Sai lets my hand go and begins easing off his own ring. He and Jude exchange glances, and when both their bands are free, they hold them out to Tian and I, together.

My breath hitches, my heart going a mile a minute. "Are you *sure?*" I ask them—all three of them.

"Yes," they say as one back to me.

I rub my wet eyes and look at Tian again. "Well…we're at least going to do this bit right," I grumble, waving at him. "Stand up, stand up."

He scrambles to his feet, his hands clutched, holding his breath.

"Christian Prior," I say, "You changed my life. I love the men you love. I love you more than I could possibly say, my beautiful baby boy. Will you marry me?"

"Yes," he cries without a moment's pause.

My heart summersaults in my chest. This is really happening.

I turn to the husbands beside us, realising that both the dogs had sat their bums down on the landing and are watching us with wagging tails. Typical that I'd have an audience to the most important, unplanned moment of my life. But I wouldn't have it any other way. I secretly hope the cats are asleep under the bed, listening to every word we're saying.

"And you two meddlesome troublemakers," I say to Jude and Sai. "Will you spend the rest of your lives with Tian and I? Because it's sort of a package deal."

Jude screams and throws his arms around my neck. "YES!" he bellows in my ear.

Sai takes one of my hands again, always my steady rock and partner. "Yes, Evan Zegler. Now and always. Husbands and Daddies forever."

I'm not sure what happens next, but I end up under a pile of bodies, human and canine. Jude rescues the magnum and is making every one drink. They all keep shouting 'YES!' at me. I close my fist so tightly around the wedding rings that they leave red marks, but when Tian and I manage to get upright again, I slip one onto his middle finger and the other onto my pinkie where they best fit.

I absolutely want to buy Tian and I our own special rings. But wearing Sai and Jude's in this moment—even on the wrong fingers—feels monumental. The four or us are entwined.

Forever, apparently.

People start counting downstairs. "Oh, shit, midnight!" I cry with a laugh, trying to get to my feet as my lovers, my partners, my *husbands,* attempt to do the same.

Sai and Jude fly down the stairs, reaching for each other's hands as they do, two dogs bounding in their wake. I go to follow them, but Tian grabs my hand, anchoring me to the landing for a moment.

"Are we really engaged, Daddy Evan?" he whispers, looking like he's going to burst with happiness.

I wrap him in my arms and kiss the top of his head. "I didn't plan any part of this relationship, baby boy. I would never have deemed myself worthy of it. But dear lord, if I have the chance to spend the rest of my life with you and Jude and Sai, I'll fight for that with everything I have. You might have accidentally overheard what I said, but that didn't make it not true. Yes, sweetheart. Please, please marry me and make me the happiest man alive."

He starts sobbing against my chest. I hold him like that, ignoring the countdown, ignoring the fireworks from the rest of the world, but enjoying as the first song on Jude's playlist resonates through the house. It's something about being young and free and beautiful that makes me want to shout with happiness from the rooftops.

"Are you okay, Tee?" I ask.

He sniffs and wipes his face with a laugh. "I've never been happier in my whole life," he says, blinking up at me. "Sorry I made you miss the new year."

I shake my head and brush his tears from his cheeks. "There are going to be three hundred and sixty-five days of this new year, and I intend on spending them all with my gorgeous men."

"But…can we go and watch the fireworks anyway?" he asks, being too adorable. "I was really looking forward to them."

I laugh and nod. "Of course, sweetheart." I start to lead us down the stairs, but he pulls me up short.

"One second!" He turns to face the bedroom, still holding my hand. "Happy new year, Beau!" he calls out. "Don't worry, you'll be at the wedding. It's going to be a big one. Love you!"

Then he's pulling me down the stairs, back to the party.

I take a second to look back to where Beau's photo is resting comfortably on our bed. I know he's watching over us. I know that in some way, he laid the path so I could find these incredible men who have filled my heart back up to the brim and repaired all the cracks.

Then we're disappearing downstairs, running towards the fireworks and the music and the people.

My ghosts will always be with me. But right now, I'm living for the living. I have forever to practice being the best husband to not one, but three of the best men alive.

And I promise to keep true to the spirit of Christmas every single day that I do.

———

Thank you so much for reading Evan, Tian, Jude and Sai's story! These four were an utter joy to write. I'm sad to let them go! If you can take a moment to leave a review on your preferred bookish site, that would mean the world to an indie author like myself.

Would you like to discover how some of the side char-

acters featured in this book found their happily ever afters?

You can find Jacob and his boys Luke, Sam, and Callum in **Three**.

You can find Bootleg's club owner, Miller, and his kitten, Charlie, in **Nine Lives**.

And you can find Jude's favourite porn star foursome in **Golden**.

––––––

Don't miss the rest of the books in the DKAG Christmas Daddies collection! This multi author series features books with Daddies, boys/littles, age gap, age play, and more. Your favourite authors are bringing all the holiday romance vibes with stories sure to warm your heart. They can be read in any order as each title is unique to the author's world. Be sure to grab them all!

His Temporary Assistant by A.W. Scott
    Daddy Santa's Snow Angel by Aria Grace
    Anson's Awakening by Anna Sparrows
    Satan's Little Helpers by Athena Steller
    Daddy's Little Drummer Boy by Della Cain
    Our Little Sebastian by Myf Wren
    A Little Cinny Latte by Kota Quinn

———

Wild Ride

When Red is chased into the woods, he seeks sanctuary at his estranged grandma's house. He doesn't expect to be rescued by his older brother's best friend, the man he was always madly in love with. Could Hunter be the Daddy of Red's wildest dreams? Especially when he unlocks a secret passion of Red's for beautiful lingerie. There's still a threat lurking in the woods, though, and Hunter realises he'll do anything to protect his beautiful boy.

———

Three

When three shy best friends sign up to a dating app to finally get some by the end of the year, they don't expect to all fall for the same gorgeous, slightly scary-looking Daddy. The only solution? Let him choose who he wants to bed. Except he doesn't. Daddy Wolf wants to spoil each little piggy, one after another. But when danger comes calling, will their love for each other be enough to save them all?
Includes Halloween bonus scene!

———

Nine Lives

When Charlie suddenly finds himself homeless and penniless, he decides to sell the only thing left he owns. Himself. For the very first time. Lucky for him he stumbles across Miller, the own of a London kink club, who saves him from those who would take advantage of him. As Miller discovers his inner Daddy, he also unlocks Charlie's kitten alter-ego. But with both their families meddling, will new love be enough to keep them together?

Click here to get the Daddy's Fairy Tales Box Set

THE FAIRY TALE COLLECTION: CONTEMPORARY MM RETELLINGS BY HELEN JULIET

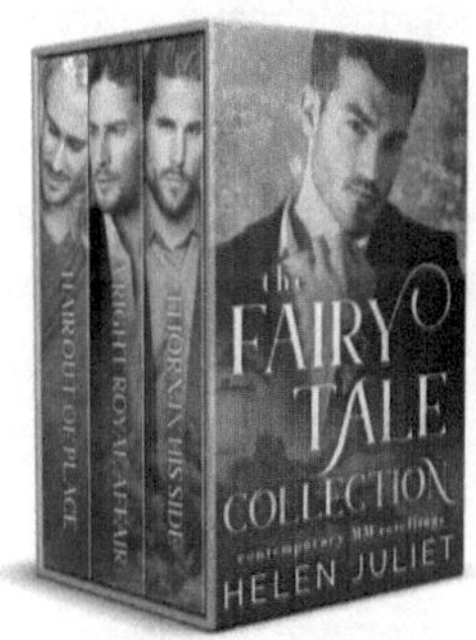

Experience Beauty and the Beast, Cinderella, and Rapunzel as you've never seen them before in this thousand page box set of contemporary adaptations! Available together for the first time, each book is a standalone with its own HEA, but watch out for familiar faces!

Click here for the Fairy Tale Collection eBook

Click here for the Fairy Tale Collection audio

Thorn in His Side

Beautiful, innocent Joshua Bellamy finds himself in an arranged marriage to the older, brutish, and scarred Darius Legrand. But in Darius's secluded mansion, Joshua begins to see that Darius isn't so scary after all. In fact, despite being a little grumpy, he's actually very protective and caring. When danger comes knocking on their door, will Joshua and Darius's blossoming love be strong enough to save each other?

―――――

A Right Royal Affair

Nobody knows that Prince James of the United Kingdom is bisexual, and as he's sixth in line to the throne, it needs to stay that way. But when he meets the cheeky, outrageously gay Essex boy, Theo Glass, everything could change. Against his better judgement, James asks Theo to help him put on a royal charity ball to remember. Can they resist their mutual attraction for a whole week alone in a picturesque castle, or will true love bloom?

―――――

Hair Out of Place

Raphael d'Oro is a secret prince who has spent his entire life exiled in a London penthouse. But now he's in a race against time to get back to his tiny European nation to claim the throne that's rightfully his and save his people. Good thing he has his insanely hot older bodyguard to take care of him. But Griff Thompson would never want someone as inexperienced as Raphie, would he? Even *if* they keep finding themselves in places with only one bed…

Click here for the Fairy Tale Collection eBook

Click here for the Fairy Tale Collection audio

JACKED UP BY HELEN JULIET

Little thief. Big problem.

JACK

When some billionaire tries to mess with my family, I decide to take personal revenge and break into his London penthouse when he's abroad to steal some compensation. The issue? He's not only very much home, but he's *huge*. Even worse, he's gorgeous and too bloody cheerful. Rather than call the police, he suggests that I stay until I've fixed what I've damaged. It's only for a few days, but I start to realise this guy isn't the villain I thought he was. In fact, he might be everything I've ever dreamed I could never have.

FELIX

It's only a little light kidnapping, so I don't feel too bad. Besides, this small, grumpy thief I've caught is too adorable. I'm drawn to his broken soul. I want to protect him from his troubles and dominate him in the bedroom. We're perfect for each other but he's determined to believe that he doesn't belong in my world. Can I convince him to stay? Or is this fairy tale doomed before it's even begun?

Jacked Up is a super steamy, standalone MM gay romance novel featuring one hell of a size difference, a romantic date in the clouds, a singing and matchmaking parrot, past wounds long overdue for healing, and a guaranteed HEA with absolutely no cliffhanger.

Click here for the Jacked Up eBook

boyfriend Dair when he gets home from work. Hold on to your horses, Marine!

———

Troubled Waters

Bodyguard Scout Duffy doesn't know what's worse: the fact that his scorching one-night-stand, Emery Klein, is his bratty new client, or the fact that he doesn't even remember Scout. But Emery's life is in danger thanks to his out and proud charity work, and once he finally recognizes Scout, their chemistry in undeniable.

———

Homeward Bound

Swift Coal just found out he's a father, and his daughter (and her cranky cat) are coming to stay. His best friend's younger brother, Micha Perkins, has nowhere to go and a wrongfully tattered reputation. He's relieved when Swift asks him to be a live-in babysitter. He just has to hide his lifelong crush. Easy, because Swift is straight—right?

———

Bright Horizon

With sixteen years between them, baker Ben Turner and lawyer Elias Solomon have no idea their crush is mutual. But when Ben inherits his long-lost family's estate and becomes an overnight millionaire, Elias swears to protect the innocent younger man from the vultures circling him. To unravel the mystery of the inheritance, they must go to England to confront Ben's estranged relatives…and their feelings for each other.

———

Crossed Paths

Raj Bhat is done living in the shadows. It's time for him to take charge of his own destiny and tell the man he's fallen for how he really feels.

————

Midnight Sky

It's the night before New Year's Eve. Taylan Demir is all alone, and he's just lost his dog. Except when his handsome customer, Hudson Perkins, comes to his rescue, Taylan doesn't just get his dog back. He's suddenly got a hot date, and maybe someone to kiss when the clock strikes midnight.

————

Memory Lane

Angel Shields saved Jay Coal's life in high school, and Jay has secretly loved his straight best friend ever since. Now Angel's back in town with amnesia after a suspicious work accident and it's Jay's turn to rescue him. He pretends to be Angel's fiancé to see him in the hospital, but with his scrambled-up memory, Angel's not sure it's fictional after all. He just knows he loves Jay more than ever.

————

Thin Ice

Kamran's ex broke his heart, tricked him into aiding a bank robbery, and now he wants him to do one last job. There's only one way to say no: seek the protective custody of the biggest, grumpiest FBI agent ever, Lee Marshall. And pretend to be his boyfriend for a week-long family reunion in their giant mansion. Wait, what?

————

Calm Shores

Gorgeous, sophisticated Dante walks into Oliver's bar and orders…a boyfriend?! Dante needs a man to keep his mother from setting him

back up with his awful, cheating ex, and Oliver is up for the
challenge.

———

Fresh Snow

Emery Klein is throwing the best Christmas party ever, but his
fiancé, Scout Duffy, and all their friends have something more
exciting in mind.

———

*Each Pine Cove book can be read as a stand alone and has its own happy
ever after. But if you read the whole series, you'll see a lot of familiar faces!*

Click here to get the Pine Cove eBook bundle

Click here to get the Pine Cove audio bundle

HOMECOMING HEARTS BOX SET BY HJ WELCH

Meet the five members of Below Zero, a boy band who have just been dropped by their record label and have to find their way back home again. Join Blake, Joey, Raiden, Trent, and Reyse as they each discover their happy ever afters! **This 1500+ page box set features all five original novels as well as three bonus epilogues that catch up with the guys after their HEAs!**

Click here to get the Homecoming Hearts eBook bundle

————

Scorch

Blake Jackson just wants to open a dance school now his pop star days are done. But his life is turned upside down by a reality TV show, and an old school friend the director has made into his fake boyfriend. Blake isn't gay, but he's happy to reconnect with barista Elion Rodriguez. However, Elion is gay, and has been secretly in love with Blake since freshman year. As the lines between fake and reality begin to blur, an obsessive stalker shadows Blake. Can he save Elion from getting burned?

- - - - - - - - - -

Reyse Hickson might be an international pop sensation, but he's also forced to remain in the closet thanks to his homophobic record label. When gorgeous Corey Sheppard saves Reyse from a mugging, Reyse can't resist falling into his bed, if only for one night. However, a family emergency calls Reyse home, and it seems like the perfect chance for him and Corey to steal some secret time together. But it can't last. Reyse's label would never allow it. Can Reyse and Corey walk away from the best thing that's ever happened to either of them? Or is this love worth going down in a blaze of glory? *Contains bonus epilogue.*

Each Homecoming Hearts book can be read as a stand alone and has its own happy ever after. But if you read the whole series, you'll see familiar faces returning, and enjoy the spectacular ending of Blaze even more!

Click here to get the Homecoming Hearts eBook bundle

PADDLE CREEK DADDIES 1-4 BOX SET BY HJ WELCH

Welcome to the underdog town of Paddle Creek, where it's always the quiet ones who get up to the best kind of trouble! Join the boys, princesses, littles, lambs – you name it! – of Paddle Creek College as they meet their Daddies and find true love…with a little help from the colorful locals, of course.

This 900 page box set features the first four full length novels of the ongoing series as well as a previously unpublished 9K word bonus prologue to Four Play.

Click here to get the Paddle Creek Daddies 1-4 eBook bundle

———

ONE – Heaven Sent

Two rival jocks. One adorable nerd. A bet that changes everything.

Seth is the captain of the Paddle Creek Panthers. Marty is the football team's slacker clown. Gabe is the shy nerd who's caught both their attention. They have nothing in common…until they get pulled into a scheme by the college bully. If Seth and Marty don't graduate, they could all lose everything unless Gabe can get the jocks' grades up. But when sparks fly between all three, sweet Gabe finds himself with two hot Daddies desperate to take his V card... and his heart.

TWO – Yes, Sir

Two men. Two secrets. Can true love set them free?

Benedict is a professor at Paddle Creek College with a hidden desire to be called Sir by willing subs. His new younger TA, Jackson, has the body of a gym rat, but under his clothes, satin and lace are waiting to be discovered. Jackson has no idea what calling his new boss Sir does to him. However, it's nothing compared to when they start some serious role playing, and he calls him Daddy as well. But Benedict is leaving at the end of the year, so their relationship can never be anything more than a secret fling...right?

THREE – Little Pleasures

One jaded Daddy. One brand new boy. A fake relationship that becomes all too real.

Xander has been in love with his older brother's best friend forever. Ruben has all but given up trying to find a sweet little to Daddy. But when a lie gets out of hand, Ruben suddenly finds himself pretending to be Xander's boyfriend to protect him at an awful family wedding. As time goes on, Ruben can't help but encourage Xander's dinosaur loving little side out, and soon enough nothing is make believe anymore.

FOUR – Four Play

Three hungry wolves. One pretty little lamb. The hunt for love is on.

Former soldiers Rick and Trey are married and devoted to their boyfriend, Brady. Primal play is what gets their blood pumping. When Brady wants to try being the hunter for once, he discovers bratty Harper is a natural at being chased. However, these three hot men aren't the only thing Harper is running from. Under this young man's bravado lurk wounds that need healing, and Daddy Rick is determined to add this sweet and sassy lamb to his wolf pack. But when Harper's past catches up to him, will four be the magic number to save him?

BONUS PROLOGUE – Be Four

Two Daddies in search of a boy. But is it for one night or forever?

After swapping military life for married life, Rick and Trey continue to enjoy an open relationship where they can both dominate in the bedroom. But when they meet gorgeous Brady at a steamy party, they soon realize that what they have is bigger than just a one-night stand. [Please note: This short story is set two years after the prologue of Four Play and two years before Chapter One of the same book. It can be read before or after Four Play—whatever you prefer!]

Each Paddle Creek Daddies book can be read as a stand alone with its own happily ever after. But if you read the whole series, you'll soon spot the grumpy owner of the cat café, a mischievous trash panda with a heart of gold, and a slightly terrifying librarian who may or may not be an actual witch. Not to mention familiar Daddies and boys!

Click here to get the Paddle Creek Daddies 1-4 eBook bundle

PADDLE CREEK DADDIES #5: HELL'S KITTEN BY HJ WELCH

One grumpy biker. One sunshine kitten. Could it be a purr-fect love?

JESSIE

Okay, so maaaayyybbee surprising my boyfriend was a bad idea, especially since apparently he already *has* a boyfriend and it isn't me. My only option for now is to sleep in my car. That is until the big, bad, tattooed biker who owns the cat café insists on letting me stay with him. I swore off men, but the way he dotes on me has me falling for him fast. My inner kitten is out of the bag, and there's no putting him back now.

NIM

I'm a terrible Daddy. My last kitten told me that. Words and emotions are tough for me. But when the perfect boy drops into my lap, how can I refuse? Rescuing strays is what I do. It's only so long that I can resist this beautiful kitten and his bubbly personality. But someone in town has it out for me and my fellow bikers, branding us troublemakers. I can't let Jessie be dragged down with me, not when it puts everything he's worked so hard for at risk. I swore I'd do anything to protect him. Even if that means letting him go.

__Hell's Kitten__ is a steamy, standalone MM romance. It's the fifth book in the __Paddle Creek Daddies series__, where it's always the quiet ones who get up to the best kind of trouble. This book features first-time kitten play, two broken hearts, a cheerleading championship, far too many black cats to count, enough love for nine whole lives, and a guaranteed HEA with absolutely no cliffhanger.

Click here to get Paddle Creek Daddies #5: Hell's Kitten eBook

PADDLE CREEK DADDIES #6: MAKE BELIEVE BY HJ WELCH

One scorned doll. His enemy's straight father. Is it revenge, or could this be true love?

KADENCE

Secretly fooling around with a closeted D-bag like Logan McKenna was always a bad idea. So I ended it, much to his fury. Retribution is swift, and his humiliation of me is devastating. I can't let him get away with it, though. That's why a chance meeting with his supposedly straight father seems like the perfect revenge scheme. I'll seduce him with my alter ego, Kiki the living doll, and once I have some juicy photos, I'll ruin the entire family.

Except Rafferty McKenna is nothing like his son. He's kind,

thoughtful, tender, and not to mention hot as all sin. I've been broken down by not only his son but my homophobic family and my callous ex-Daddy. But as Rafferty starts to piece me back together with love and care, can I really go through with this plan of mine?

RAFFERTY

When a living doll throws himself at me, it doesn't matter that he's a boy not a girl. He's simply *mine* and I can do whatever I want with him. One passionate encounter at a party won't do, so I invite him to stay with me for a weekend, but even that's not enough. He makes me feel alive in a way my failed marriage never has. However, as our connection gets deeper, I can tell he's keeping secrets. This is just a fling, and I can't seriously be thinking about burning my whole life down for something that's not even real. Right?

*Make Believe is a steamy, standalone MM romance. It's the sixth book in the **Paddle Creek Daddies series**, where it's always the quiet ones who get up to the best kind of trouble. This book features Kiki the fabulous, bratty doll who will do anything for her Daddy, an extremely naughty conference call, a romantic picnic, two hearts in need of mending, plenty of secrets that need to come out, and a guaranteed HEA with absolutely no cliffhanger.*

Content warnings: This book features a scene of consensual sharing, as well as a loveless marriage with both husband and wife knowingly cheating on one another. However, Kadence and Rafferty never cheat on each other.

Click here to get Paddle Creek Daddies #6: Make Believe eBook

Helen Juliet is a British author of contemporary MM fairy tale adaptations, including the international bestselling Beauty and the Beast retelling, Thorn in His Side. She lives just outside of London with her husband and three balls of fluff that occasionally pretend to be cats.

She began writing at an early age, later honing her craft online in the world of fanfiction on sites like Wattpad. Fifteen years and over half a million words later, she sought out original MM novels to read. By the end of 2016 she had written her first book of her own, and in 2017 she achieved her lifelong dream of becoming a full-time author.

When she's not writing she's usually dancing, singing, filming music videos, taking long walks, working on jigsaw puzzles, drinking prosecco, or talking about Taylor Swift.

She also writes contemporary American small town MM series as HJ Welch, including Pine Cove, Homecoming Hearts, and Paddle Creek Daddies.

––––––––

You can contact Helen Juliet via social media:

Newsletter (never miss a release!) – https://www.subscribepage.com/helenjuliet

Website (with FREE original stories) – www.helen-juliet.com

Facebook Group – Helen's Jewels

Facebook Page – @helenjulietauthor
Instagram – @helenjwrites
Bluesky – @helenjuliet.bsky.social
Book Bub – @helenjuliet